# TRUST ME

Nell Grey

# CONTENTS

# CHAPTER 1

---------✹---------

His feet, one slippered and one covered in a grey sock, swayed pendular in the icy January wind that whipped mercilessly around the old three-walled stone barn.

The medical examiner moved methodically, photographing each angle and every detail of the corpse hanging from the ancient pitch-pine beam.

The body.

The stepladder kicked flat below it.

The black rope tied efficiently with a knot, which would later be identified as a double running bowline.

"Any idea on time of death?"

The medical examiner turned to face the detective.

"He's stiffened up. If I had to hazard a guess, I'd say he died twelve, thirteen hours ago. But don't quote me."

Detective Ellis Roberts edged himself beneath the eaves; sheltering from the stinging rain, but keeping out of the way of forensics. That would make it seven or eight o'clock last night.

"Anything else?"

"Ligature marks. Probably a fractured hyoid and thyroid. I'll need to confirm that when I get him on the slab."

Ellis could see inside the building now. The daylight lit up the shadowy corners that lay beyond the weak halo of the naked light bulb, hanging like the body from the beam.

In a couple of months, this shed would be full of new life. Nursing ewes and new-born lambs. This morning though, there was only death here. Empty pens and a swinging man.

The face was reddened and bloated. The eyes bulged from the pressure of the drop and the snapping of the neck.

"Definitely suicide, then?"

The medical examiner pointed with his camera towards the toppled stepladder below the corpse, alongside which the other slipper lay.

"Looks that way."

Ellis studied the rocking body. This was the third farmer suicide he'd seen in as many years. At least this one hadn't decided to splatter his brains across the shed. Those were the worst.

"You talked to the Missus yet?"

Ellis snapped back to attention.

"Uh… briefly. Diane from Family Liaison's with her."

The wife had raised the alarm at around six a.m.

"Thought he'd be downstairs sleeping it off on the sofa after coming back from The Cross Keys. Instead, she found him in here. Looks like he never made it there, after all."

"If he was off to the pub, why was he in his slippers?"

The medic raised an eyebrow.

"And why check the outbuildings in the dark? Did she suspect that he might've topped himself?"

He paused, and Ellis chewed his lip thoughtfully.

"Hey, you're the detective, I just cut 'em open. Is there a note?"

"No. Nothing so far."

Inside the farmhouse, Ellis and Diane sat across the kitchen table from Maureen, wife of Glyn Evans, the deceased.

She looked drawn, the detective thought. There wasn't much of her, and her face had a pearl-like translucence, no doubt from the shock.

Sat alongside her was a male, who Ellis estimated to be around thirty, and who he quickly established wasn't Maureen's son. Six foot, lean and muscular. He looked like he could handle himself.

"I called Jac after phoning you."

She stuffed the crumpled tissue she was holding, up the sleeve of her cardigan.

"He's my nearest neighbour."

"I'm renting the farm," he added by way of introduction.

The detective jotted it down. Jac Jones lived in the white cottage, around a half a mile away in the direction of the pub.

"Where were you last night?"

"In The Cross Keys."

"All evening?"

"Pretty much. Played pool with a couple of the boys."

He'd check that later.

"Was Glyn there?"

"No."

"You sure?"

Ellis studied Jac steadily.

"Certain."

"Do you still need me, or can I get on? I've some silage to put out for the sheep in the top fields."

"If we need you, we'll be in touch. Got a mobile?"

"Yes, but you're best calling the landline. There's no signal around here. If I'm not in, leave a message and I'll get back to you."

He gave the detective both of his numbers, then touched Maureen's hand.

"I'll be back 'round in a bit. See how things are."

"He's a good lad," she mouthed to Diane, the family liaison officer after he'd disappeared to the porch to put on his boots.

She fished out the tissue from her cuff and dabbed away another tear.

The detective's eyes strayed towards the porch.

"'Scuse me a sec."

Thankfully, the rain had stopped, but the bitter winter wind still sliced into his cheeks as he raced onto the yard.

"Hold up!"

Jac turned around as Ellis jogged over to him.

"Detective?"

Ellis shivered. In his rush, he'd left his coat on the chair.

"Glyn?" he asked, catching his breath.

"D'you think he was depressed?"

"You mean, were there any signs he'd do this?"

"Pretty much, yeah."

"Everyone knows he's gotta…," Jac corrected himself, "He *had* a problem with the drink."

Ellis noted the slight emotional crack in his voice.

"That's why I'm renting the land, it had gotten too much for him… But, yeah, I'd say he had his ups and downs. Maureen can tell you more. She was a nurse."

Ellis scribbled it down. He'd check out Glyn's medical records later.

"Anything else? Money worries?… Marriage issues?"

Jac coughed.

"I dunno."

"And Glyn definitely wasn't in The Cross Keys last night?"

"No. I told you."

"D'you think it's odd that he was wearing his slippers to go to the shed?"

"It's bloody odd, if ya ask me, that he's in there hanging off a beam."

"They've taken him down now."

Jac nodded grimly.

"Any other next of kin, apart from his wife?"

Jac looked down at the concrete.

"There's a daughter. Annie."

Ellis got out his notepad and scrawled down her name.

"Where's she?"

"London."

"Stace, tell me I'm not being a total fool."

We've slipped out to a popular Italian coffee shop near the office for a morning catch-up. Tongue-in-cheek, I call it our weekly one-to-one, as I'm technically Stacey's line manager. But that doesn't get in the way of us being mates.

She's been there for me through thick and thin since I got back from New York. We meet up on the weekends, go shopping or out for drinks, the usual stuff.

She contemplates my dilemma, spooning the top off her cappuccino.

"The best bit," she grins, savouring the chocolate-sprinkled froth. "You *were* a fool, Annie, but honestly, hun, you're doing the right thing now."

"Hmm, you're probably right."

"*Definitely*. Remember last week, yeah?"

Thinking about *that* again makes me cringe.

I was convinced that everyone in the restaurant was pitying me as I played with my phone for a whole hour, until he finally answered my numerous texts to tell me he wasn't coming.

"But, what about New York? It was so much fun at the start."

Stacey rolls her eyes at me.

"Don't give me all that New York rom-com crap. Ice-skating in Central Park, listening to jazz, eating cream-cheese-bagels, bollocks."

She yawns.

"It was exciting 'cos Seb breezed in from the London office for a couple of days, took you out and banged you senseless... Honey, he was on a mini-break from his marriage, and you were his New York office fling."

"Sounds kinda sleazy when you put it like that. But it wasn't, Stace, honest."

The company we work for has a strict 'no relationships' policy, and there is no doubt that this has added to our affair. The thrill of forbidden fruit.

"Sorry if I'm being a bit brutal."

She smiles at me apologetically.

"D'you love him, Annie?"

That was quite a question.

"No."

The answer flies out of my mouth without hesitation or consideration. The truth.

"I was smitten, but I was never in love. I thought he was cool... He wore good clothes."

"As do lots of men who *aren't* married, and who isn't now your line manager."

I drain my espresso.

"*Argh*... Moving back to London, it's made everything so complicated."

"At least, now you see it as it really is."

"Yeah... That he's a married man and I'm his booty call, you mean?"

I can't begin to tell her how awkward it is working with him every day.

I hide my head in my hands.

"Stace, I need to end it. Before someone finds out."

"They won't. Trust me, babe. Go call him."

"What? Right now?"

"If not now, when will you?"

Blowing out a deep breath, I realise she's right.

"Crap! My phone's on five percent battery."

"Just do it, alright?"

"Okay!"

I roll my eyes at her for being so pushy.

"I'm going outside so you can't eavesdrop or pull faces at me."

"Don't worry, I'll actually be doing some work. I've got our monthly customer survey stats for you to look at, when you get back."

I squeeze out from our table, and Stacey produces a paper report from her bag.

"We can add it to this meeting's agenda."

I push past queuing customers to the pavement outside, where I make the call.

"Annie?"

Seb's got a phone especially for me. And I can tell immediately, from the curt way he says my name, that he's irritated that I've called him.

"Is this important? I'm going into the boardroom in ten."

"It is actually, Seb."

I'm trying not to lose my nerve.

"I'm sorry, but it's over between us."

The phone line is silent for a second or two.

"Just like that? Look, Annie, let's discuss this later, after work? We could go for a drink? Or, how about we meet up in the archive room again?"

Very classy.

I shudder with the realisation that I'm not even worth a hotel room, these days.

I steel myself.

"No, Seb. We're through."

Stace studies my face as I squeeze to sit down at our table.

"It's over."

# CHAPTER 2

--------- ✳ ---------

Diane was on the farmhouse telephone, trying to get family liaison officers in London to pay the daughter a visit. This Annie wasn't answering her mobile.

The body had been removed, and Detective Roberts had gone. She'd stay another hour and then go too, she decided, as she returned to the kitchen.

The wife was doing fine; considering. As a nurse, she'd no doubt seen a dead body or two. But still, she couldn't imagine how terrible it must have been, to find him hanging like that.

She was still ghostly pale.

"Do you have anyone who can stay with you tonight?"

"Annie'll be coming home soon."

"Hmm... D'you have a sister, or a friend who could stay?"

"I'll be fine."

The hard edge in her voice told Diane not to push it.

"Alright. But, I'm giving you my number. Call me anytime. I mean it. Day or night."

The officer handed her a business card.

"Maureen?"

Diane watched as Mrs Evans got up from her chair to greet another young man who'd strolled into the kitchen without knocking.

"Sion."

"Jac told me. I'm sorry for your loss."

He embraced the grieving widow, holding on to her when she let out a loud sob.

"Sorry."

"Hey, it's okay."

She dabbed at her face with her tatty tissue, recovering her composure.

"He'd been threatening to do it for years. But still, I'm not gonna lie, Sion. When I saw him hanging there, it was still a terrible shock, it was."

She had told the detective all about her husband's manic depression. Apparently, she'd talked him out of it before. Ellis had taken down the details of his condition and medication. They'd be checking that now, back at the station.

Maureen started moving towards the kettle.

"Cup of tea?"

Sion stepped around her and guided her back towards the chairs.

"No. No. You go sit down. I'll do it."

He pointed to her mug, "Wanna fresh one?"

"Oh, yes please, love."

Who was this other young man to Mrs Evans, Diane wondered?

He was about the same age as the other fellow, Jac, and had a similar confident air about him.

He waved a mug at Diane and she nodded back.

"Bet you get through some tea, in your job?" he said casually.

"Occupational hazard. But I've made a pact with myself never to touch the biscuits."

"You still haven't got hold of Annie yet?" Maureen cut in.

"No. The officers are going over to her workplace and her flat. There's no answer on her mobile."

"I'm not sure I can tell her."

Maureen's voice cracked.

Diane went over, sat beside her and held her hand as Maureen whimpered quietly, fighting back her tears.

"Hey, that's perfectly understandable. Would you like anyone

9

else from the family to call her?"

Sion handed Maureen a box of tissues.

She took a fresh one and blew her nose.

"What about *Jac*?"

"What *about* me?"

Jac stood in the kitchen door jamb with a casserole dish in his hand.

"For your tea," he said, placing it on the worktop near the stove. "It's still frozen."

Maureen stared uncertainly at him.

"Jac, would you mind calling Annie for me? The police haven't had any luck so far."

"She's not answering her phone," Diane chipped in. "Can you keep trying through the day? Or try social media? Or text?"

"I dunno if she'll speak to me."

It had been twelve years. She hated his guts. But, who else was there?

He rubbed his hand across his stubbled chin and exhaled.

"Give me her number."

Maureen rose and shuffled over to the antique dresser drawer. Opening it, she took out a large address book and wrote Annie's mobile number carefully on a scrap of recycled envelope.

Her eyes teared up again as she handed it to him.

"Tell her to come home, Jac."

He nodded solemnly and stored the number safely in his shirt pocket.

Diane looked puzzled as she struggled to work things out.

"So, how exactly do you two lads know each other?"

It was a thinly disguised cop question.

"From our army days," Sion answered. "I'm a contractor now."

"Where?"

"All over the place."

"Doin' what?"

"Computer networks. IT security, mainly."

Sion gave her a disarming smile.

"Jac lets me stay at the cottage between jobs. Saves me renting, and this part of the world is heaven for adrenaline junkies like me."

"Really? What kinda sports d'ya do?"

"Kayaking, mountain biking, coasteering…"

He took in her blank expression.

"Y'know? Jumping off cliffs into the sea for the fun of it."

Diane pulled a face.

"Not sure that's my kind of fun. Sounds cold, wet and dangerous to me."

"He's a handy man with the plumbing tools, too."

Maureen pushed a plate of biscuits towards Sion, urging him to take one.

"Sorted my old boiler out for me, didn't you, love? And it's still goin' fine, fair play."

"Glad to hear it."

Sion popped the second half of his chocolate bourbon into his mouth.

"I'm off to London in a bit. Got a job down there. That's why I came 'round now. I'm not sure if I'll be back for the funeral. D'you know when it'll be?"

Maureen looked to the Family Liaison Officer.

"They need to do the post-mortem first," Diane confirmed. "After that, the coroner will release the body for the funeral. Usually takes a couple of weeks."

Maureen pushed the plate towards them, and Sion took another biscuit.

"I'll try my best, but you'll understand if I'm not there?"

"That's alright, love."

She smiled gratefully at Sion.

"You've done so much for me, already."

"Can we talk, Annie? You're making a big mistake."

Seb is leaning over my desk a little too closely into my personal space.

My eyes dart around to check that no one's watching us, and he takes the hint. After dropping a file onto my desk, he steps away.

For the benefit of my co-workers near my corner office space, he projects publicly,

"Come through to my office please, Annie."

He turns impatiently on his heels, beckoning me to follow.

From the twentieth floor of his glass-lined office, the views stretch out far across the City mile.

Seb shuts the door, then stalks towards me.

I edge back.

"Do I need to remind you of our company policy?"

His face turns flinty.

Passing me without eye contact, he anchors himself behind his desk.

Desperate to retain the formality, I do the same, sitting stiffly in front of him.

"If this is about the other night and the restaurant, Marnie's in a bad place right now. She's very suspicious. In the end, I couldn't stay late in town... You knew how hard it would be, when you decided to come back from New York."

My stomach twists. It's bad enough, already.

Bringing up his wife, only adds more fuel to my already huge pyre of guilt. I'm the other woman. The hussy who had a fling with a married man. The home breaker. No one else needs judge me, I'm already doing a great job of it, all by myself.

"Seb, it doesn't matter about the other night. We're done. It wasn't working out between us."

His eyes are fixed in a stony stare. He's not used to not being in control.

"Very well," he sighs. "If that's what you want?"

"It is."

He switches roles. Just like that. From lover to line manager.

His eyes cut into me like a hot knife through refrigerated butter.

"I need to raise something with you. From the People Empowerment Division."

"Who?"

"Human Resources. HR. They say, they've found discrepancies in an appointment you made."

As Director of Customer Happiness (or Customer Services as we were called up until a month ago) I control all my division's appointments. In my head, I begin sifting through all the new staff we've taken on recently. I can't think why there'd be issues with any of them.

From my rabbit in the headlights stare, Seb can tell that I haven't got the foggiest notion of what he's on about.

"Lottie Mathews? Ring any bells?"

"Lottie?"

We were at university together.

"She's fab. She's brought in heaps of new ideas. We've made some key changes already."

The large retail company Lottie worked for was downsizing, and I'd snapped her up for a junior leader role.

"HR say, you didn't follow protocol. That you interviewed her but didn't declare that you were friends."

The look he gives me reminds me of a stoat I once saw on the farm as a kid. I caught it slicing its teeth into the neck of one of our chickens, sucking out the blood.

"It shouldn't be a problem. *I'll see what I can do.* I'll have a word."

A shiver runs through me.

"It's alright," I counter, "I'll go up there myself, and set things straight."

He flicks his gaze towards his computer screen, and I get up quickly, taking my cue to leave.

"Annie?"

My eyes slam head-on into his frosty glare.

"I'll call them too."

Giving him a cursory smile through gritted teeth, I head hastily for the door.

I'm not sure how long I'll be able to carry on like this. New York suddenly seems quite appealing again, even though I'm glad to be back in London. Maybe, it is time to look for a new job?

One thing's for sure about our relationship, or rather fling; because let's be honest, it was little more than sex. Whatever this 'affair' was called, it's been a huge mistake.

"Everything okay in there?"

Stacey stops by my desk as she saunters past.

"Yeah, just a glitch. People Empowerment are after me about Lottie's appointment."

I feel a headache coming on as I sit back down.

"People, who?"

"You didn't read the email, either?"

I rub my temples as a shooting pain begins to pulse right behind my left eye.

"I'm gonna need one of their mindfulness sessions after this stress, that's for sure."

"The hand that giveth and taketh away. Tell me how you get on."

"Sorry, she's not here."

Chantelle pops her head up from her workstation, as I knock on the Director of People Empowerment's office door.

"She's uh… got a wellbeing appointment."

"You feelin' empowered enough to help me, then?"

"Don't even go there, Annie. And how's life in Customer Happiness?"

"Oh, y'know; painting the world with rainbows, every call we answer."

"Can you tell me if there's been a query on Lottie Mathews' appointment?"

"Lottie Matthews?"

Chantelle looks confused.

"Not that I know of, and I handle all the recruitment issues."

She types her name into her computer database.

"Let me have a little look… *Ooh.*"

She draws up some record, then pulls her computer screen discreetly out of my eyeline.

Hold on a sec, I'll just see if Imran knows anything."

She clicks out of the record, then goes over the main office area, where she speaks in hushed tones to another advisor, who I presume to be Imran. They're glancing briefly over in my direction as they whisper together.

Then, I see Chantelle discreetly putting in a call from Imran's desk.

When she comes back over to me, her face has changed. Gone is the chatty banter. She's all corporate and business now.

"Sorry about that, Annie. The Director's been dealing with this."

Seb was right. There is an issue.

Chantelle eyes me cagily as she sits back at her desk.

"But, Lottie's the best appointment I've made this year."

She scans the screen.

"So it seems. Her reviews have been exemplary."

She glances up at me.

"Did *you* write those?"

"Yes."

It takes me a second to catch her insinuation.

"Hold on..."

"And *you* headhunted her? This friend of yours... from university?"

Flustered, I try to protest.

"Well, yes, I knew her at uni... but...we're hardly friends... I mean we don't..."

"There's no easy way to put this, Annie. There are irregularities."

"I don't understand."

"The Director recommends that you're suspended, until we investigate the matter fully."

"Suspended?"

"We were intending to call you in for a meeting this afternoon. It's in the diary."

"But, I haven't..."

"I know it's sudden. But, suspension; it's like a no-fault position."

Chantelle sees me gawping at her. Possibly about to blow. Shout. Cry. Make a scene.

"Don't worry, Annie. These things happen. Think of it as a free holiday."

Back at my desk, I gather my stuff together in a stunned daze.

And as the shock subsides, my anger begins to build. *This is so unfair!*

I'm such a rule-taker. I would never try to cheat or do something I shouldn't. I've never once over-claimed my expenses. Never pulled a sickie. Or been late. For God's sake, I've never even filched a biro.

I take three out of my desk drawer and stuff them into my bag.

No, my only transgression ever, was Seb.

There are no family photos on my desk. I always keep it clear.

At least, I won't have to walk the plank with the cardboard box of shame in my arms. They can keep my straggly spider plant, and my personalised to-do list from the office Secret Santa.

I throw the three biros back onto the desk.

*Stuff the lot of them!*

I've turned off my computer, and I'm grabbing my bag to leave when Seb saunters over to my office space.

I can feel my head beginning to pound again. He's the very last person I want to see right now.

"I thought you were gonna sort it," I fling at him under my breath.

"Annie, honestly I tried, but they wouldn't listen."

His whispering smarminess makes my nostrils flare. What did I ever see in him?

"This whole thing's bloody ridiculous."

My fingers scour my bag for my security pass, so I can get out of there.

"That's what I told them too."

I fling the lanyard around my neck.

"I really don't understand why I can't work whilst they're looking into it?"

"I know, it's ridiculous... But, apparently, it's *company policy*?"

I stare at him hard.

"Yeah, right."

I slam the desk drawer shut.

"And we all know how good you are at sticking to that."

His eyes flash me a warning, as a couple of staff peek at us from behind their workstations.

Why *should* I keep it together?

But, people are beginning to take an interest in us. If I leave calmly, there'll be nothing to gossip about. Annie Evans has left the building. For a late lunch, or a client meeting.

"Use the time to take a break. You look tired."

Great! First, I get suspended, and now he tells me I'm looking like shit.

"It'll only be for a week, or so. They'll be in touch when they're done."

"Lottie's a super appointment. You said so yourself."

"I'll keep working on it for you."

He reassures me with an emollient smile.

"Trust me."

# CHAPTER 3

---------*---------

It feels odd, finding myself midweek in the middle of a mall.

I've spent the last couple of hours aimlessly mooching around. Trying on clothes I've no intention of buying, spraying myself with free perfume samples, waiting for Stacey who's meeting me as soon as she finishes work.

How has this happened? And, so fast?

I sit across from Stacey in the pseudo Italian-American restaurant chain, sampling happy hour cocktails. Mojitos, to be precise. Which I'm drinking way too fast. The deep crooning of Dean Martin fits my mood perfectly, as he sings on a loop in the background.

"What I don't understand is, who told HR about Lottie?"

I prod my straw maliciously at the bruised and wilted mint in the crushed ice.

"Only Seb knew that we were at uni together."

Stacey checks her phone.

It slams into me hard. What an idiot I've been for not seeing it.

Has he engineered all of this?

Did Seb flag the appointment to HR, as soon as I'd ended it with him?

Because I'm now a problem he's trying to get rid of?

Stacey watches the penny drop.

"So?... He's a shit."

She grabs two menus from the holder and tosses one to me.

"What d'you fancy?"

"No idea."

I'm so mad with him that I can't focus on the ketchup-caked menu in front of me, let alone decide which carb-laden offering to choose.

"I'll just order another one of these."

I deliver another mortal wound to the mojito-flavoured slush.

Stacey's menu squelches shut.

"Annie, you need to eat or you'll be ill."

"I'm already sick. Sick to the back teeth of the bullshit that's just gotten me suspended."

She pulls a face, and I try to swallow my bitterness.

"Have they said who'll be looking after the division while I'm off?"

Stacey squirms and plays with her necklace.

"That was quick."

"Seb called me this afternoon and asked if I'd step up for a while."

Draining the last watery dregs, I try to process all of this.

In a way, it's a relief. Stacey's a safe pair of hands and I won't have to worry about work. But if I'm not worrying about that, what am I going to be doing? Sitting in my flat, watching day-time television?

Or, God forbid, going home?

I was there for three days at Christmas, and that was long enough, with my Dad in the state he was in.

I shut that out of my mind. I don't need any more guilt. Not today.

I give Stacey a weak smile. It's not her fault that she's got dragged into this.

"Hey, it's okay. I'm glad it's you. I hope you asked for a pay rise?"

Stacey's mouth curls. She has.

"Use the time to take a break."

"Doing what?"

"I dunno. Take a holiday? Clean your flat?"

"I s'pose."

"Apply for other positions? There are plenty of senior customer services roles with much better pay," she adds hastily.

"Hmm... but not one where I get to shag my boss."

We both start to giggle.

"I didn't like to say this before, Annie, but you *have heard* the rumours about Seb, right?"

I had. There was a marketing manager who'd left suddenly a couple of years back.

"*Oh God*, Stace! Is that what everyone's saying about *me* too?"

Stacey sucks noisily on her straw.

It's confirmed. Our fling has not gone unnoticed.

"So, how long will you be here for?"

Jason gave Sion a hand to unload the luggage from the Volvo Estate parked tightly on the South London suburban street.

"A couple of weeks, tops. Is that alright?"

"Yeah, 'course, mate."

It was late, and he had to be up ridiculously early the next day.

Sion shut the boot of the car and Jason carried the two sports bags to the house. Sion handled the two reinforced metal cases himself.

"Stay as long as you like. I'm not gonna be here much, though. Got a couple of runs to Vegas this week."

"Sin City, eh? I quite fancy a night at the tables," Sion said, stacking the luggage neatly in the spare bedroom. "Catch a few rays. Crash a pool party or two."

"One day, my friend. But this time, I'll be laid over in an airport hotel, far away from the roulette wheels and the Cirque du Soleil."

Sion grinned at his old special forces buddy.

"Still, doesn't sound too bad. I bet, getting laid over in Vegas is a regular occupational hazard for you guys?"

Jason shook his head.

"Yeah. And I haven't heard that before."

Sion patted his friend warmly on the shoulder.

"Great to see you, man."

Jason's eyes met his warily.

"You here speccing out another job?"

Sion took off his jacket and jumper. The flat was positively tropical after the dampness of the old Welsh cottage.

"Yeah. This one's a bit on the risky side. But, y'know how I like the top end jobs."

"Interesting. Fill me in on the details."

"The less you know, the better."

They both knew that was true.

"Ever think of doing a normal job?" Jason yawned, "Like the rest of us?"

"What, like Farmer Jac? Or like you, Mr Big-Bucks Commercial Airline Pilot?"

"Okay, whatever."

Jason went to the fridge and grabbed them both a beer. Prising off the tops, he handed one to his friend and they both slumped onto the sofas in the living area.

"I mean it, Sion. One day, mate, they're gonna catch up with you."

"Not while I'm still two steps ahead of 'em… Cheers!"

Sion's short-sleeved t-shirt revealed the lower edge of his tattoo as he took a swig. A large Welsh Guards battalion emblem that Jac and Sion had done, before their first tour of duty.

It had been Jac's idea.

A week before they flew out to Camp Bastion, Jac took one for the team and Sion got a cover-up for his scars. In particular, the thick blue carved-in marks that the older boys had given him on his first night in the children's home. It was a deletion of the inked-in reminder of the worst time in Sion's life.

The worst, that was, until he'd done six months in the dusty deserts of Helmand. There, he gained new scars that couldn't ever be etched away. Unless you could tattoo your brain.

"Jac sends his regards, by the way."

"How's he doing'?"

"Fine when I left, but I'm not so sure how he'll be in the coming days."

"Why's that?"

"Annie's dad, the guy he rents the farm off, he topped himself last night. They've been trying to get in touch with her, to come home."

"Annie?"

Jason took a swig.

"As in *THE* Annie?"

Sion nodded.

"The one he wasted three years over."

"Jees."

Jason's eyes burned into Sion's.

"He topped himself, you say?"

"Yeah."

Sion pulled at the loose label on his beer bottle.

"He was an alcoholic. He was depressed."

Jac had tried all afternoon to get hold of her from his landline. He could only think that her phone must be switched off or out of charge.

When he called Maureen back later to tell her that he'd failed, she said that the police had drawn a blank too. She wasn't in her apartment, and she'd left work early. Her line manager hadn't said why, and he didn't know where she was.

This was his last shot. Otherwise, he'd have to rely on Callista. But, something told him that he needed to speak with Annie first.

The Cross Keys had a good mobile phone signal. He'd send her a text, he decided, locking the cottage door behind him. Then he'd wait in the pub to see if she called him back.

As soon as he walked into the back bar of The Cross Keys, Claire's eyes were on him. She gave him a friendly smile, then looked searchingly over his shoulder, towards the door. By the time he reached the bar, she was already pouring him a pint of real ale.

She put the amber-filled glass between them onto the polished top.

"Your usual, Jac."

"What if I'd have wanted a pink gin?"

"Unlikely. A tough army boy like you."

"Not that tough these days."

"Your mate Sion not with you tonight, then?"

Jac's mouth curled. He thought that she'd been taking an interest in Sion. It seemed he was right.

"He's in London for a few days. Job came up. Short notice."

"Police were in here earlier, asking about you."

Jac looked at her levelly.

"Yeah? Askin' 'bout what?"

"About where you were last night?"

"And what did y'say?"

"That you were here all evening."

"Which I was."

"He took down the names of the two you were playin' pool with."

The police were welcome to go down as many rabbit holes as they liked. He had nothing to hide. Once they read up on Glyn's history they'd be satisfied it was suicide, he was sure.

"How's Maureen doin'?"

"Bearing up, considering."

Claire wiped the top of the bar down with a beer towel.

"So sad. Still can't believe it, to be honest with you. Goes to show ya never can tell what's goin' on in people's heads.

"True enough."

"Poor old Glyn. Absolute legend, he was."

Jac said nothing.

"Used to have me in fits all night, he did. *Ah!* And that voice of his. When he sang Myfanwy in the bar that time; d'ya remember? I'm sure he could've gone professional back in the day."

The bell from the kitchen sounded.

"'Scuse us, for a second."

Claire disappeared into the kitchen to take food to a couple sitting at a table near the bar, giving Jac the opportunity to escape with his pint to the small table near the fire.

He would, no doubt, be hearing lots of similar sentiments over the next few days, now the word was out about Glyn.

*Angel Pen Ffordd a Diawl Pen Pentan.* That was what they said around here. An old Welsh saying. An angel in the community, the devil himself at home.

Glyn Evans, the life and soul of the party. The hard-drinking, sweet-singing, loud-laughing, larger-than-life character that he was.

Jac took out the crumpled scrap of envelope and thought about what he was about to do.

Taking a gulp of his ale, he began carefully tapping out the message on his mobile phone.

They'd be the first words of his that she'd actually read.

# CHAPTER 4

---------*---------

I stare hard at the text that has pinged in on my charging phone, trying to focus on the words.

I notice there are lots of missed calls too. One from Seb, some also from home, and from another number with the same area code.

Something has happened and I feel too tipsy to deal with it. More than tipsy. Things are spinning slightly as I try to focus on the text.

*'Annie, it's about your Dad. Call me. Please. Jac.'*

Jac.

Before I think about it, I press to call the number, buoyed up by my mojito buzz.

"Annie? Is that you?"

"Yes."

I can hardly breathe. Hearing him say my name, after all these years, sends a shudder of electricity through me.

This is ridiculous. I hate Jac, I remind myself.

"Uh… have you been trying to get hold of me? I've loads of missed calls. What's happened?"

"Hold on… Don't hang up."

He sounds like he's in a bar.

The line goes silent for a minute, then I hear his voice again.

"Annie, how are you?"

It's quieter now; like he's gone outside. His voice is strangely reassuring after my God-awful day.

"I'm fine."

"You sound odd. Kinda slurred."

I clear my throat and try to speak slower; articulating my words more roundly, trying to sound sober.

"I'm tired, that's all. How are you, Jac? How are you liking farming?"

He cuts across the pleasantries.

"Annie, it's Glyn. The police have been trying to contact you. He's... he's dead, Annie. He killed himself."

"I..."

I can't speak and it's silent at his end too.

We listen to each other in the silence, until I'm sure he hears me crack as the news sinks in. It's a slight whimper escaping from somewhere deep, and I cough it away.

"Jac..."

"I'm sending Callista 'round. She'll be with you soon."

Did he hang up or did he lose signal?

Either way, the call's ended; and the dizziness is back with a vengeance.

Is it from the alcohol and lack of food? Is it from hearing about Dad? Or, is it from hearing Jac's voice again, after all this time?

He didn't say what happened, and I can't call Mam. Not like this.

I lie down on the sofa, still in the dark.

Taking in the news.

Thinking about Dad.

Mam.

Home...

A shrill buzzing makes me jump awake; disoriented, but sober now.

Wiping the dribble off my face, and smoothing down my hair, I get up off the sofa.

It's still dark, and I stumble to grab my phone as I go to answer the door.

It's only eleven. Not quite the wee small hours yet. The early drinking with Stacey makes it feel much later.

The buzzer sounds again.

"Alright... I'm coming."

It's probably a pizza delivery for someone in the other flats.

"Annie, let me in."

Callista's voice calls through the intercom and I buzz her in.

The news hits me again, like a mid-afternoon hangover. Dad.

"Annie! My darling. Come here."

Callista's arms feel warm and familiar as she holds me, letting the wave of emotion that smashes into me ride out as I break down in her arms.

"How did you...?"

"Jac called me."

I try to recover, brushing away the hair that has become plastered on my wet face. Wiping my eyes with the back of my hand.

Callista goes to the bathroom to get me a tissue.

"D'you know what... how he...?"

Callista shifts a little uncomfortably.

"No, sweetie. Just that he ended it."

I feel her eyes on me. Like her son Jac's; they are dark and impenetrable, making her appear deep and thoughtful.

"How was he at Christmas?"

"He was in a low phase, depressed. Spent most of his time getting pissed."

"And your mother?"

"*Ah*, ya know, Mam's Mam."

I don't mean to sound dismissive. Callista's rushed across London to be with me. It's the least I can do to be nice. She's one of the few people who know us. The real us. The real Glyn. The real Maureen. The real me.

"She looked tired. She's lost a lot of weight since I was home last."

It had been the same old story at Christmas. We'd spent most of the time skirting around the elephant in the room. The elephant sitting next door drinking in front of the TV, to be exact. Dad.

On Christmas Eve, after he'd left for The Cross Keys, I sat in the kitchen with her, trying to persuade her to leave him. To come live with me, or even Callista, here in London.

But, Mam had just smiled and carried on obsessively with her knitting. She makes hats and cardigans for premature babies, and still visits the hospital to catch up with her old workmates.

Callista goes over to the kitchen area in search of coffee. She's sussed that I've been drinking.

"How's the married man?"

"I ended it today."

I shrug.

"Probably cost me my job."

"How's that?"

"It's a long story."

She frowns.

"Well, whatever happens, I'm glad you finally came to your senses. He sounded like a self-absorbed prat to me. You deserve so much better, sweetie."

She knows everything about me. Too much, really. But she always has. It was Callista who picked up the pieces after Jac, her son, left. In many ways, and not just geographically, she's been closer to me than my mother's ever been.

"So what you gonna do?"

"Call Mam first thing. Get the train home."

She senses me tensing.

"And how do you feel, about seeing Jac again?"

"Cal!"

Callista is usually careful never to mention her son, unless I ask first.

"Annie, you need to face it. You've been ignoring the fact that Jac is back at the farm. He's gonna be there. On the yard. You'll probably see him tomorrow."

I chew it over. This ridiculous block that I've built up in my mind about him.

"Hmm."

"And, you'll probably need a lift from the station, now your Dad's…"

She didn't finish.

I sob and look away.

"Sorry."

"Annie; don't fight it. You must grieve. And it's perfectly natural to feel mixed emotions, after what he's done to you and your mother."

"It's hard. Is it wrong to love him, in spite of everything? And to feel relieved too… that he's gone?"

"No honey, it's not. Whatever you do, don't feel guilty about the things he did to you."

But I do. And while I've been away in New York and London, I've left Mam to deal with him all on her own.

"Cal… Seeing Jac again, terrifies me."

Callista takes our coffees and places them on the side table. With her arm around me again, she hushes me, like I'm a small child.

"It's been twelve years. You've both changed so much. Give him a chance to be your friend again."

I calm down and we sit for a while in silence, drinking our coffee.

"Annie, he'd joined up. He had to go."

"He should have told me he was going. Not slip away like he did, in the middle of the night."

"Darling, you have to let it go. Jac needed to get out, see the world as much as you did."

"It still hurts. The way it happened. The way he did it."

"The way you let him go too, you mean?"

Exactly. Trust Callista to see right through me.

"You're scared… in case he's still angry with you?"

She hugs me tight.

"You both need to talk about it."

I've never opened any of his letters.

For over two long years, he'd written them regularly from the army base. And they sit in their sealed envelopes. Mam's piled them in a neat stack on the antique dresser. He must have seen them when he's been in the kitchen.

Callista changes the subject, trying to cheer me up by telling me all the latest about her charity supporting vulnerable women in North London, where she lives now.

I'm a little embarrassed because it's been so long since I was over there, helping her fundraise. The stories of some of the women are so inspirational. Especially the ones who've been brave enough to leave abusive relationships.

I've run away too, but there's only been cowardice on my part. I've been too chickenshit to go back and help Mam.

Callista mentions Sam, her new partner. Jac met her at Christmas. He was in London when I was in Wales. We must have passed each other on the train.

"Does Jac ever ask about me?"

Callista gazes at me wisely.

"He's as stubborn as you are, darling. And just as curious. Though, like you, he'd never admit it."

# CHAPTER 5

---------✳---------

My grief is messy, but Callista has helped me to realise that it was bound to be like this.

We stayed up talking through the night and I cried some more. Much more.

And by the morning, I'm a little wrung out and strung out, but it has definitely helped me to sort my tangle of emotions about Dad.

My father, the vulnerable man battling with alcoholism and his mental health, and Daddy the monster with the belt strap. I can't help but love him and hate him at the same time. But above all, I feel immense pity for him. How depressed and isolated must he have been.

He had manic times. The sleepless nights and the crazy projects. Like, the three days and nights he spent knocking stuff together in the far shed, making a commercial chicken unit. Of course, he finally crashed. The shed was never finished, and chicken farming was never mentioned again.

But, the depression was far worse. Then, he'd be hitting the bottle hard at home, and that was when the belt came out. He'd flare up at the slightest thing.

Callista used to call him a functioning alcoholic. He never had hangovers and was still doing farm jobs and getting about, if he wasn't at his blackest. The farm gradually deteriorated as Dad got worse. The stock numbers declined every year. The fencing needed patching up, and the fields became poached and weedy.

I speak briefly with Mam on my way to the train station. I can tell she's teary as she tells me the news, and she's pleased I'm coming home.

I hate to admit it, but I can't deny it either. Part of me is glad that Glyn has passed. The other part of me grieves for the man I worked with every day on the farm. Lambing, driving the tractor, feeding the sheep.

Then, as if I wasn't already feeling enough emotional turmoil, Callista casually drops the bombshell that Jac is picking me up from the station. Telling me it's cold turkey. We have to meet, and it may as well be like this, so I'll just have to suck it up.

Brutal but true.

I can't go on hiding from him forever, I suppose. Still, it doesn't stop my stomach from clenching as I stare out of the train window, getting ever closer to the end of the line.

Exhausted from lack of sleep, I've bunched my jacket into a pillow. But every time I close my eyes, Jac's there, floating through my thoughts.

Us, messing around together on the farm. Swimming in the river. Hanging out on our last day together. Before he deserted me.

I remember climbing up to the craggy outcrop. The highest point on our farm. Through the bracken, up onto the mountain tops. From there, you can see for miles. It was always our favourite place to go, and I'd spotted him sitting up there, on our ledge, as I'd driven around the fields.

There was something different about him. And as I got closer, I could see what it was; he'd shaved his head.

Of course, that was a sign, I totally missed.

I sat down beside him and studied the pencil sketch he was busy drawing. A lapwing. My favourite bird. They were nesting in the heathers and tufts of grass below the rocks.

He bit his lip as his pencil lightly brushed the paper, carefully shading in the feathers of the wing.

"Hey!... D'you like it?"

I rubbed his head playfully with my hand, feeling its prickliness. It made him look tougher.

"What? The drawing? Or this?"

He carried on etching with focussed intent.

"What happened to the hippy drifter look?"

Callista and her son Jac had rocked up at our hill farm five years before, looking to rent somewhere remote and rural. Off the grid.

"Does Ellie like it?"

"Dunno. Split up with her last month."

He shot me a look, a grin I can still remember. It made me squirm. The secret crush I had for him had been killing me.

I recovered myself.

"And, you never told me? Thought I was your mate?"

His head bent over again, his eyes focussed hard on the sketch.

"So... How's it going with Lizard Man?"

It's what I'd been calling Alun, the next-door neighbour's son I'd been dating more off than on since Christmas.

"Trying to avoid him."

Alun's hands were always cold and clammy, and his overly eager tongue made me feel like I was kissing something vaguely reptilian.

Jac carried on making light strokes, creating depth to the plumage.

"You're bonkers not going to Art School. You could still apply."

High school had been over for a couple of weeks. Our final exam papers had been sent off; our fate was being decided with a red pen.

"Your A in Art's already in the bag."

"What you been up to?"

"Dad's got me on maggot watch."

"Found any?"

"Yeah, I've treated three lambs."

I eased myself up off the rocky ledge onto my feet.

"Wanna come for a ride?"

33

Nodding, Jac packed his sketchpad and pencils in his bag; but stayed sat where he was, gazing out at the mountains around us.

Reaching up, he suddenly grabbed my hand, pulling me back down to sit with him. Making me giggle.

"Annie... This view... This place... Here... It's so special to me."

Waves of green, rugged Welsh mountains stretched around us. Out west, in the distance, we could see the grey-blue sea.

He still held onto my hand.

But, then he was always tactile. Putting his arm around me when we walked or watched a film together in the static caravan, where he lived with Callista. And it was my favourite place to be, with my head on his chest as we sat stretched out watching TV.

I'd always been closer to him than anyone else. Even the numerous girls he'd gone out with.

And yet, thinking back, how well did I know him? Really?

He faced me. And stared at me; curiously, intensely, making me blush.

His deep chocolate eyes sent my pulse secretly racing as I felt the charge between us. Did he feel it too?

"What's up, Jac?"

He squeezed my hand.

"Nothing. It's nothing. Come on."

He jumped up. Standing, he pulled me to my feet too, and we raced and skidded down the rocky scree back to the quad.

Hopping on, we did the usual tour of the fields on the farm bike, and Jac helped me feed the fat lambs in the lower paddock that had been drawn for early sale.

"You up for shearing next week?" I called over my shoulder as I steered the quad back towards the static.

He didn't reply, so I took it as a yes.

Dad had been giving him paid jobs. I knew only too well that Dad wasn't the easiest to work for, but he said Jac was a good worker. Plus, he made a refreshing change from all the bloody women around the farm, he half-joked.

I pulled the quad up.

The outside of their place was lined with pots of pink geraniums and Buddhist prayer flags. Inside was as colourful too, with bright crocheted blankets and tie-dyed cushions that Callista had made herself.

I always felt much happier there than at the farm.

Callista was doing yoga naked on a mat behind the caravan. Neither of us raised an eyebrow. We'd seen it all before. Plenty of times.

"See ya tomorrow, Jac."

Jac hopped off the back of the bike.

"Ya doin' anything tonight?"

"Making tea. Avoiding Dad 'til he goes out or passes out. Whichever comes first."

Jac shrugged. His mother. My father.

"How about meeting up at the cottage?"

I pulled a face.

We'd been there a few times, but not since the time we drank too much cider and he'd kissed me.

"I'm not sure."

It had made things super-awkward between us for a good while until eventually, I'd told him it was all a huge mistake, a big regret on my part.

We were just friends after. But, I'd often wondered what would have happened if I'd have told him the truth. That I thought about that kiss every day. There was no way at the time, though, that I was going to be another one of Jac Jones' conquests.

It feels ironic now, when I think about that. I should have trusted my gut.

"Come on, Annie," Jac persuaded me. "We're not little kids anymore. You're off to uni soon, and I'm… *hey*, you're my best mate, I need to talk to you. It's important."

I caved in.

"Okay. But no cider."

His cheeky grin back at me made my heart thump even harder.

I remember feeling so nervous about meeting him that evening. Perhaps, deep down, I suspected what was going to happen?

In retrospect, it had been building up; him and me. No way, were we ever purely friends. And, I was praying something would happen too, even though the powerful feelings I had for him scared me.

I put on my new denim shorts, a vest top with a cute shirt hanging loosely around it. I wanted to look good, without him realising I'd made an effort. The humiliation of being rejected would have been too much to bear.

"I'm off out," I called to Mam as I passed through the kitchen. "Dad's had his lasagne and there's a plate for you in the oven."

"Thanks, love."

She'd just come in from a busy shift at the hospital, and the theme tune of her favourite soap was playing on the television in the kitchen. Both of us avoided the living room. I'd learned the hard way not to disturb Dad when he was tanked up.

I was glad to be escaping soon, and I honestly wasn't sure if I'd come back.

In the end, I didn't.

From the footpath, I saw Jac sitting on the garden wall by the whitewashed cottage. A bag by his side.

"What you got there? *Ah, no!* Please don't tell me you've brought cider?"

I landed a playful thump on his back and snatched the bag off him.

He wrestled it back, and then took the large front door key from my hand, opening the bright-red cottage door.

"You sure you wanna sit in here?" I grumbled, rubbing my nose to relieve the peppery itchiness triggered by the sooty air.

"It's lovely out. Why d'you wanna sit in this damp place?"

He retrieved a box of matches from the bag.

"It'll be better once I get a fire going."

Soon, Jac had a small collection of dry sticks alight in the old stove. The flames crackled as the fire took hold. The air in the cottage quickly lifted, and the thick stone walls started to heat. It began to feel cosy.

We sat on an ancient chesterfield sofa. There were cushions and an old Welsh woollen blanket. The place was still furnished as my uncle had left it. It had been rented out a few times over the years, but no one stayed long. Callista said she preferred the static.

Opening his backpack, Jac revealed his swag.

"Oh Jesus, Jac. Is that Cal's elderberry wine? Even Dad won't touch that stuff."

"Chicken."

Rising to the challenge, I fished out the two tin mugs that he'd stashed in the bag.

Sitting, huddled up together on the scratched green leather sofa, we drank Callista's potent homebrew, chatting and laughing about people from school.

And still, he said nothing. Even though I could sense his mood darkening, growing more pensive.

"This is great."

Shifting to face me, that curious look had come over him again. My eyes met his, and I shuddered. But I held his gaze, emboldened by the wine, enjoying the spark that always crackled between us like the sticks in the fire. I was pretty certain this time, he was feeling it too.

"What's up, Jac? You've been acting weird today."

He gazed into my eyes but didn't answer.

His fingers lightly caressed my cheek. His arm encircled me, pulling us closer.

"You're the only one for me, Annie."

As I tried to comprehend what that meant, his lips grazed softly against mine. They felt warm and familiar.

The kiss deepened.

This is what I'd been longing for. My stomach flipped. New thrilling emotions, as I sensed the passion for him rising within me, stirring me in a way that only he ever made happen.

And I felt his hands on me, as we kissed, tentatively exploring my vest top. His mouth moving to my neck and ear, flooding me with such lust it drove me on too. My hands touched his skin, grazing the contours of his chest underneath his t-shirt.

He pulled it off.

"Jac!"

"Annie, d'ya wanna stop?"

"No."

Nevertheless, my words slipped out nervously as he began where he'd left off, trailing his mouth along my collarbone.

"I just don't want it to be like last time."

He stopped.

"Annie, we were both confused back then. But I've wanted this for a long time."

"You have?"

"Yeah."

"And you?"

I can't lie.

"Yeah. Me too."

"No regrets this time, then?"

I quivered, overcome.

"No. No regrets."

His forehead touched mine.

"The time wasn't right before."

"It is now?"

"It has to be."

We kissed again, his hands removing my shirt, my top, unhooking my bra.

"Annie, have you ever…?" he whispered huskily.

I felt my cheeks burn up. His bare chest was enough of a distraction, but now this.

I hadn't. And he knew it.

"D'ya wanna?"

I kissed him deeply in affirmation.

"Tell anyone you popped my cherry and I'll tell everyone your full name, Jacaranda Jones."

He winced, and I covered my breasts with my arm.

He moved it gently away.

"You're so beautiful, Annie. Let me see you, properly."

He put his lips to my skin. My arm, my shoulder, the nape of my neck, my back.

"What are these?"

I tensed up, suddenly self-conscious as his mouth found the deeply indented marks on my shoulder blade where the belt buckle had caught and dug deep into my flesh.

I shook my head. Tears were threatening to well up.

"It's okay. Don't be ashamed, Annie. But, you gotta get out of there. Promise me, you will?"

Placing the blanket and cushions on the floor by the stove fire, he took me by the hand down onto them. And lying there together, he steered me with him into uncharted waters.

It was very late when we finally made our way back across the fields, our fingers entwined tightly together.

The moon was high in the sky, its full light eerily peaceful. I remember thinking about what we'd done; a surge of new emotions racing through me.

He walked me to the farmhouse door, then pulled me close to him for one long, knowing kiss.

"I'll never forget tonight, Annie. It's a promise between us. Trust me."

"I do," I replied breezily, trying to play down everything I felt for him. "See ya tomorrow."

He kissed me passionately as if he never wanted to let me go.

I held his face and brought my lips to his, one last time.

Tearing myself away from his magnetic arms, I left him standing on the doorstep.

And I snuck up to bed, wrapped in blissful smugness, completely unaware that by morning he'd be gone.

Waiting for me as the dawn broke, propped up by the front door, was an A4 envelope. Inside, was the lapwing perfectly sketched, and a letter.

I was his soulmate, he said. He loved me. But he had to go. He'd joined the army, and he wasn't coming back.

Callista dealt with me that day too.

And the poor lapwing. It lay strewn across my bedroom floor in soggy ripped-up fragments, alongside his shredded words.

The train begins to slow down. It's the end of the line. As far west as you can get without ending up in the Irish Sea.

People are beginning to shift in their seats, getting their stuff together, putting on their coats.

But, I sit tight.

My heart is thumping, and I feel like I might vomit.

I'm about to see him again.

# CHAPTER 6

--------- ✴ ---------

I sneak a sideways glance at him as we sit alongside each other in the Land Rover. I'm trying to act casual, and failing miserably.

It's been an awkward first meet up, and then a mad dash through the freezing rain. And I can sense his eyes still on me.

"What you staring at?"

"Nothing. Sorry; it's odd, that's all… seeing you after all this time. You're looking well."

What does 'well' mean?

"I'm looking like a drowned rat, more like."

My emotions are all over the place, and I'm quelling the instinct rising up in me to bolt.

Of course, he's different now.

He's filled into his height, and he's broad and much more muscular. And he has stubble. It suits him. Gives him that sexy just-got-out-of-bed look.

I check myself. *What am I doing?*

I venture another glance his way, and his mouth curls.

"What?"

"Your accent. You sound almost English."

"Hmph."

I take my soggy coat off and place it on my knee, right next to the man I've been avoiding for so long.

The rain batters onto the windscreen, and we're both sitting awkwardly; half-drenched, shivering, unsure of what to say.

Twelve years apart is a long time. And Callista's right. He has changed.

We both have.

He switches the wipers on full speed and takes an old tea-towel to the steamed-up windows. Then, turning on the ignition, he sticks the Land Rover into reverse, and I catch him sneaking another peek at me as he checks his rear-view and side mirrors.

"Your hair. It's different. Smoother."

"It's called straighteners, Jac."

That sounded stuck-up.

"Bet it's curling in all directions, like it used to do," I add, trying to soften what I'd said.

"I liked it that way."

We drive in sticky silence through the town, then out onto the open road towards the hills.

"Glyn? How'd it happen?" I finally pipe up.

No one's told me the details, and I couldn't ask Mam when I phoned.

"He hung himself off the beam in the shed."

"And Mam? How's she?"

"The police stayed with her most of yesterday. She's holding up. Starting to get calls from neighbours."

I stare out of the window.

"Thank you, Jac."

It pierces the tension between us.

"What for?"

His voice sounds gravelly.

"For picking me up today. For always going out of your way to help them both. For sending Callista 'round to look after me last night."

The lump in my throat makes it hard to talk.

Stretching across, he presses my hand, his eyes still on the road.

His touch shocks me; I recoil on reflex, and he fixes it firmly onto the steering wheel, focussing on the road.

"Don't thank me," he utters gruffly. "Your mam asked me to

call Cal. And anyway, I'm your parents' tenant and they've been good to me."

He's slapped me down. He's very clear. He's helped me as an obligation to them.

We switch to farm talk. Safer ground.

"How's the stock?"

"I'm up to a thousand ewes now."

"Not bad."

"Yeah, it's double what I had last year. And with better fencing, reseeding and rotation, I think I can double it again. How many other ex-squaddies would have a chance like this?"

"Sounds like you've got it all figured out."

"Only when it comes to sheep."

Momentarily, his eyes move off the road and onto me.

Dark and unfathomable, the same as before.

He can still stir me in ways he has no idea about, and my nerves jangle the whole journey back to the farm.

Mam is waiting at the front door as the Land Rover pulls up onto the yard. I'm sure that she's been watching out for our arrival.

I hold my breath.

"It'll be alright, Annie."

His gentle voice makes my pulse race, and I quickly get out of the cab.

"Thanks again for the lift."

Jac watched Annie as she got out of the Land Rover.

The rain was petering out, and the yard was strewn with shiny puddles from the heavy downpour. Even wet from the rain, Annie was stunning.

This Annie was a far cry from the motorbike-riding tomboy he'd known before. London had rubbed off on her. Her smooth highlighted hair, and her manicured nails. That expensive-looking cashmere sweater she was wearing. He'd noticed how perfectly it fitted around the contours of her breasts. And the pair of tight jeans she had on. His eyes had feasted appreciatively on the way they hugged her shapely curves.

There was no denying it, this new polished Annie looked fantastic.

He climbed out of the cab to give her a hand with her things.

Stowed away behind his seat, was a plastic bag full of the unopened letters he'd written to her. He'd asked Maureen for them that morning. They'd sat on the dresser waiting for her to read them for a decade. It was too late now.

But still, he couldn't leave things like this.

"Come and see me. At the cottage."

"I don't think that's a good idea."

He caught the hint of a smirk on her lips. She remembered.

"Just tea or coffee this time. Scout's honour."

She returned him a sassy smile and met his gaze with a confidence that she'd not had before.

"Jac Jones, you were *never* a Boy Scout."

It was still there.

His heart bounced as they stood transfixed by each other. The air sizzling between them. Neither of them willing to look away.

"Annie!"

She screwed her nose up a fraction and gave Jac a smile. Then, rushing across the yard to find Maureen, she dropped her bag onto the wet concrete and hugged her mother tightly.

Maureen, in turn, held on to Annie, not letting her go.

There were no words to end their embrace, just the lightest touch of her mother's hand on Annie's face, as she beckoned her inside.

Driving away, Jac watched through the mirror as Annie disappeared with Maureen into the farmhouse.

Before the door closed behind them, he was sure that she'd turned to watch his Land Rover go.

"I'm very sorry about your father."

"Thank you. Come on in."

I hold the door open, but the scruffy-looking detective remains fixed on the front doorstep. I'm not sure if he's checking me out, or if he thinks I might be a vampire inviting him over the threshold to steal his soul. Something is holding him back.

"When did you get here?"

"Yesterday."

"You've got company?"

He gestures at the two cars parked up by the house.

"Is now a good time to talk?"

"It's fine. I think having people visit is helping Mam."

Ellis nods. He understands how close the community is around here. Mainly farming families.

"Can you give me an update?"

"Sure," he says a little stiffly. "If you like, I can show you where *he*... where *it* happened?"

I'm glad of the chance to get out of the house.

"Hold on, while I get my coat."

We set off across the yard and he seems to relax a little.

"You get home often?"

"No. Not much at all. I've been busy with work," I answer a little guiltily. "I don't get much time off."

"Your mother says you were living in New York?"

"Yes, for three years. I've lived in London, mainly. After uni, I never came back."

I pause; then add by way of explanation, "There wasn't much keeping me here."

"Your father? Did he ever try to get help?"

I'm not sure how much he knows.

"You mean medical?"

"For his depression."

That's what this is about. His reticence. He's fishing about Glyn.

I'm not going to sugar-coat it. The policeman needs to hear the truth.

"Glyn was ill. He was bi-polar and that's a difficult condition for anyone to manage. But, my father was a nasty bastard too."

The detective's eyes widen.

"In what way?"

I can tell Mam's not told him. Typical.

"You didn't want to cross him when he was drinking heavily. And Mam, me, even the poor old dog, got the scars to prove it. I can show you if you want?"

"Did you ever report it? Call the police?"

The look on my face, answers the question for him.

He changes tack.

"Did he ever try to kill himself before?"

"No idea. Mam would never have told me."

"No?"

I find myself staring at my nails.

"No. She… uh… she likes to keep things private. That's part of the problem."

If we didn't talk about it, it never happened.

"So, people 'round here didn't know what Glyn Evans was really like? Is that what you're saying?"

"Pretty much. His mates in The Cross Keys, bet they said  he was the life and soul of the party. A real character."

"Did your dad go into town often?"

"Why?"

"Just establishing his routines, that's all."

It's a bit of a random question. I'm getting the sense that this isn't just a casual chat.

"He went every week. Since Mam retired, they do a trip into town together for supplies on market day. He liked to go to the mart to see his farmer buddies, while Mam did the shopping."

"Your mother seems close to Jac?"

"We've known Jac for years. Lived in that static over there as a kid."

I point to the ramshackle mobile home at the far end of the track. It probably needs scrapping by now.

"And, do you know a Callista Jones?"

"Yes."

Again it's unrelated. How did he know Callista?

"She's Jac's mother. Lives in London. She stayed with me the night I found out about Dad."

The detective scribbles in his pad.

"Hmm... that explains the call. You're still in touch."

He's not making much sense.

"So, where did it...?" I ask, looking around.

"There."

He points up to the old grey beam.

"How?"

"With a rope. He used a stepladder to climb up. Then, kicked it away."

I stare coldly at the space.

I feel nothing. Just the chill from the realisation that death has happened here.

"Was your dad ever in the navy?"

"No. Why?"

The detective stares up at the beam as he floats the question.

"The knot he used. It's not a common one."

"He was a practical man. Had to be, farming this place. And bloody-minded too. If he decided he wanted to end it, he would've planned it out. Found the best knot."

"Planned it enough to have thought about the rope?"

"I imagine so. Why?"

"It was a specialist climbing rope, that's all. Strong enough to hold his weight."

"Yes. Glyn would have thought through the details. Made sure he did it properly."

The detective turns and stares at me searchingly.

"Why then, d'you think he was still wearing his slippers?"

"If he was gonna end it, why would he care what he was wearing?"

"Fair point."

He turns to leave the shed and I follow him out.

"The post-mortem results show probable cause of death as hanging. There'll be an inquest, but the coroner should release the body soon."

Back to reality, and the practical matter of dealing with Dad's body, and the funeral.

Ellis Roberts leaves me by the farmhouse door. I blustered through his questions, but what he'd said about the climbing rope doesn't sit right. It wasn't Dad's style.

Something's off, but I won't be losing any sleep over it.

Mam's looking pale, I think, as we eat supper together.

She's pushing the food around the plate and has been chewing the same mouthful for an age.

"Come on, Mam. You've lost weight since Christmas. You need to eat."

"Don't you be worrying about me, cariad."

A lump forms in my throat when I hear her use the Welsh word for 'love'. No one calls me 'cariad', except her.

"You're looking thin."

"I'm fine."

It's the same steely impenetrable wall I've faced for years.

"Okay, Mam. What do I know? You're the nurse."

I thought Dad's death might have changed things. But no, the defences are back up again. Something's going on with her too, I'm sure of it.

I take our plates over to the sink.

"I'm going out after."

The bowl fills with hot soapy water.

"I'm gonna see Jac. For a catch-up."

"About time too."

She grabs a tea towel to dry the dishes.

"He took his letters back, Annie."

"What?"

The top of the dresser's clear. I hadn't even noticed that they'd gone.

"When?"

"The day you arrived."

"You were too hard on him for all those years. Remember, Annie; you left too."

"Fancy coming out for a drink?"

As I stand at the door in front of him, my traitorous heart skips a beat.

He's surprised to see me.

"Yeah, okay," he says huskily.

I must have woken him up. Or, maybe I've called it wrong, and he was only being polite? He didn't mean it when he said to come over and see him.

Nervous, my mouth rattles on, "I figured it was safer to go out, than stay here drinking your mother's elderberry homebrew."

I instantly feel my cheeks redden, and my pulse races as his mouth forms a quizzical smile.

*Dammit!* Now, he thinks I'm chasing him.

The pub's busy. It's Friday night and there's a crowd in for food.

Jac stands by the bar trying to get served, and I use the opportunity to check my phone and emails. It's annoying that this is the only place where I can do that. It doesn't take long. No one's called, and there's nothing of interest in my inbox.

Jac comes back from the bar, placing two pints of real ale on the table. And suddenly, I've absolutely no idea what to talk about.

"How's Maureen doing?" he asks, kicking off the convo.

It's as good a place to start as any, and I don't pull any punches.

"I'm worried about her, Jac. She seems different."

"We both know why that is."

He understands the tensions of living with my father's unpredictable mood swings.

"I mean, she's warmer with me than she's been in years. But, there's something she's hiding from me, Jac... D'ya think she's lost weight?"

"Hard to tell, 'cos I see her most days. But, now you mention it, yes she has."

"And she's tired all the time… what if she's sick?"

"Don't worry. It's sure to be all the stress and grief. She's mixed up too. She must have loved him. She stayed with him for all those years."

What he says makes perfect sense.

"The police came to see me today. A young detective."

"Ellis Roberts?"

"Yeah, that's him."

"He spoke to me too… What did he say?"

"Couldn't work out why Dad used climbing rope to hang himself."

Jac pulls a face, but I shrug it off.

"Ah well. That's my dad for you. Nothing was ever straightforward. The post-mortem confirms suicide."

"It'll be better once the funeral's been."

"That's what everyone says."

Jac looks down into his pint glass.

"So, how's Callista? You see her more than me."

I can't help but smile.

"She says hello… She tells me that you used to ask about me."

"It was the only way I could find out how you were. You never answered my letters. Or even bothered to read them."

There it is. The sucker punch. He's still angry with me.

I play nervously with a beer mat, as his judgement weighs down on me. Words dry up and we both resort to drinking our beer.

Finally, he breaks the drought.

"Game of pool?"

As the pub closes, we walk slowly back along the lane towards the cottage. We've had a nice time, and I'm surprised. I thought it'd be more difficult. Playing pool helped, even though he pretty much thrashed me every game.

Reaching the cottage, I turn from him to go up the footpath through the fields. It's a muddy shortcut back to the farm.

"See you, Jac. You've gotten a whole lot better at pool, since I saw you last."

He gazes down at me, wrapped up in my padded coat and woolly hat.

"Wanna coffee?"

The invitation comes out of nowhere. Even Jac looks shocked he's said it.

I think about it for a second. We do need to clear the air, even though the safer thing would be to go home.

"Alright... A coffee'd be good."

As Jac goes through into the kitchen, I sit on that same old chesterfield. The fire has just about kept in and the place is cosy. I place some kindling on it and rake it with the poker until the orange embers reignite, bursting into yellow flames.

Grazing my knuckles over the mustard Welsh tapestry blanket, its woollen harshness on my skin jolts me back to the time I was here last.

The place is different now, though. It's cosy. The living room is freshly painted and there are radiators. And the back wall is covered in black-framed pictures, mainly of birds.

Walking over to one, my breath catches. Another lapwing. Identical to the one he drew for me.

"Your favourite bird," he says softly, behind my shoulder.

I shudder and turn. He's holding our coffees.

"You still draw?"

"Yeah. A bit."

"That's good... I'm sorry about your lapwing."

He looks at me puzzled.

"The one you drew for me? I ripped it up, together with your letter, when I was mad at you."

"You still mad at me?" he rasps.

"No," I breathe. "Not anymore."

"That's okay, then. I can pop them out to order. You can have that one if you like?"

"I daren't risk it."

He sets down his coffee, and I go back to the sofa.

"Excuse me for a minute, while I go and see if Jess is alright?"

"Jess?"

It never even occurred to me that he might have a girlfriend. Why didn't Callista tell me?

His face breaks into a smug grin.

"Jess… my dog."

I smile down at my coffee, embarrassed for the jealous wave that washed over me. And for being so easy to read.

"I should go."

The dog gives me an excuse to leave, but I don't want to either.

"Stay. I'll be two seconds."

"Can I use your bathroom?"

"Yeah, sure. Upstairs on the left."

Putting my coffee down, I go through to the kitchen. He's put in new units and the wooden worktops are spotless and clear.

I drift upstairs to use the toilet. It's a man's bathroom. There are no female items in the cabinet.

There are two bedrooms, and the door to one is open.

His bedroom?

The bed is immaculately made. Smooth and tightly tucked in. All his clothes are stowed away. Army training, I presume.

Then, I catch sight of them. On top of the chest of drawers lie a neatly stacked pile of letters.

His letters to me.

All those years that they've sat unopened on our kitchen dresser. Like a battle of wills, Jac versus me. And suddenly… *now*… I have an overwhelming urge to read them.

Deep down, I know it's because he doesn't want me to.

Listening out to make certain that he's not back, I steal impulsively into the bedroom and snatch the top letter, stuffing it hastily into the back pocket of my jeans.

At least I will read one, I convince myself.

Moving swiftly back down the stairs, I sit on the sofa waiting for him, slightly out of breath but casually drinking my coffee as he comes back in.

"I should go, Jac."

I conceal the letter in my back pocket with my coat.

"Let me walk you back."

"Don't be silly. Anyhow, I like the dark."

I'm a little disappointed that he doesn't try to persuade me to stay.

"You sure?"

His deep chocolate eyes are gazing down at me again.

"Absolutely. It's just me, the owls and the stars."

"I'll show you around the farm tomorrow morning if you want?"

"I'd like that."

I squash down the guilt, and an impetuous urge to kiss him. The electricity between us; it's thrilling and terrifying. Does he still feel it too?

"Annie, I'm sorry for leaving you."

My eyes fill up in spite of my resolve, and I look away.

"It's okay, Jac. I understand now that you had to go."

I make a hasty exit too.

# CHAPTER 7

---------✳---------

I can hardly wait to get home. It's late and Mam's already in bed; so I creep around the kitchen, getting a knife and slicing open the envelope.

Why did I leave it so long to read his words?

*September 25th, 2007*

*Dear Annie,*

*I hope that this has got to you before you leave for uni. If it hasn't, Happy Christmas!*

*I haven't been able to write to you sooner because I've been on my first ten-week block of training. And it's been hard. I thought I was fit, but you'd never believe the things they've been having me do. I won't bore you with the details, but it's tough, Annie. And if you fail. I can tell you, it's not worth failing. So, I try to keep my head down and get on with the job.*

*So far, I've passed everything with flying colours. And, you know what? Even though it's bloody hard work, I'm really enjoying being in the army, most of the time. Cal would have a fit if I told her that. But, I've got a great bunch of lads with me. And we stick together and help each other get through the stuff that they keep throwing at us.*

*It's dead strict here. A bit of a shocker for the free-ranging son of an eco-warrior, like me. And Sion, my best mate, is the same. The poor sod's been in children's homes since he was twelve. At the start, he put on a big front, like he was this tough guy who'd been on the streets, seen a bit of action. And Boss Man, our corporal, had his eye on him.*

*Last week, Boss Man caught him shooting his mouth off, and he had him spending all of Sunday cleaning the toilet block with a toothbrush. But, we both went at it. When everyone else had some R&R, Sion and me were on our hands and knees scrubbing all day long. That was a bitch. But he's back in the clear, and he's learned to keep his mouth shut when Boss Man's about.*

*I think of you, Annie, all the time. Especially at night. I think about our ledge; the mountains and the sunsets. Of us curled up watching a film. And of us together that night.*

*Thinking about seeing you again keeps me going.*

*Now, for the big stuff. I'm embarrassed to write this, and if you EVER take the Mick out of me, I'll never say it again.*

*Annie, I love you. I always have and I always will.*

*I'm pretty sure that you're still mad at me for going without telling you. I'm sorry. That night was perfect, I couldn't spoil it by telling you I was leaving.*

*The army's good for me. Running around, doing fitness and learning new stuff. It's exciting. Cal freaked out about it, but I was never brainy enough to go to uni, unlike you (smarty pants). And when Cal started talking about going back to the commune for a bit, I went into town and joined up, there and then. And I'm glad I did.*

*Trust me, Annie. Just because I've left the farm, doesn't mean that we can't be together. I hope you can still be my girl, because no matter what, I'll always be there for you.*

*And we can see each other when I get leave.*

*I could come up to see you at uni?*

*I've written down my address.*

*Please write and tell me that everything's still good between us.*

*I'll be waiting for you, Annie.*

*Always.*

*Love you,*

*Jac x*

I reread the letter over again.

And then again.

I find this out now? After all this time.

*Argh!* What an idiot I've been!

My stupid temper and my stubborn pride meant that Jac slipped through my fingers.

I glance up with a start.

Mam's standing there in her nightie, ashen-white in the door frame.

"What you doing up?"

"I could ask you the same thing, love. How was Jac?"

"Good. Helped clear the air a bit. We had a nice time. He's got much better at pool."

"Did he give you one of his letters, then?"

Rubbing my eyes, I'm feeling a little ashamed of myself.

"Don't judge me, Mam. I had to read one."

"Annie! You helped yourself? You had no right."

"Why did you let him take them back?"

"You had your chance."

She's right. I stare at his handwritten words of love in front of me.

"He won't be happy when he finds out you've read them."

"It was just the one. The first one he wrote."

Maureen comes over and lays her hands on my shoulders. It feels so good. A simple touch. A touch that she's denied me for so long. It's like Dad's death has melted her, brought us finally together.

"I should never have left you alone with Dad."

"Shush, love. I wanted you to go. I did my best to make you leave. To get you away from here. Away from him."

"You did?"

She hugs me close and I hold her tight. Making up for the times I was without a mother, even when she was there.

"D'you want a cuppa?"

"I'd say we both need something stronger."

She fetches out a bottle of brandy that's been stashed behind the flour at the back of the cupboard and hands me a glass.

"What if he notices the letter's gone?"

"I think what'll be, will be."

She takes a sip.

"Callista and me, we always laugh about you the two of you. You're both as pig-headed as each other."

"Cal?"

The detective mentioned that she'd called her.

"Yes. Cal's always been there. My rock, she is; bless her. Can't tell you how many times she tried to get me to leave him. You know, when he was sober, he could be very loving too. And what with his illness, and all; he needed me, Annie. I couldn't just up sticks, and go live with Cal. He'd never have coped."

This is all news to me.

"Cal's never told me you were still friends."

"I asked her to keep our little chats to herself. The stuff about your dad. Didn't want the whole world clacking on about it. And she kept me up to date with what you were up to in London. I wanted to come out to New York to see you. But your dad wouldn't have it."

"Ah, Mam, that would've been fun."

Having said that, she'd hardly ever been down to London. There was always an excuse. Work. Dad. The farm. Perhaps, he'd stopped her from going?

"And, what's this she tells me, about a married man?"

My mouth moves like a goldfish.

"Annie! What were you thinking, love?"

I'm stumped, and more than a little bit miffed with Callista for blabbing.

"It's over."

"Good."

She looks at me, her lips curving mischievously.

"Jac used to ask after you."

"Don't get your hopes up there."

I'm eager to scotch any matchmaking before she starts. I gesture to the letter in front of me.

"That ship's sailed, believe me."

His first letter was the heartfelt sentiment of young love, but over the two years of unanswered letters, things will no doubt change.

He'll probably be bitter and twisted by the last one. Full of anger and hate for me. Betrayal, even, by then? I'm sure that there must have been many other women in Jac's life.

And again, I realise how little I know about him.

Sion rubbed his eyes. It was nine am and Jason was long gone; high in the skies over the Atlantic.

Sitting on the leather sofa in the empty London flat, he opened the encrypted message on his laptop.

Every job took meticulous preparation. That was why his clients and his handlers were satisfied. And, why no one had ever been suspicious.

The jobs were coming in regularly, all through trusted recommendations. Then, contact was made; encrypted messaging and burner phones.

He worked hard on being unremarkable. Someone you'd see in a bar and not look twice at. He didn't consider himself especially good looking or ugly. He wasn't especially tall or short, quiet or loud, obnoxious or charming. His forgettable features were his advantage.

He lived with trusted friends. Friends who'd been with him through the fire of combat. His brothers in arms. And when he wasn't with them, he moved around, staying in budget hotels.

He told people he was in computers. It was perfect. No one ever took any interest in what that meant.

When he wasn't away working, he challenged himself with outdoor sports. Hiking, kayaking, climbing. He did odd jobs too. Painting, plumbing, joinery; mainly for friends. He'd helped Jac renovate the old cottage. He'd mended Maureen's boiler and done work around the farmhouse for her.

This job, and most of the others he'd done recently, had been for the main Liverpool outfit, the Scousers. His contact's username was Irish. And from what he could determine, the gang were moving south and were starting to knock heads with some pretty nasty London firms.

The Scousers were early innovators of county lines, a genius business model where drug dealers set up small user networks through provincial towns. They had their foot soldiers all across the North West. Using burner phones, they messaged customers and sent drugs out for delivery, usually via vulnerable kids on bikes.

Kids like he'd once been. The kind of kids that hang around on the street all hours of the day and night, probably in local authority care, or neglected by their dysfunctional families.

The army had saved him. And the street and children's homes had given him the skills to survive. Even if his line of work now was a little unconventional.

He opened the secure link from Irish and read through the information.

His instincts had been right. This job that the Scousers wanted him to do was high risk.

The man's picture in front of him was one Leon Prifti, leader of London's notorious Helbanianz gang. Though he didn't know of Prifti, Sion had heard of the Helbanianz. They'd muscled into the East End of London around ten years back.

Originally from Albania and with established bases in most of the big European capitals, they'd developed a reputation for being a set of serious psychos who you didn't mess with.

Prifti would be a hard man to get at. He carefully read through more background on his operations. It was sketchy stuff at this stage, but at least there was no condition to make it look like an accident.

This job had to be a single clear shot. A sniper's bullet.

Information on the Helbanianz was easy to find. They didn't seem to care about their online profile. With a quick search,

Sion could see that they were prolific on social media. A gun-inspired logo worn like a badge of honour. Gang members paraded openly for selfies, flaunting flashy sports cars. They even made rap videos, for God's sake.

It might be doable.

But the background information described another side to the Albanians too. These guys were nimble multi-country poly-criminals. The gang culture was a distraction, a front. There were brains hiding behind the muscle, and it wouldn't be easy to get at Prifti from the street.

It was a far cry from the East-End gangs of old. The Krays. The Richardsons. The old firms were long gone.

London today was a postcode battleground for the spoils, and the Scousers wanted to send a simple message to the Albanians to get off the patch. They wanted a cut and a sniff of London's five billion pound cocaine trade too. It was bold, he gave them that. It had never been said, but Irish had to be the brains behind the Scouser outfit; he was sure of it.

He got up and opened the cases to examine the kit he'd brought with him. He chose the Barrett M82 semi-automatic with the magnification scope. The sniper's weapon of choice.

Before he'd agree to anything, he would check out a suitable viewing point where he'd study the habits of Prifti, his mark.

And if he couldn't do it? He'd walk away.

"Need a hand? I could do with some fresh air."

Annie strolled over towards Jac and the quad bike.

"You came."

He wasn't sure if she'd show. He wasn't sure why he'd asked her, either. When it came to Annie, his mouth and brain weren't always connected.

And last night, he'd felt an intensity between them that he was sure made her feel uncomfortable too. Afterwards, he'd lain in bed for ages thinking about it. About her.

"Let's go."

The day was fresh and cold. The best that January could offer before the first glimpses of spring arrived. The frost coated the grass, and the morning sun lit the verdant valley in a pale yoke-yellow light. The perfect day to show Annie what he'd done on the farm.

It felt odd. It had always been the other way round. Her on the front, and him riding pillion.

And now, the feeling of her behind him, her thighs brushing against his, it disturbed him. He'd extinguished all hopes, dreams about Annie long ago. Her return was reawakening something he hadn't felt for years. And he didn't like it at all.

Thankfully, Jess hopped on between them, and they set off up the fields; the bags of feed on the back.

"I've forgotten how much I love being out here."

She took a deep breath of the crisp air. Scanning the rolling fields, she pointed towards the new taut pig wire lining the perimeters.

"You've done a lot of fencing."

"Jess was sick of fetching the sheep off the road all the time."

Jac grabbed a bag of sheep nuts off the back of the quad and she did the same, giving him a hand to fill the feeding troughs.

"Have you reseeded those pastures too?"

Jac put the bag down.

"Yes. I have," he said impressed, "And spent all last spring chain harrowing and liming the other fields. They'd gone real rough. The reeds had come back and they'd gotten boggy and wild."

"You've done a great job, Jac."

"Thanks."

He couldn't help but feel a pang of pride as she noticed the results of all the hard work he'd put in.

"Still much more to do, though," he said, clearing his throat.

Out in the fresh air, she'd more colour in her cheeks. Her skin was glowing. She'd always been outdoorsy. London and New York must have been a real culture shock for her.

He told her about the stock he'd bought in the autumn sales and the new breed of rams he'd put in.

"Bigger lambs will help raise profitability."

"But they'll cost you more in feed. And they'll be more tricky to lamb."

She was right. There was that.

"How are those hands of yours?" she joked.

Jac held them up for her.

"Ah! Too big."

She playfully held up her own.

"Now these… these hands here are perfect for lambing."

"I'll bear that in mind when I need help with the night shifts in the lambing shed. Those glued on nails might not be so popular with the ewes."

"*Uch!* There's mud and muck underneath them already."

She laughed at the sorry state of her hands.

"Oh, and one's snapped off."

It was nice talking farming. Bouncing around ideas. He didn't have much opportunity to do that. And Sion didn't know one end of a sheep from the other.

They worked together filling up the creep feeders in the frosty fields and checking on the stock. Lambing was a couple of months away, but the ewes were getting heavier and needed a regular top-up of food.

In her waterproofs and wellies, no one would ever guess that it was the same woman who'd got off the train.

"Do you miss the army?" she asked as they got back onto the yard by the farmhouse.

"Yeah. I was good at it. I miss the boys, more than anything else. Still see some of them from time to time. Sion stays with me a lot. They're like brothers to me. But, I'm glad I left when I did. I always wanted to come back and farm."

"Did you do any tours of duty?"

"Afghanistan twice."

He didn't want to elaborate. There was the good, the bad and the very ugly in his memories of that place.

"Best deployments were Cyprus and Belize."

"Wow. They must have been wonderful experiences."

"Definitely. Especially Belize. I learned to dive out there. The sea's incredible. Different shades of turquoise. So clear. And, marine life... I can't even begin to describe it. Shoals and shoals of fish, all shapes and colours. And turtles. I've got some sketches, if you wanna see?"

He clammed up. He'd gotten carried away.

"I'd like that."

She grinned at him and his gut twisted.

"Bring them over and I'll make you some supper tonight. As a thank you for the lift from the station."

"Annie, you don't need to."

"Don't be daft, I want to."

"Okay. I'll see you later, then."

She was still standing there, like she was reluctant to go.

His pulse was racing, in spite of himself.

"Jac, you apologised last night for leaving me."

He heard her voice faltering as she struggled to find her words.

"I'm sorry too. Sorry, that I never read your letters and that I didn't keep in touch. I know it's no excuse, but I was angry with you."

His throat felt raspy and dry, his heart in his mouth.

"It was a long time ago. Things have changed since then."

The way she'd looked back at him, like she was a little hurt, puzzled him after.

Until he went back to the cottage for lunch. He needed to go to the agricultural merchants, and it was only as he was changing out of his farm clothes, that he noticed.

The letters had been moved.

Not by much, but they weren't stacked as neatly as he'd left them. And upon closer inspection, he realised that there was one letter missing. The one on top. The first.

She'd been there, and she'd helped herself when he'd been out tending to Jess.

All those years when she could have opened them, and yet, she chose to do it now. The day he'd taken them away from her. That was so Annie.

Picking up the pile, he took them downstairs and fed them one by one into the woodburner's fire. Angrily pushing them with the poker, until all his words were eaten up by the flames.

There was only one letter left now. The last one he wrote.

He printed his bitterness onto the back of the envelope.

This thing between them had to end. Now. Before it messed anymore with his head. And his heart.

Slipping it into his coat, he made his way up to the farmhouse and silently posted the final letter through the letterbox. It landed on the hall floor, joining the pile of sympathy cards that had been delivered by the postman.

# CHAPTER 8

---------*---------

Sitting alone in his unmarked police car, Detective Ellis Roberts considered his morning and his lunch as he peeled back the cellophane. Two limp-looking triangles. They didn't quite hold the promise of the label; mature cheddar cheese ploughman's on malted granary bread.

He'd been to all the shops in town that sold climbing rope and none of them stocked it in black. It wasn't an uncommon item, apparently. Just that most climbers used the more colourful ropes. They were easier to see, and sell.

If he had the time to trawl through Glyn Evans' bank accounts, would he find any details of a payment to an outdoor shop? As the farmhouse didn't have any internet, he could hardly have ordered it online.

He could have bought it anywhere. And there'd be no chance of getting the time or manpower he needed to sift through Glyn Evans' farm receipts. Farmers used cash. It could have been bought off the back of a van in the market? Or from a stall in an agricultural show? There were too many possibilities.

And all farmers around here liked a deal. A length of rope on special would be appealing to some. Even if it wasn't to be used for its intended purpose, it'd still be a useful item on the farm.

His daughter hadn't been surprised about it. As she'd said, he was a farmer, he was resourceful.

It wasn't worth spending more time on the rope, he decided, as he took another bite of his soggy sandwich.

Plus, his boss had already told him in no uncertain terms to wrap this one up quickly. The coroner was going with a suicide verdict. The pathologist had confirmed death by hanging. The toxicology reports had come back clear, and Glyn Evans had a long record of medically diagnosed mental illness. His liver was sclerotic, and he had undiagnosed diabetes too. Not uncommon in long-term alcoholics, the pathologist had confirmed when he'd called about the results.

Plus, he was a domestic abuser, by all accounts.

There was no more digging to be done.

Loose ends, like the rope and the slippers, they always bothered him. But not everything in real life could be tidily explained away.

I'm making food in the kitchen when I hear the familiar click of the letterbox.

Wiping my hands, I go into the hall to pick up the post off the floor.

Mam's in the lounge with Auntie Pat. It's been another full-on day of visitors.

I can see a couple of bank letters addressed to Dad, but mostly it's sympathy cards.

And then my heart sinks.

In the middle of the envelopes, there's another one of Jac's letters.

Picking it up, I read the neat writing on the back.

*'You took what didn't belong to you. But, seeing as you've finally started reading my letters, here's the last one. The others are burned.'*

His curt tone is a slap in the face. But, unable to curb my curiosity either, I take it to my bedroom to read.

*June 2010*

*Dear Annie,*

*It's been over two years and I've not had a reply from you. I get the hint, don't worry. You're still angry with me, and Callista tells me you're not reading my letters.*

*You've obviously moved on, and I mean nothing to you. If you can't be bothered, then I'm not going to be some creep who's stalking you. I'm getting on with my life too.*

*I'm off to Afghanistan next week. So, this is goodbye. For real.*

*You were my best mate, Annie, and I loved you. But I was kidding myself. You never felt the same way about me.*

*I'm never being that sucker again.*

*My rule is that I'm taking all my opportunities now. And I've had plenty, Annie. Girls throwing themselves at me. They all love army boys 'round here. Never any numbers. Never get in deep.*

*Cal told me how hurt you were.*

*You're so unbelievably stubborn, you know that?*

*Never bothering to read any of my letters has hurt me too. And this letter's a complete waste of time, anyway. But, I'm writing it for me, not you.*

*I guess, we're quits.*

*Now Cal's moved, I don't suppose I'll see you again.*

*All the best in your life, Annie.*

*Jac*

I stare at the angry and bitter words. My stomach knots; and the empty hollowness, the sadness that's consuming me, makes me sigh out loud.

"This is ridiculous."

I shake myself.

It was years ago. So, why am I doing everything to stop myself from crying?

I've been dumped.

*Argh!* It was me who opened this particular Pandora's box of letters, and here I am getting a taste of my own medicine.

At least I know what happened to Jac Jones. Wounded by me, he turned into a tart. Taking his opporunities. Isn't that what he did with me?

But, putting that aside, what really gets me is that he'd gone off into combat believing that I didn't care about him. I had no idea how much I'd hurt him. Thank God, he came back unharmed.

Wiping my eyes, still bruised and remorseful, I go back downstairs, to the food I'm preparing for us, to put the chicken casserole I've made into the oven.

Not that there's any point. After posting that letter, writing those words, there's absolutely no chance, he'll turn up tonight for a cosy meal for two.

Sion waited on the South Bank by the crowded McDonald's restaurant. London's Embankment was teeming with tourists, even on a grey and drizzly winter's day, like this one.

"Wanna coffee?"

A tall man in jeans and a padded jacket sidled up to him.

"You paying? Or are you still struggling with Government cutbacks?"

"Alright, alright. I agree, it's not exactly The Ivy, but if you wanna go mad I'm sure I can stretch to a cheeseburger."

With the code word *'The Ivy'* confirmed, they sat down at a table in a corner by a group of Japanese students.

It was the perfect venue, so public that people wouldn't pay a blind bit of notice to them. The practised art of intelligence.

He'd been sending in details of his jobs, as instructed, since the start. But, this was the first intervention, and he wasn't entirely comfortable with the development.

The assassination of the Albanian gang leader would be tricky enough, without the added pressure that MI5 wanted a new 'hands-on' approach in his operations. This job was no longer purely about gangs and crime. It was now a question of British national security.

"Why now?"

The spook ignored Sion's question and stirred a sweetener into the paper cup.

"Have you found a place to do the job yet?"

"Yeah. The front of Prifti's property's well-secured. Pretty much impregnable. But they've been very slack at the back. There's no high wire fencing, alarm system or cameras. And best of all, no dogs."

Sion hadn't found anywhere opposite the house. This wasn't like the films, where the sniper set themselves up on a flat rooftop, or across the street in a conveniently located derelict flat. The cocky Albanians had bought a large detached house in London's suburban South Woodford, with electric gates and a big drive filled with a range of premium cars.

"I've been trialling it out. The shrubbery at the back's pretty dense, and there's easy access over a five-foot wooden fence to a back cutting. I can leave a vehicle two streets away, so no problem getting from there quickly. The only hassle is the weight and size of the sniper rifle."

His handler listened carefully.

"You'll need to be outta there fast. Once they spot you, it'll be mayhem. These guys are properly tooled up. Flashy cars ain't the only things they've been collecting."

"Did you see the Tesla?" Sion smirked, "Good to see that they're taking their carbon footprint seriously."

"Yeah. Green gangsters. We've had eyes on Prifti too. He's got minions all over the patch servicing him. Some use cover outfits; fast food shops, that sort of stuff, for laundering. Others swagger around like a biker gang. They're thugs, mostly; doing his dirty work for him."

Concealed in the bushes, Sion had watched the gang through

the large conservatory windows.

"Prifti's a little shy. He doesn't do much out and about stuff, except in the evenings. In general, people tend to visit him at the house."

Over the course of each day, several of the men, including Prifti had used the patio out back to smoke their cigarettes and vapes.

They had strict house rules, it appeared.

The spook looked around uneasily. The Japanese students were taking selfies. The last thing he wanted was him and Sion in shot.

"What'll be interesting is the Scousers' next move after you do the job."

"Think it'll start a turf war?"

"We're depending on it. With Prifti out of the way, the Albanians'll fold like a bad poker hand. We want them out of London, and we'll use all our powers to make that happen."

So, that was why Sion was being pulled in now.

A double whammy.

MI5 wanted to rid London of the Albanians, and the National Crime Agency wanted to see how far up the chain they could go with the Scousers.

Would the Scousers be able to put two and two together?

"Can you guarantee that this won't work its way back to me?"

The spook looked directly at him, reassuringly, "We'll look after you; trust me."

Easy enough for him to say. Sion was the one who was up to his balls in it with the nutters. The fall guy, if this went tits up.

It was a win-win for MI5. If it ever came out, they could brush Sion off as another ex-squaddie diversifying into private security, hired by a criminal gang. MI5 would melt away and Sion would be left high and dry.

Or dead, more likely. And very wet. At the bottom of the river Mersey.

For now, he didn't have to worry about that. All he had to do was to fire the shot, and then get the Hell outta Dodge.

"You came?"

I'm confused. His note on the letter was pretty damning. And the letter he chose, a goodbye.

"Uh... yeah."

He's carrying a folder full of drawings and a bottle of red wine. He stares at me.

"Oh! You didn't think I'd... Look, it's not a problem... I can come another time...don't be..."

"No, no, don't be silly. There's plenty of food. I wasn't sure that's all."

He holds the red wine out towards me. His edginess is making me tense too.

This evening's already a disaster, and I'm sure he's regretting turning up. I can't, for the life of me, work out why he came.

Struggling what to say, I check the rice boiling in the saucepan, hoping I can make it stretch to three.

"Where's Maureen?"

"In the lounge. She wants dinner in front of the telly."

An awkward silence.

He turns his attention to the wine, avoiding the strained atmosphere building between us.

"Corkscrew?"

"Top drawer."

He opens cupboard doors until he has two wine glasses in his hand. He pours one for me.

"You've got a tattoo."

"Yeah, my battalion. Welsh Guards. Got it before my first tour."

He rolls up his T-shirt sleeve for me to see it all. It's inked across on his large bicep.

"Cymru am byth? *Wales forever?* On an English boy like you?"

"Not so English these days," he says warily.

We're skirting around each other, but it's brewing. And I'm struggling, so I check the food and get the plates out.

"Annie?"

His stormy tone sets me even more on edge.

"Hmm?"

"You opened up the past when you decided to help yourself to my stuff."

I can feel my cheeks burning.

"Yeah, about that…"

I take the rice over to the sink and begin draining it through a sieve.

"I shouldn't have…"

"No. You shouldn't," his voice rumbles.

There it is.

Being told off riles me.

I can feel my temper rising.

He's the one that buggered off, right after he screwed me.

A notch on the bedpost.

Like all the other girls he went with after.

"They were *my* letters, Jac! You sent them to *me*."

I start loading the plates noisily with the chicken casserole and rice.

"After ten years of you *not being arsed* to read them, it was only right that they got returned to sender."

I turn to face him full on, a plate of food in my hand.

"*Not being arsed*?" I thunder.

He has no right to talk to me like that.

"That wasn't how it was."

He glowers back at me and I refuse to look away.

"How *was it*, then? Exactly?"

"You broke my heart."

"So… you decided to break mine too."

I look away.

I did step over the line taking the letter… and I've nothing else to say except…

I mutter the words moodily; finally relenting.

"I'm sorry."

The corners of his mouth twitch. He knows only too well how

hard it is for me to ever back down.

He takes the plate of food from me, sets it on the table and hugs me.

His arms wrap around me, enveloping me. My head is buried in his chest as he holds onto me tightly, the tension between us melting away.

"Wanna start over?"

Neither of us let go. Until I remember the food.

"Dinner'll be getting cold."

We pull ourselves apart.

"Is this plate for Maureen?"

He takes it through to the darkened lounge where Mam is watching a soap.

She's coughing as we go in.

I catch my breath. In the pale light of the television, her face is drawn.

"You still got that tickle?"

"I can't seem to shift it."

"I'll get you some water."

I come back with the glass and Jac moves the side table for her.

"You sure, you don't want to join us?"

"No, cariad, talking all afternoon's done me in, it has."

There's no other choice, but to have dinner with him, alone. Sitting across the kitchen table from him feels strange. A little too formal, especially after our fight.

He watches my fork playing with the rice in the casserole juice.

"You alright?"

"Bit sad, that's all. I wish we'd have kept in touch."

"Me too."

He's suddenly studying his plate too.

"I'm sorry that you went into battle and I never wrote back. If anything had happened, I'd never have forgiven myself."

Jac cuts across.

"It didn't Annie, so don't beat yourself up."

I brood on it for a bit.

"It's not just that. Callista came to see me in New York. You could've come over too. It would've been a laugh."

"You could've come to Belize. Swam in the coral, seen the turtles."

We talk about these places for a while.

I clear the plates and we look at the drawings he's brought with him. Finely drawn pen and ink etchings of tropical fish and turtles.

Emboldened by the wine, it slips out.

"So… you waited for me. For how long?"

He shakes his head.

"Too long. Idiot that I was."

"And how did that rule work out for you, after? Were you the complete tart you said you'd be in the letter?"

He's amused to see me fishing.

"I was twenty when I wrote that. Put it this way, it'd been a very long, dry spell. There've been plenty of women in my life, Annie, don't you worry. Just as you've men had in yours."

I take another sip of wine.

Had Callista been blabbing to him too?

Suddenly, I don't want to dredge up the ghosts of lovers past either.

"You're right. Let's leave it be. Old friends. Fresh starts, what d'you say?"

I take a sip of wine.

With a quirky look on his face, he drinks too.

"Yeah. The future."

# CHAPTER 9

----------✷----------

He'd been hidden from their view every day and evening for a week; spotting the characteristics of the men, learning their habits. Sion had lain flat for hours. Watching. Hidden from view in the dense shrubbery, fighting the creeping cold that moved through his muscles into his bones. Staying silent and still, blending in with the vegetation around him.

He'd spotted Prifti easily. He was a smoker. Sion had studied him closely as he stood by the back door enjoying his cigarette. And he was a creature of habit.

The gang members were all armed, from what he could see. Each carried at least a handgun. And they were brazen about it too, wearing their holsters in plain sight. It wasn't something he'd seen before in the UK. No wonder the security services wanted these bad boys gone.

As the MI5 agent had said, his main challenge would be getting out of there quickly, before the fireworks went off. With the weight of the sniper gun on his back, there was a real possibility of a pot shot from one of Prifti's heavies. If he went for a smaller rifle, his range and accuracy would be compromised. And that could also cost him his life.

So, he practised his escape over the fence each night. And a week of practice later, he was confident that he could move fast out of there when he came under pressure and fire.

He'd been in touch with Irish, his Scouser contact, and they'd agreed on a price for the job. It'd be wired to his offshore account.

Earlier that day, he'd texted him the coded confirmation.

*'I've taken a look at the holiday you recommended and will make the booking later today. I'll be in touch when the payment goes through.'*

Now it was all up to him.

He had no choice but to do it.

It was Monday afternoon; the best time for his mark to be there, with only a few of his homies hanging around.

He was dressed in black, his face obscured by a balaclava. The gun was set up on its bipod, camouflaged in a dense laurel bush. He had a clear view of the patio where the men smoked, and he was as close as possible to the perimeter for his escape. The silencer was on.

Prifti had been having a smoke on the patio each day at around three. In the week that Sion had watched him, Prifti's nicotine cravings had shown surprising regularity.

The February gloom suited his purpose well, as he sat and waited patiently. He could see the men clearly in the lit-up conservatory. They were playing pool. He considered venturing a shot through the window, but the angles weren't ideal. Best stick to the plan and wait for Prifti to appear. He hoped he'd be alone.

Keeping patient, he practised his breathing as he looked down the sight, his finger poised on the trigger, ready to squeeze.

When that trigger was pulled, all manner of shit was going to be flying from the fan. And he didn't want any of it hitting him.

He'd go back to Jac's place, his safe haven where no one would ever find him. And then, there was Claire from The Cross Keys. She was the other reason why he stayed with Jac. Claire was unfinished business. Not even started. But, chatting to her every evening was fast becoming the best part of his day.

He couldn't get her out of his head. She was exotic; different to the other girls around there. Almond-shaped eyes. Long, dark, wavy hair. She was slender but with curves in all the right places. And behind her chatty banter, he could tell she was shy, reserved even. And she had that edge to her. You can't kid a kidder. She hadn't been dealt an easy hand in life, either.

He snapped to attention.

There was a movement at the back door.

Positioning himself, with his eye focussing through the telescopic sight, he fixed on the face of the man who emerged onto the patio.

Prifti.

He was alone. There was no holster or belt to be seen about his black jeans. He looked relaxed, a little tired even.

Sion's luck was in. He studied him intently through the crosshairs as Prifti took a cigarette out of the packet he was holding, moving his hand to his back trouser pocket to retrieve his lighter.

He took a long satisfying first drag.

His last, Sion thought glibly.

Prifti suddenly tilted his head back towards the house.

Was someone else coming outside to join him? Or, was he being called back inside?

Sion froze statue-still, hunched intently over the sight.

Exhaling steadily to regulate his breathing, he had a clear shot. The time had to be now. Now.

Sion coolly pulsed the trigger.

To the trained ear, a faint whistle could be heard as the bullet sliced through the air. And, with one swift, fluid move, Sion had already half disassembled the gun as Leon Prifti keeled backwards.

A dull thud.

The cigarette slipped from his mouth, as Prifti's head banged against the patio flag. He lay lifeless on his back, shot cleanly between the eyes.

Crunch time.

Slinging the cumbersome gun over his shoulder, Sion crouched and stalked smoothly and rapidly back through the bushes, speedily reaching the perimeter fence.

Faint shouts began to ring out as Sion leapt and vaulted himself cleanly over the wooden trellis, as he'd practised. Not looking back.

Clearing the cutting, his balaclava removed; he stored the gun back in the case he'd concealed in the shrubbery by the fence.

As he walked swiftly along the street, he heard the first shots ringing out. The hired white transit van was parked around the corner.

Calmly, he stowed the cased gun out of view, behind the driver's seat. Not that anyone was paying any attention to him. Slipping on a high visibility jacket and placing a clipboard on the dashboard, he became just another delivery van in the London suburban street.

Moving casually into the traffic, he drove past Prifti's place, slowing down slightly to subtly assess the situation.

In the front driveway, the electric gates were open, and several of Prifti's muscle were waving their handguns about. He saw them jumping into their luxury cars and shouting at each other.

But, Sion wasn't worried. He'd already slipped into anonymity.

With the van returned to the hire company, he headed back to Jason's South London apartment, where he reversed parked the Volvo into a free space.

He reached for his phone and sent a text to Irish.

*'I've made the booking and the payment's gone through.'*

Inside the flat, he clicked into his other encrypted message space and sent another message. A thumbs-up emoji. Another job for Queen and country. The security services now had the Albanians in disarray. Next up, the Scousers would be in their sights.

Quickly and methodically, Sion packed up his things. With the weapons safely stored in the boot of his Volvo, it was time for him, as predicted, to get out. Get off the grid.

His heart thumped with excitement as he thought about it. About seeing Claire again.

It had been going through Jac's restless mind all night. And then all morning, he went over and over it again, as he drove the tractor.

He agonised about whether he should ask her or not, as he took the silage up to the fields. And how she'd react, and what she'd say to him, as he unloaded the bales into the feeding rings.

Spreading the fermented grass out evenly to the sides with a fork, he worried about being rejected. He'd been too hard on her over those letters. He'd rubbed her face in it. But then, she'd deserved it.

He smirked to himself. Once he'd taken the letters away she couldn't help herself, she'd been desperate to read them.

He thought about how her eyes had flashed in temper. It stirred something deep within him. He hated to admit it, but he loved that stubborn spiritedness he brought out in her. It was part of who they were together, it sparked the electricity that coursed between them.

The wasted years. That was a damn shame. But, all the more reason to go for it now.

Things had moved on. They'd agreed to start over.

Moving the bales was a mucky job. It meant wading around the feeders where the animals had trampled the ground into a sea of mud. By lunchtime, his waterproofs and wellies were caked in sludge, and a sweet cloying odour clung heavily about him.

There was no way he could ask her like this. He'd get a shower and then go up to the farmhouse to see her. Ask her out to dinner. The prospect excited him in a way he hadn't felt for years.

He never did dating. It wasn't his style. As he'd told her in that last letter, he was more of a get-with-a-woman-on-a-night-out kinda guy. There was rarely a second date. If he was being honest, over the last decade he'd stuck to his rule fairly religiously. He hadn't felt the need for a relationship. He'd always had his army buddies for friends. They'd been all the family he'd needed. But, that was then.

Since he'd been back at the farm, he'd had nights out from time to time. He'd meet women; stay over, if he had half a chance. And he was always meticulously careful. The army had taught him that too. But, he'd not found anyone he'd wanted to spend longer than a night with.

And that was the problem with Annie. Even though he didn't mean to, he measured every other woman against her.

He'd been kidding himself.

He wasn't over her.

He never had been. Not even close.

What Glyn did was tragic, but he was glad that it had brought Annie back to him. Perhaps, it was meant to be? Like fate? Not that he believed in all that guff. What mattered, was that she was here now, and he had a second chance. He couldn't and wouldn't pass that up.

Shaved and smartly dressed, it was early afternoon when Jac found himself in the farmhouse kitchen. As he walked in, Annie was busy making tea and cutting up cake.

Her face lit up flirtily at him, giving him a little hope.

"You look good. Off out?"

"Err... no."

Her nose crinkled at his abrupt response.

It was a bad start. He was nervous as Hell.

Annie, thankfully, seemed oblivious to his tongue-tied state.

"Dad's body's been released by the coroner. The minister's in the living room."

She arranged the plates and cups onto a tray to take through.

"We can arrange his funeral, at last."

"Want me to come back later? I can see you're busy."

For the first time in his life, he was bottling it.

"No, don't be daft. I'll be right back."

Annie grabbed the laden tray.

"Anyway, they were having a bit of a heart to heart when I popped my head in before. Best leave 'em to it. Make yourself a brew, while I take this through."

He went over his game plan again. It had seemed straightforward, when he was on the tractor. But here, now, he wasn't so sure.

He felt foolish. And, what would he do if she said no? She might be angry with him, still. And there'd been no indication at all that she wanted to be more than friends. Except, perhaps, when she'd been angling about other women. And when she'd been jealous of Jess.

The other hope he had, and he might have imagined it, was the look on her face when he'd shown up for dinner. Before they'd argued about the letters. She'd looked a little hurt. Like he'd just broken up with her. Which, technically, he had.

"You're looking serious."

The chirpy tone of her voice cut through his thoughts.

"*Uh*... I was thinking... about lambing."

"Yeah, you've got your work cut out this time, pal, that's for sure."

He leaned back against the kitchen unit. This was a bad idea. He put his mug down. He was chickening out.

She stood by the side of him, leaning against the worktop too.

"Will you be needing help?"

"Probably."

Annie was quiet for a moment.

He could seriously use her if she was up for it.

"Wanna give me a hand?"

"If I'm here."

She bumped her shoulder against his arm playfully.

"Depends on how much you're gonna pay me?"

He bumped her back.

"Depends on your experience."

She pivoted around sparkily.

"Got more experience than you, mate. And much better

hands."

She held them up against his, measuring their daintiness against his big paws.

Her eyes danced as they met his, but her voice shook slightly.

"See… much better."

Stealing himself, he interlaced her small fingers with his.

"Annie?"

Her emerald eyes gazed up searchingly, drawing him magnetically in towards her.

"Yes?"

He couldn't help himself.

Her breathing quickened as he leaned in close.

"Would you…? D'you wanna…?"

The front doorbell cut shrilly across his inarticulate utterances as he struggled to ask her out. Or kiss her. One of the two. Or both.

It rang impatiently again.

Letting out a small sigh, she moved apart from him.

"I'd better get the door. It might be a visitor for Mam."

The bell rang out insistently for a third time as if whoever it was, was keeping their finger on it until somebody answered.

"Bloody rude."

Jac raked a hand through his hair. The moment was broken, and he'd failed.

"If it's a delivery driver, I'm gonna tell them where they can go."

Straightening herself up, she walked through the hall to the front door.

"Okay, okay, I'm coming."

Jac sloped after her.

"Annie."

She was standing, mouth open, staring at a tall, well-groomed stranger on the doorstep.

"Seb."

Jac could see the man's taxi disappearing down the track.

"Can I come in?"

"What you doing here?"

"I need to talk to you."

"Could you not have phoned?"

"I did. There was no answer."

She shrugged resignedly and stepped to one side to let the stranger into the hallway.

From the shadows, Jac studied this 'Seb'. He was older than her. In his early forties, Jac guessed. His dark hair was beginning to pepper with a little grey at the sides. But there was an air of sophistication about him that made Jac think that he could have stepped straight out of a department store clothing advert.

There was no doubt that he was perfectly put together, but there was something shallow about him too. He couldn't put his finger on it, but it was to do with his smile. It didn't match the steely intent of his eyes.

Stepping up to embrace her, Annie froze. Taking the hint, he settled for a perfunctory peck on each cheek.

They both moved through to the kitchen, and Jac slunk awkwardly behind.

He needed to get out of there.

He didn't know who this bloke was, but if Annie had a boyfriend, then he'd had a lucky escape not asking her out.

There'd clearly been a thing between the two of them, although judging by Annie's reaction to him now, it didn't look as if they were still friends.

He could still read her well enough to sense that she wasn't pleased at all that he'd turned up unannounced at the door.

"Seb, this is Jac. He lives next door. Seb's my boss in London."

He eyeballed Jac.

"And Annie's good friend."

The fiery glare she hurled back at Seb after he said that, made Jac smirk.

He was right. She wasn't a happy bunny.

"I'd better be off."

Jac grabbed his coat.

"I'll leave you to it. Good to meet you Seb."

Her boss didn't grace Jac with a response.

Annie looked torn as she guided Seb to sit down at the table, following Jac with her eyes as he went to the porch to put on his boots.

Neighbour? Is that all he was to her?

"Jac, wait up. Please."

She rushed through to the porch as he was finishing tying his laces. He straightened up as he saw her approaching. Her face was flushed and her bright green eyes sparkled angrily.

"This. It's not what you think. I've no idea why Seb's here. And he's not *bloody well* staying, either."

Placing his hands on her shoulders, he steadied her.

"Why would he come here, Annie? There's obviously some un-finished business between you two."

Running her teeth over her bottom lip, she stared up at him, her eyes pleading.

"We're not together. I mean, we were once, but it wasn't any-thing. Except a big mistake. I'm not sure what he wants… But, whatever it is, I don't want *him*."

His pulse raced.

Unable to help himself, he ran his palm gently across her soft, reddened cheek.

Inexplicably drawn, he felt himself bending towards her. His lips, at last, gently finding hers for the lightest, fleetest of kisses.

She didn't resist. Or recoil, this time.

She was trembling.

"Jac, what did you want to ask me?"

"It's alright, Annie. Go sort this, first."

His lips brushed over hers again, resting there a while longer. He felt her mouth parting, but he pulled away.

"We'll talk again."

Taking a deep breath, Annie shook her head, and made her way slowly back into the kitchen, to face whatever it was, with Seb.

# CHAPTER 10

----------✳----------

Seb tells me from the outset that he isn't staying, and I drive him to the station myself, to make sure that he catches the last train back to London.

The visit hasn't been about our relationship. I'm not sure why he felt the need to wind Jac up like he did; he said himself that we're well and truly over. Now it's sunk in, he's relieved about that too.

No, this visit is all about him. Or more explicitly, about him saving his own neck.

Trusty Rusty, our ancient SUV, isn't exactly the style of travel he's accustomed to. At first, I'm ashamed about the state of it, myself. Dad was never very tidy. But, it's hilarious watching him trying to save his expensive woollen coat from the bits of dirt on the tiger seat cover.

"Don't tell them, Annie. I beg you."

I switch off the engine.

Even though I've told him, I don't know how many times, what I'm going to do; he still seems distrustful of my intentions. And I'm quite enjoying watching him squirm.

"I've got a huge mortgage and school fees to pay."

His whining is pathetic.

"If I lose my job, Marnie will leave me, for sure."

"She should've left you long ago."

My voice sounds more bitter than I feel. In truth, the only thing I feel is irritation that he's invaded my world.

Hands rigid on the steering wheel, I stare forward at the windscreen.

"I told you. I'll do it."

He takes that as a dismissal.

And it is.

I never want to look at him or speak to him again.

He hops out of the rusty truck without another word, shutting the door on his coat. Wrestling it free, he slams the door hard behind him for a second time, then dashes off for the train.

I watch Seb disappear out of my life, but my mind is full of Jac.

And how my heart thumped as his lips found mine.

Before I head back home, and while I've got a phone signal, I decide to make the call.

It clicks through to Lisa; Director of People Empowerment.

"Annie."

She sounds surprised to hear from me.

"We're in the process of writing to you about a matter. How *are* you?"

I'm pretty wound up as it is. And the way she stresses the fake emphasis of concern lights the fuse. In fact, it takes me all my self-control not to scream.

I just about manage that, but I can't suppress an unstoppable urge to shock her out of that corporate smugness of hers.

"I'm not so good actually, Lisa. My father hanged himself on the same day you suspended me." Boom.

Silence.

Lisa's flummoxed.

It was a pretty crappy thing to fling at her.

"You're entitled to compassionate leave," she says quietly.

"Does that mean, I'm not suspended?"

"I'm afraid not."

Another silence.

"So, this silly misunderstanding still hasn't been resolved?"

Hesitation again.

Like the sea sucking backwards from the shore.

Luckily, Seb has given me the heads up.

"Annie."

Her tone is cold.

"We've had some further allegations made since your suspension. About your personal conduct, that goes against organisational policy... with an unnamed member of staff."

"*What!* Who made those allegations?"

Lisa confirms what Seb has told me, but I want to find out where it's come from, so I'm playing along.

"A formal complaint has been made by one of your subordinates. She says that she was forced to cover for you and to listen to your unprofessional comments at work."

This is more than Seb has told me.

He said that they'd been told that I was having an office affair. Breaking their relationships policy. He said nothing about unprofessional behaviour.

Covering up? Unprofessional comments? Allegations by one of my team?

My mind races.

Who could it be?

Someone who'd benefit from me gone.

The tsunami hits land, and its realisation sweeps me away.

It couldn't be, could it?

Not Stacey, surely?

Not my friend?

"There's no easy way to say this," Lisa continues, "We need to set up a full disciplinary hearing about your professional conduct. I'll email you with a date, probably next month now, due to your personal circumstances."

I can't take it all in.

"Who told you these things?"

She doesn't answer.

The betrayal floors me.

"What about him?"

"We need to know who it is you had a relationship at work

with, Annie. You need to tell us."

This is why he came.

There's a full minute's silence on the phone between us.

This is for Marnie. Although we've never met, the woman has now attained sainthood, in my mind.

I don't give a toss about him.

"We'll pick this up at the hearing," Lisa drones on. "In the meantime, you must clear your mind of work. Your wellbeing is important to us, Annie. Make time to grieve. If you need to talk to anybody, we can arrange for a counsellor. Try some yoga."

"*Fuck* your yoga!"

I end the call.

My wellbeing was fine until she suspended me.

It's confirmed. Seb has cost me my job.

The evening was drawing in when Jac saw her again.

After taking the time off in the afternoon, he'd plunged himself into a fencing job in the far paddock. Thumping in the posts was the only useful thing he could do to keep his mind off Annie and Seb. He was a slimeball. He could tell. She deserved way better than him.

It was dusk before he was done. And it was as he was riding back, that he spotted her. Wearing a head-torch, she'd marched across the fields and was now climbing up through the bracken line.

In the twilight, he saw her, pounding on. Trampling the small leafy promises of spring under her feet. She was past the ancient hawthorn now. The lonely tree they'd called it, when they were kids.

"*Shit!*"

She always did this when something was up. Go off to their place. And the high ledge she was aiming for, and the scree below it, they were damn slippery at this time of year. Even with a headtorch, it was getting properly dark by now.

He turned the quad bike and rode as far up as he could after her.

Cutting the engine, he followed on foot as she pushed on up. Through the heathers and the gorse, pounding over the rocks, climbing up the scree slope until finally, she reached it. Their old spot at the top of the mountain.

He saw her silhouette on the ledge, the moon above her. And he was near the ridge too, when he heard her first cry out.

She screamed again, this time standing up, shouting angrily at the sky.

"*Arghh!* How could I have been *so fuckin' stupid!*"

Breaking down then, she cried ugly, noisy, private tears.

"Annie."

He startled her. She looked embarrassed as he came up beside her onto the ledge.

Wrapping his arms around her, he let her get it out.

It took a while, and he held her tightly as she broke down again, her wet face buried deep in his coat, against his chest. His heart.

A proper, full-on hysterical meltdown. Her jagged stuttering when she'd finished reminded him of a toddler recovering from a tantrum.

Pulling away, she slumped down onto the rock.

"You weren't meant to see that."

Sitting down, he put his arm around her. His other hand stroked her hand gently with his thumb as the darkness cloaked the mountains.

Shaking her head, she wiped at her face with her sleeve.

He didn't say a word.

Instead, he took her hand, led her carefully back down the scree to the quad and drove them back to the cottage.

Still a little puffy-eyed, she smiled weakly at him as she came down from the bathroom.

"Wanna talk about it?"

"I s'pose I owe you an explanation. Seeing as you scraped me up off the floor."

He took her through to the living room and they sat on the old sofa together.

"I dunno. It's been building up. First, Dad. And Mam, she's not right and she's shutting me out as usual...and then, there's you..."

She shot him a look.

"And now Seb; tosser, that he is. And the cherry on top of the shit-cake that is my life is I've just found out I'm gonna get the sack."

"Why?"

"*Oh God!*"

She stared at the fire.

"Jac, I'm not sure I wanna tell you all this."

"You don't have to."

She shrugged, focusing intently on the cup of tea in her hand.

"I had a thing with Seb when I was in New York. And when I came back."

"So?"

"It's against the rules. What, with him being my boss, and all."

She chewed the side of her bottom lip with her teeth.

"I finished it. He's a self-absorbed, arrogant bastard...Plus, he's married."

She flicked a look at him, expecting at least a frown. Instead, he was smirking.

"D'you find this funny?"

He pressed his hand on her thigh as she jumped up to leave.

"No! Stay! I was only laughin' cos, I've done stuff I'm not proud of. But, you're no angel, either. You and me, we're more similar than you think, that's all."

Her shoulders dropped and she settled back down.

"Why're you gonna get fired?"

She rubbed her hands over her face.

"The only other person who knew about me and Seb, was my mate, Stacey. She's doing my job while I'm away."

"Your friend told them?"

She nodded.

He was trying to keep up.

"Seb betrayed me first. He wanted me gone, so he flagged up

some bullshit irregularities to HR. He started it all."

"Jees, Annie."

"Yeah. It backfired on him, big time, when Stacey ratted me out. That's why he showed up today. To get me to keep my mouth shut, so he wouldn't lose his job too."

Jac scratched his head.

"What you gonna do?"

She shrugged and they sat quietly together for a while.

"Annie, you need to face the facts. Your job in that company's over. Use this time to plan what you want to do next."

He felt her pain as her eyes glistened.

"I've been such a fool."

"Maybe… But, this Seb's no straight shooter either."

"And Stacey?"

"Her too. She took her chance."

"By destroying me?"

"You do have some lousy friends."

"Yeah," she breathed, "Everyone I trust always ends up betraying me."

Her words burned him.

A key, rattling in the lock, broke the silence.

"You expecting someone?"

Getting up from the sofa, he went to the back door.

"Sion, man!"

He embraced his friend.

Sion and Jason, he counted them as brothers. Each one would go through the fire for him.

Sion had done.

In Afghanistan, when their truck hit an explosive device, Sion had pulled him out of there unharmed. Seconds before it burst into flames. Others weren't so lucky that day.

And Jason had gotten them out of sticky situations too, more than once.

What a difference to Annie's friends.

Annie was putting on her coat as Sion strolled into the living room, Jac behind him.

"This is Sion, my army brother."

"Hi."

She smiled at Sion shyly.

"I better be going."

"You don't have to."

"I do. I've got to book the funeral tea."

She gave Jac a watery smile, "And then start applying for jobs."

"Who's *she*?" Sion asked as soon as Jac had closed the door behind her.

"That's Annie."

"What? As in *the* Annie?"

"Leave it out."

"You back with her?"

"No."

"You wanna be?"

"It's complicated."

"I thought you liked things simple, mate? What about that rule of yours, the one you keep banging on about when you're pissed."

"Yeah, whatever."

"If she's free then, I might have a crack myself," Sion winked, trying to wind him up.

"You keep away from her."

And by the intent on his friend's face, Jac was deadly serious. And in deep.

After embarrassing myself with Jac, I slip down to The Cross Keys.

It's an understatement when I say I'm mortified that he caught me in such a state. And now I've told him everything. *Oh God!* What must he think of me?

"Hey, Annie!"

Claire, my old school friend, comes around from the bar and gives me a warm hug. I'd waved hello to her the other night, but she'd been flat out, serving at the bar.

"Great to see you, hun… *Ahh!* I'm so sorry about your dad. Case and a half, he was. We all miss him."

I flash her the same plastered-on smile I give everyone who says that about Dad. The last thing I need right now is hearing more of Glyn's legendary shenanigans. Mam's had a belly-full of it too.

Claire writes the arrangements for the funeral tea into the diary. Then, Kevin, the new bar manager comes over, cross-checking everything she's already written down.

"The brewery moved him here last week," Claire whispers.

His loud Liverpudlian voice carries over the noise of the bar, and I can see a couple of locals already rolling their eyes, every time he speaks.

Kevin lets Claire have a short break, and we go sit down at a table in the corner.

"You staying here for a while, then?" Claire asks.

"Yeah. For now."

"What've you been up to? You married? Got kids?"

I take a sip of my small beer.

"No. You?"

She looks towards the door as Jac, and his friend Sion, walk into the bar.

"Yeah. Single too."

I can't mistake the interest that she shows in them.

Is she staking her claim on Jac?

It wouldn't surprise me. The girls at school were all after him, and I'd always be the one mocking him for being so clueless.

Now, it's me who's the clueless one, with friends and lovers who'd happily stab me in the back.

If my judgement's that off, it's possible then that I've totally misjudged '*Jac the Lad*' too?

Claire's a pretty girl, and Jac's single. Probably still applying that rule of his. Ending relationships before they get too clingy and messy.

I cringe as Jac sees me. I've been about as clingy and messy as it gets.

He comes casually up to our table.

"Wanna join us tonight?"

"No. It's alright. I'd better get back and see Mam."

I'm not going to stay to watch him flirting with Claire.

"Earlier on," I say quietly. "You caught me at a bad time."

"No worries."

"Thank you."

"For what?"

"I'm not doing so well on the friends' front at the moment." I feel a lump in my throat. "Thanks for being there."

"Any time," he rasps.

"What was it you wanted to ask me? Before Seb turned up this afternoon?"

"Nothing," he says gruffly. "It'll keep."

When Sion suggested he treat Jac to a meal at The Cross Keys that evening, he thought he'd snap his hand off.

But after Annie left, Jac didn't seem that keen. Instead, he offered to cook, but Sion insisted they go out. He needed to check his phone; and see Claire.

He'd missed her.

Being away made him realise how much he looked forward to their evening chats. She was chippy with him, but she wasn't as tough as she pretended to be.

His eyes locked onto hers when they walked into the bar; and seeing him, she got up from the table where she was sitting with Annie, to go and serve them.

Predictably, Jac slunk over to Annie, while Sion stayed at the bar.

He ignored the new piggy-eyed barman who asked him what he wanted to drink. And Claire quickly took charge, serving them their pints.

"Who's he?" Sion asked her discreetly, leaning over the bar.

"That's knobhead."

Sion let out a loud laugh.

The little man shot them a suspicious glare. She had pretty much summed up Sion's first impression of him too.

"The brewery shipped him in."

The new manager was now talking to a couple of young men, strangers, who'd just walked in. Taking his cigarette packet off the back bar, he followed them outside.

There was something decidedly dodgy about him, Sion decided. Not a good fit for a rural pub, like this one.

Jac was sitting at the table in deep conversation with Annie, the good-looking blonde who'd been sitting on the sofa when he arrived.

He felt bad about that. He'd clearly interrupted something.

He couldn't remember ever seeing his old army buddy so doe-eyed. Even though she didn't realise it, she'd got Jac by the balls, alright.

And he was a goner.

Sion helped himself to a couple of menus and waited for Claire to finish serving a round of drinks to another customer.

Her long raven hair shone under the lights on the bar, and her face was set in concentration as she pulled the pump and got the head of froth just right.

She moved back over to him.

"So, how was the job?"

"Boring. Patched up the network after a virus and got it all working again. Did you miss me?"

"A bit."

Her mouth curved into a grin.

"Like I missed the verruca I had burned off my foot last week."

"Aw, come on, Claire. You love our nightly chats."

"I do. Every time we speak, I make a point of writing it down. Word for word."

"You do?"

"Uh-huh," she smiled sweetly. "So as I can use it in the 'harassment at work' case I'm filing against you."

"Oh okay, I'll leave you alone, then, if that's what you want?"

Her flirty smile told him that was the last thing she wanted him to do.

"You're kiddin' right?"

"P'raps. I haven't made my mind up about you yet."

The new landlord called her over to take food out, and Sion took the drinks and menus over to the far table, where Jac now sat alone.

"Scared Annie off, did you?"

"No. I warned her about you, and she took fright."

"Yeah, right."

"Truth is, I didn't want you filling Annie's head with sordid tall tales about our army days," Jac half-joked.

"About your army days, you mean. And there's a fair few tales I could tell about you."

Sion handed him a menu.

"That weekend in Amsterdam?"

Jac winced.

"Fair enough... Don't you miss it?"

"Miss what?... Amsterdam? I know *you* did. What was that Swedish girl's name again?"

"No, ya prick. Not Amsterdam. Don't you miss operations? You were always the brains. The action man. I'm not being funny, mate, but this computer stuff you're doing these days, it ain't you."

"What *is* me? I'd never have fitted you up for a sheep farmer, either... I'm gonna have the steak pie special. How about you?"

Jac's attention turned to the menu, and Sion was relieved. The less Jac knew about what he did, the better.

His weapons were stored safely under his outdoor gear in the cottage's little shed. Even though he considered Jac his best and truest friend, it was for his own good that he kept him in the dark. He needed this bolt hole. Now, more than ever.

"I'm gonna do some climbing in Snowdonia next week."

"Cool."

"Sorry, about earlier on. I didn't mean to come across you and Annie."

"You didn't. She was upset, that's all. About her job."

"Does that mean she's staying?"

"No idea, mate. But the longer she's here, the more she's messin' with my head."

# CHAPTER 11

----------*----------

Callista's arriving on the train later; and killing two birds with one stone, Mam and I have come into town to get something to wear for Dad's funeral. Most of my clothes are back in London, and Mam wants something smart.

She looks exhausted already, as she shuffles slowly around the shopping centre, browsing for something suitably sombre and warm.

"Let's have a breather."

We've paused outside a large coffee chain.

"Why don't you have a sit down, while I find us something to wear? How about a turtle-neck jumper and a straight skirt from Marks?"

Mam smiles at me gratefully.

"Just the job."

Something's wrong. She's only sixty-five, but the weight loss, lack of appetite and energy, together with that constant cough she has, it's not normal. It's been gnawing at me for days.

Setting our two lattes on the table, I pluck up the courage to ask her.

She's a nurse, surely she must have picked up the symptoms. Seen a doctor?

"Mam, what's up?"

She stares blankly back at me. The look she's been giving me her whole life.

"I'm fine."

"You're not *fine*."

My voice catches.

"Stop pretending. We've done enough of that. Tell me the truth… Please… Are you ill?"

Mam sniffs and scours her bag.

I reach over to the next table for a crunchy paper serviette, and then hold her hand as she takes it from me. It's icy cold.

"I didn't want to worry you, love."

She clears her throat and tells me.

And it's bad.

She went to the doctors with her cough before Christmas, and the tests they did confirmed the worst. Primary bladder cancer metastasised with secondaries. They've offered her palliative chemo, but she's refused it.

The irony is, that she's never had so much as a urine infection. She felt perfectly healthy until the weight loss started in the autumn, and then that persistent tickly cough.

I'm reeling. I have to stay strong, but it's hard.

Callista will be here later. She'll help me get through to her. We need to make her see sense.

"We'll go back to the doctors. There must be treatments available? I'll do some research online. See what's out there."

"You're a good girl. I really will be fine," she smiles, taking my hand. Not upset at all.

"And when you go back, Jac'll be here."

"No way am I going back to London, until you're sorted."

"But, Annie! What about your job? You're a senior manager. You need to get back."

"Don't fret about that, they'll give me a leave of absence, I'm sure."

I can't bring myself to tell her the truth.

"Cal!"

Jac greets his mother on the yard.

"Jac, my darling. Come here."

"Cal, I'm not fit."

"Rubbish."

Mam and I chuckle as Callista grabs her son, ignoring his dirty clothes, and covers him with mother-hen kisses.

"I've missed you so much."

He gives in to her and lets her drag him into the house. Bringing in the shopping, there's a pair of large wellies with the water-proof over-trousers tucked into them at the porch door.

"Sorry, I stink of silage," he apologises, grabbing the shopping bags from me to put on the table.

It's the only spare space. The kitchen unit tops are stacked with boxes full of sponges and fruitcake. The window ledges are filled with cards, and there are three bunches of flowers in the kitchen alone.

"Ah, no bother. I'm used to it. You and Sion have gotta help me out with this cake. People are so kind, but I'm gonna have to freeze most of it. I'll drop some off at the cottage later."

Callista helps me unpack too, while she chats to her son.

She's threaded her long grey hair with colourful lacing since I last saw her. And her waist-length dreadlocks are held off her face and tied back with a pastel-striped headscarf.

She looks great, and I've always admired how effortlessly well she layers. Today she's wearing a tubular grey skirt with a floaty white cotton shirt over a tight black vest top. For warmth, she's paired it with a grey boyfriend cardigan. And she's covered in lots of chunky silver jewellery.

Her clothes are Bohemian and expensive. As the daughter of a successful oil executive from a wealthy family, she's lived off trust funds and inheritance her whole life. She's never had to earn a crust like the rest of us.

She told me how, as a youngster, she'd rebelled. Rejected university and went off on a year-long road trip in a hippy bus. It lasted far longer than a year. She ended up travelling around the world, then living with a group of like-minded friends; going to festivals and getting involved in political activism. Eventually, she settled down so Jac could go to high school, living off-grid here.

Many would be right when they argued that it was easy for her. Money had never meant much to Callista because she'd always had it. She wasn't flashy, but you could tell that she never had to make choices about what she could afford.

What I like most about Callista, though, is that she's passionate. She always fights for what she believes in. And, I've not met anyone with a more generous heart than her's.

Standing side by side with Jac, I'm taken by their similarity. Both are tall and striking. And both have those same dark, unfathomable eyes.

The crematorium service has been well attended, and Maureen has held up well.

It was only me that heard her sigh of relief when the coffin disappeared behind the curtains. She gripped my hand tightly and I squeezed it back. I didn't want to ever let her go.

Afterwards, The Cross Keys is jam-packed with friends, family and neighbours. Some that we haven't seen in years. Everyone likes a funeral tea around these parts. It's a chance for a good catch up.

A handsome man with sandy hair approaches me purposefully through the funeral-goers, with a cup of tea and a plate of food in his hands.

"Alun."

"Annie. I'm sorry about your father."

I nod back in acknowledgement.

I haven't seen him in twelve years. Alun Lewis, my neighbour. Lizard Man.

He's looking well. Very well, in fact. Muscular and trim.

We make small talk, mainly about his large farm, that lies next to ours. He's running his own machinery contracting business from there, too. His quick eyes flick over me, making me bristle. Or, maybe the hairs on my neck are standing up because I can feel Jac's eyes on me the whole time that Alun and I are talking together.

He's with Sion, chatting to some old school friends.

I turn around for a second, glancing towards the bar, and my eyes slam into his.

He nods back at me.

*Dammit!* It was like I was checking him out.

Feeling my cheeks burning up, I switch my attention back to Alun.

Thankfully, Alun is oblivious. He's wrapped up in a long conversation about himself. And by his manner of speaking, it feels like an opening gambit.

He's laying his cards out for me. How many acres he's farming. How many cows he's milking. The number of sheep he has. Ask any farmer, and with that kind of information, their heads will be instantly filled with calculations of how much he's earning.

Alun Lewis is telling me that he's quite a catch.

"I'll call by sometime, if you're going to be around for a while."

It's a statement, not a question.

"For a cuppa."

"Yes, alright."

I hope he takes the hint from my non-committal tone.

Alun Lewis is not a 'call-round-for-a-cuppa' kinda guy.

I search for Mam. She must be getting tired by now, and Callista has promised me that she will take her home whenever she's ready to go.

Cal already knew about Mam's diagnosis. I'm coming to realise that there are a lot of things that Callista knows, that she's not told me.

And it's only me in the dark. Again.

I hang on through the afternoon until most of the funeral-goers have drifted away. Jac is long gone. He left to check the stock. And Callista's taken Mam home, so I give Claire a hand to clear up.

Discarded crockery and glasses lie everywhere, and Kevin the manager is nowhere to be seen.

"Need some help?"

Sion pops a cold sausage roll into his mouth as Claire comes past, arms laden with a stack of dirty plates.

"What with eating? Or clearing up?" she jokes, throwing me a look.

"Both."

But, to be fair, Sion's good. Before long, most of the dishes are in a pile on the buffet table, ready to be taken through to the kitchen. Then, he goes at it again, helping me collect the glasses.

"She loves me really," he whispers, nodding over to where Claire is stacking the dishwasher. "She just doesn't know it yet."

"You sure about that, pal? I thought she fancied Jac?"

Sion looks at me curiously.

"I hope not. If she does, she's gonna get her heart broken."

I shrug it off.

"*Ahh*, Jac's rule, you mean?"

"You know about that?"

I put the final lot of glasses onto the bar.

"I'm gonna head off in a minute. It's been a pretty full-on day."

Sion takes the last of the dishes through to Claire, then joins me as I get my coat.

"Want some company on the walk home?'

After he's stayed to help, I don't have the heart to tell him that I'm all out of conversation and want to be on my own for a bit.

With a goodbye to Claire, he follows me out of the pub into the chilly late February afternoon.

"They always say it gets better after the funeral."

I don't reply, and we walk on in silence.

"I've been there too."

I've heard more than enough 'time heals' platitudes today.

"Annie," Sion tries again after a minute or so. "I *really do* know what you've gone through. Maureen told me."

I stop in my tracks and stare at him.

"She did?"

"I saw the scars on her arm. Got a couple of impressive burn marks myself. From my old man."

"How?"

"Cigarettes. You?"

"Belt," I shrug. "For coming back late from Jac's one time. Another, for looking at him the wrong way. Once, for breathing."

He walks quietly alongside me.

"I got in the way," he says. "Mainly when he was going after my mam. She was too pissed to care."

"What happened?"

"Social services took me from there. I joined up as soon as I could. Mam's dead. Dad's gone, not sure where. Jac and Jase are my family now."

I touch his arm. I can tell he understands how tangled my head is about my father. Because his is too.

"I only wanted to tell you, that you're not alone."

# CHAPTER 12

----------*----------

In the end, Mam only lasts three weeks. I can't believe how quickly everything's happened. The funeral marked a turning point, and it wasn't long after that she took to her bed. The doctor came out to see her, but it was palliative care that they set up, not the treatment plan I'd hoped for.

"She made her peace once your father was gone," Callista reflects, holding my hand as the funeral director's van moves slowly off the yard with Mam inside it.

She'd died in the early hours of the morning.

A palliative care nurse has been with us too. And between us all, we've given Mam the dignity and care she wanted in her final days; in her own bed.

"I don't know what I'd have done without you, Cal. Again."

She hugs me.

"Thanks for putting your life on hold for me. For being here."

"I'll always be here for you, sweetie. I promised your mother that."

This loss is different. I'm exhausted but strangely calm.

And there are no more tears.

The few weeks I've had with Mam have been so precious. It's a small comfort now that she's gone, but I was never so close to her as I was over this past month, and I'm eternally grateful for the time we had together.

We both go back indoors for some rest before we tell anyone. I'm not up to more rounds of visitors, tea and cake just yet.

I need a nap, then a long walk.

Every day, I've been getting out in the afternoon for a break, while Callista sat with Mam.

I needed the fresh air and the exercise after being in the house. So, I walked the fields and footpaths around the farm.

The first day I came across Jac fencing in the lower field.

The second, I found him in the pens worming the sheep before they lambed. I stayed longer than I'd intended, giving him a hand moving the sheep through the holding race for him to feed them the dose of wormer more quickly. It was fun, like old times, and what I needed to clear my head.

On the third day, I saw him early in the yard. He joked that if I bumped into him that afternoon he'd start thinking that I was his stalker, so he made points instead to meet me, so I could give him a hand with moving the sheep.

He's put the heaviest sheep, the ones in lamb with twins, in the fields around the cottage. He can keep a closer eye on them there over the next month. Then, he'll transfer them into the lambing sheds once they're closer to their due date at the end of March.

And that's how it's been. Every afternoon since then, I've been doing farm jobs with Jac.

We don't discuss anything profound. We don't do much talking at all. He lets me be and understands that I need some time out. Time to breathe.

Jac's offered to cook.

I was a little reluctant when Callista first mentioned it, but by the time we've both had a sleep and a shower, I admit to Callista that I'm glad to be getting out of the house. The place feels odd, and it's our first evening without Mam around.

And when we arrive at the cottage, things are in full flow. Jac pulls himself away from the stove to give me a hug. In the end, I slept all afternoon, and so I haven't seen him since Mam passed this morning.

"I needed that."

Jac seems to sense the rawness I'm feeling, and doesn't mention her. He's already said it all in that long hug he's just given me.

"Make yourself at home."

He takes our coats.

"Mi casa es su casa."

I clock the look Callista throws him.

The cottage. The farm. Perhaps, Jac hasn't worked it out yet, but it's all mine now.

That's quite a lot for me to take in too.

What on earth am I going to do with it?

Callista reads my mind.

"So, what next?"

I give her a blank look.

"After the funeral, I'll need to sort out my flat in London. Clear out all the new life-forms that are growing in my fridge."

"Did you write back to your employer?"

An email had come through setting a date for a disciplinary hearing, and I'd agonised about what to do.

"You know my thoughts on that. You absolutely have to fight it. It's nothing less than sexual politics in the workplace. Why should, this Seb, get away with it? He's used his power, and you're rolling over."

But, I've no appetite for a fight. I don't tell Callista that I've already made my mind up. I'm going to resign quietly and walk away.

The bigger question for me, is whether I'm going to try and get another job in London, or stay here in Wales?

I haven't made up my mind yet.

It's too much.

All I can face right now are small steps.

Resign.

Sort my flat.

Jac has made us a vegetable lasagne, and the kitchen is filled with the mouth-watering smell of the focaccia loaf smothered in garlic butter, that's finishing off in the oven.

My stomach is growling.

Sion makes an appearance and gets everyone drinks. It's a bit of a squash, but it feels cosy as the four of us sit down to eat in the tiny kitchen.

"Good effort, Jac. This is delicious," Callista declares, eating another piece of his homemade Italian bread.

"Sion's made the pudding."

"Don't get excited, it's only a crumble."

"You're like a married couple," Cal jokes, and Jac gives her a look that makes everyone laugh.

"It's true," she chuckles, "I always wanted a gay son."

Jac shakes his head.

"As you kept telling me. All through my teens. It was very confusing."

"You staying for a while?" I ask Sion, as he finishes the last of his lasagne.

"Yes, until my next job comes up."

"What've you been up to?" Callista pursues.

"Mainly kayaking and some hill-walking. Spent a night camping in Snowdonia."

"Camping? In February?"

"Yeah. It's a little cold at night, I'm not gonna lie, but I was climbing in an old quarry up there. Something to do between jobs."

"I hear you're pretty handy around the place?" I fish. "Any good with a screwdriver and a paintbrush?"

"Why?"

"I could use some help in the farmhouse. I'll pay you."

"Yeah. Okay. Sounds good."

Draining the final drops of his red wine, Sion makes his excuses to leave.

"You sure it's your emails you're checking out in The Cross Keys?" Jac teases.

I ask him with my eyes, and he mouths the name 'Claire' to me.

"I thought she liked you?"

He pulls a face at me, to tell me how stupid I am for missing something so blindingly obvious.

"I'm whacked," Callista announces. "I'll give you a hand to clear up, and then I'll be off too."

"I'll do that," I offer. "I've been asleep all afternoon. I'm good to go clubbing all night, if anyone's up for it."

Jac starts loading the dishwasher.

"Not sure about clubbing, but we could watch a DVD? I'll take you both back. We can watch it at yours."

"Yeah. Okay. Something mindless, with explosions and fast cars?"

"Deal."

Jac drives us back to the farm.

Callista goes off to bed, while Jac and I sit down together in the living room.

It feels like old times again, as I snuggle down under a throw with Jac to watch the movie.

And somehow, as we get into the action-adventure film, I've found that his arm is around me, as my head has come to rest on his shoulder. And it feels so comforting lying up against him, like we did as kids, watching the movie's set-piece action sequences and city car chases.

"It's strange being here without Mam."

He squeezes my shoulder, and his breath on my head sends a disturbing thrill through me that I try desperately to squash.

But then, he sets me tingling again as I sense his mouth quietly brushing the top of my head, and it's all I can do not to tilt my face towards his lips, like a flower to the sun.

He's only being nice to me.

Repeating that as a mantra in my head, helps steady my pulse.

"You're not alone, Annie. We're all here for you."

You were right, I tell myself. He is only comforting you.

But it's at that moment too, that I finally admit it to myself. My teen crush isn't over.

I'm still in love with Jac Jones.

"How's my favourite bar worker this evening?"

Claire placed a perfectly poured pint of lager onto the bar.

"Who, Kevin?" Claire fired back with a quirky grin. "If you wanna know, he's being his usual dickhead self."

"What's he done now?"

Pulling out the plastic bag that she'd dumped under the bar, she produced from it a tiny cutaway vest top with a beer brand across it.

"He just wants me to wear this as my uniform. He says we need to boost sales."

"What? And does he wanna stick a couple of poles in the corner too?"

Kevin was starting to get up his nose.

"Where's he tonight?"

"Liverpool. Probably seeing those dodgy mates of his, who were in here last week. I'm gonna tell him to stick his job. I like it here, but there's plenty of bar work on the coast. And I'm definitely not wearing that."

"I'll miss you if you go."

"I thought you were only here for the wifi?"

He took a sip of his drink.

"But, if you did wanna go out some time?"

"I don't date customers."

"What if I stop coming in?"

He held her gaze.

"What if you stop working here?"

"Go check your emails, Sion."

He grinned.

She hadn't said no.

She looked really good this evening, in her black Nirvana t-shirt and tight black jeans. She was far too cool for this place. She didn't need that pillock harassing her.

The payment from the Scousers was in, and there was an update from Irish in his encrypted emails. He'd been lying low for five weeks, and he'd stay here for a couple of weeks more. It had been a wise plan. Things, he could see, had been kicking off in London.

The Helbanianz were on the warpath. There'd been a couple of hits on other gangs, and then retaliations from that. A turf war. But without Prifti, as predicted, the Helbanianz were weak and disorganised.

And most importantly, Sion was still a ghost to them.

And as forecast by his handler, the Scousers had used the confusion to quickly muscle into the area and set up supply and distribution chains.

These guys were logistics experts. Better than Amazon.

Snapping shut his laptop and stowing it away, he took himself back over to the bar.

So far, it had been plain sailing. A couple more weeks and he could start considering jobs again.

# CHAPTER 13

----------*----------

"I need to get back. People in London will have forgotten who I am. And besides, I miss Sam."

Jac and Callista wandered through the fields, her arm in his.

"You sure that old thing of Annie's will get us there? Do you mind checking it over for us, darling?"

"Yeah, no worries," Jac agreed, "The last thing you need, is a blow-out on the motorway. If that old banger does break down, at least Annie'll have you to keep her company on the hard shoulder."

Annie had offered to drive Callista back to London with her. The old SUV hadn't been further than the nearest town in the whole time Jac had been there. And he was sure, Trusty Rusty, as Annie called it, was the same old truck Glyn had when Jac was a kid. Glyn was far too mean to spend money on garage servicing, preferring to tinker with his motors himself.

They'd had a cold snap since Maureen's funeral, and the weather was holding dry and frosty. The ground hadn't thawed for days, and the frozen grass crunched under Cal's borrowed wellies. Jac went around the stock with her, explaining what he'd been doing and showing her his plans.

Callista listened with interest.

"The cold weather means they need more silage."

"My son, the farmer."

She patted his arm.

"Better than your son, the soldier?"

"Much better. I was never happy about that, as you know. Though, you're also well versed on my views on meat production."

Her exasperation made Jac laugh.

"How can I forget that memorable day when you caught your vegan son scoffing down a double cheeseburger."

"All this work... What happens if Annie sells the place? Alun was in a deep convo with her at Maureen's funeral. He's after the land. And her too, I wouldn't be surprised. His eyes were on her the whole time."

Sensing she'd touched a nerve, Callista stopped.

"Son, if you like her, you need to tell her."

"It's not that easy."

"You're too scared to take a risk, you mean?"

"It's complicated. I don't wanna muck things up between us."

"Jac, you can't help who you love. Look at me and your father. And now with Sam, we have this deep..."

"Cal!"

He wasn't going there. Delving into the depths of his mother's pansexual love life.

"When you find real love, and I'm not talking about sex, I mean real *knock-you-sidewards-so-full-on-you-can't-even-breathe* kinda love; it's like a truth. And, however much you try, there's no denying it."

He studied the ground and his boots.

"You've always loved Annie. This is only as difficult as you want it to be. Think about it, son."

He did. He thought about nothing else.

Bringing in the wood for the fire. Feeding Jess. Making dinner.

He remembered her in his arms, watching that film. And the smell of toffee from her shampoo as his lips touched her soft, golden hair. He needed to see her before she went back to London. To tell her how much she meant to him; that he loved her.

It was dark by the time he finally decided to go for it.

Grabbing his coat and toolbox, he headed up to the farmhouse to check Trusty out and see Annie before she left.

From the back porch, he could hear her voice drifting in from the farmhouse kitchen.

"Uh-uh. Strip back what you can and cover everything in a cream colour. If you could paint the kitchen units and screw those loose doors back on tight, that'd be great too. I'll be back in three or four days, so all that should keep you busy 'til then. At least the kitchen will look fresh if I have viewings."

"Viewings?"

Jac was taken aback. She'd not mentioned anything to him about selling up.

And where did that leave him and the farm?

"That's fine, I can do that for you," Sion carried on as Jac stormed in. "I'll keep receipts and we can settle up when you get back."

"I'm sorry if I'm interrupting you both," Jac rumbled. His throat cracked and dry.

"We… we… we were going through…"

"No need to explain. You don't even need to tell me, you're selling the farm. In fact, don't tell me anything…"

His voice rose.

"Considering, I'm only the *bloody tenant.*"

"I think I'll get going," Sion said, assessing the situation. "I'll come by first thing in the morning."

Jac watched his old buddy leave. He moved out of there quicker than a plate of beans through a vegan. So much for having his back.

"See ya, bro'," Jac called after him, snarkily.

Annie's eyes slammed into his with a defiant glare.

"Don't you go having a pop at Sion, for helping me out," she railed at him. "I'm just considering my options, that's all."

"Keys?" he growled at her. "Cal asked me to check the truck. I'm doing it for her."

Her temper was up too now, and her green eyes flashed at him ferociously. Snatching the keys off the hook, she flung them at him.

"It's my farm, Jac. I can do what I want with it. And if I do decide to sell the land, I'll *bloody well* sell it."

When she saw him scowling back at her, she added, "Don't worry, I'll give you first refusal."

"Gee, thanks."

He turned to charge away but halted in his tracks.

"And just how do you think, an ex-squaddie like me is gonna get hold of the multi-million pound price-tag on this farm?" His sarcastic tone, infuriating her. "Rob a bank? Or better still, I'll look down the back of that old sofa."

"You could always ask Mummy?" she said mockingly.

"No."

The thunderous finality in his voice ended all conversation. She threw him the heavy-duty torch, then slammed the door.

He was still seething, as he turned the key in the ignition and started it up. The SUV's engine sounded fine, but the ride would be a boneshaker.

Good. It served her right.

Selling the farm. He hadn't seen that coming.

When I've simmered down, I'm feeling pretty bad with myself. His outburst surprised me.

I should have been more sensitive to him and explained it to him first. Plans? I've no idea what I'm doing myself yet, but I do tend to go off like a bull at a gate.

Like redecorating the farmhouse.

Jac's got Trusty's bonnet open when I come out onto the yard. It's freezing, even though I've wrapped up against the cold.

I approach the Isuzu gingerly.

"Thanks for checking her over."

"Got a tissue for this?" he grunts, his head in the engine, not looking up.

I go get some kitchen roll from the house and he snatches it out of my hand to wipe the dipstick.

"Tyres are good. Oil's fine," he says flatly, stepping away from the truck, still refusing to look me in the eye. "Should be alright."

"I hope so. She's all I've got."

He leans against the driver's door and I follow suit, standing in moody silence for a couple of minutes stewing on the words we've thrown at each other. Wondering who'll give in first?

This time, Jac folds.

"You can't sell up, Annie. You love this place."

"I do. But what's here for me, Jac? There's no jobs."

He considers it, wiping his hands clean of oil.

"Look, it's your place, you need to do what's best for you."

"Yeah," I shrug, holding my chin high.

"But... I don't want you to go."

"You don't?"

My stomach flips.

"No."

Our eyes meet.

Whether it's from us fighting, I'm not sure. But, that electricity we have, it's definitely crackling between us now. And its heady, heart-thumping anticipation makes it so I can hardly breathe.

My body fizzes as he suddenly pulls me into him, caging himself roughly around me and covering my lips in a dizzyingly passionate, claiming kiss.

I can't help myself. Consumed with desire for each other, I arch my body up against his strong torso as he presses me back hard up against the Isuzu; still wrapped together, his mouth on mine, our tongues dancing.

Suddenly, my mushed-up brain kicks into overdrive.

What's he doing? Kissing me like this, the night before I'm leaving? The same evening he finds out that I might sell the farm?

It's happening to me again.

*The bastard!*

He's playing me.

Pulling away, I suddenly can't breathe; and I push him back

with the palm of my hands against his chest.

"Annie! What's up?"

He's good, alright.

Making his eyes appear clouded with lust, then confusion.

"You were amazing. Can't you feel this thing we have between us?"

"Don't you dare!"

"What?"

Jac rubs his face.

"What've I done?"

"You've taken me for a fool, Jac Jones."

"What?"

His fake innocence maddens me even more.

"Don't give me, '*what*'. I mention selling the farm and you snog me, like that."

"*Snog?*"

"What d'ya take me for, some gullible fool?"

"*Uh?*"

"D'ya think I'll melt in your arms and do whatever you want me to do?"

"Annie… Please… You've got this all wrong."

"Have I?"

I push him back angrily again with the flat of my hand.

"You make no moves until now? *Now*. When I'm considering selling up. D'ya think I'm daft?"

"Hold on," his voice rises in anger. "You're suggesting I'd *use* you like that? For the farm?"

"Well, wouldn't you? Mr Love'm'n'leave'em?"

"Mr *What?*" he sneers, making my blood boil. "Are you, like, twelve or something? Grow up, Annie!"

"What about your rule, Jac?" I hurl back at him furiously.

"Yeah, bloody good rule, if ya ask me," he snaps, slamming the bonnet down shut and storming away.

"See ya around."

"You gonna be quiet the whole journey, Missy? I thought we were gonna have some fun? What happened to Thelma and Louise?"

"Sorry, Cal. I'm tired, that's all. I didn't sleep much last night."

I've been in a foul mood since I woke up, having spent most of the night sniping and grousing to myself about Jac.

Cal stares blankly out of the window.

It's not turning out to be anything like the road trip we'd cooked up together. But we drive on, covering the miles as I brood silently about Jac.

That kiss. The rush of excitement, and the temper we both have when we fight.

"You're doing it again."

"What?"

"Thinking and sighing."

"Am I?"

"Uh-huh."

"Tell me about Sam," I say, trying to sound upbeat, switching the conversation.

"What about her? She's a lecturer."

"In?"

"Printmaking. We met at an art retreat in Spain."

"Cool."

"Hmm. It *was* heavenly. We were in this remote finca in the Sierra Nevada, miles from anywhere, surrounded by the spring flowers and the birds," Callista explains wistfully. "We were up high in the mountains, but it felt like Wales too, like the farm. Except that they had almond and lemon trees, of course."

"What d'you mean *like the farm*?"

"Peaceful, sweetie. There aren't many places left where you're totally unplugged and surrounded by nature. It's very special."

I chew that over later.

I've never thought about the farm in that way before. The lack of connectivity has always been a huge hassle for me, and a convenient excuse to get back to London.

But, I get what Callista means. Being out of touch with all the stresses of work has helped put my career into perspective.

The truth is, my job had become tedious. The move from New York to London was me trying to find new challenges, re-energise. But it wasn't the geography, that was the problem.

From the events of the last few weeks, I've learned too, that work is only one part of my life. It used to be everything. And my career must never define me. Because, if it's taken away, then what will be left? It took being perched on my ledge, gazing at the magnificent Welsh mountains, to finally figure that one out.

"Where did you stay on the retreat?"

"They'd turned the farm buildings into bunk rooms, and there was a living area where we could cook and sit together. They had a large art studio there too. And they had yurts. Very romantic," Callista chuckles.

"I hope I get to meet Sam, soon."

"You will. I've told her all about you."

"Did Jac like her?"

"Yes, of course, sweetie... Now, how about we stop beating around the bush," she says finally, as we filter onto the motorway. "What on earth is going on between you two?"

I focus hard on the traffic, trying not to engage.

"It's complicated."

"*Ha!* That's *exactly* what he said."

"When?"

"Yesterday afternoon, when I went for a walk with him."

"Yesterday *afternoon*?"

"Yes. He likes you, Annie. A lot. More than likes. He always has. But, he's afraid to mess things up with you. I told him to go for it and tell you how he felt."

"You *did*?"

"Yes. Why?"

I turn to look at Callista and then hit the brake hard as the traffic slows up sharply in front of me.

"*Crap!*"

"What's up?"

"He went for it."

"And?"

I chew on my bottom lip. I've messed things up.

"He kissed me, Cal. And we had a big fight. Two actually. I thought he was only kissing me, so I'd keep the farm."

"What?"

"I was confused. It made sense at the time."

"You're thinking of selling the farm?"

"Yes... No... I dunno yet... I asked Sion to help me paint up the place and Jac overheard."

"And, you believe that Jac was trying to manipulate you?"

"*Oh, God!*" I cringe. "When you put it like that."

"Why would Jac do such a thing?"

She's right.

"He's like me, he doesn't give a hoot about material things."

"*Argh!* I'm over-analysing everybody's motives these days."

"Don't be so hard on yourself, my dear."

"But, I'm getting it wrong all the time, Cal. How can I trust anybody ever again, when I don't even trust my own judgement?"

"Do you still feel something for him?"

My pained expression and the sigh escaping my lips tells her all she needs to know.

"Trust your heart then, sweetie. Try listening to that."

# CHAPTER 14

----------✳----------

"Want another one?"

Jac was going for it, slamming down the tequila shots.

"We better be heading soon."

They were the only two of the original gang of friends left in the club on the pier, and Sion was ready for home.

"Taxi's booked for one o'clock, mate. It won't wait. And it'll be a bitch to try and get another one to go all the way to our back of beyond."

"Take a chill pill, Sion. Worst case scenario, we kip on a sofa. Best case, we get a bed."

"Easy tiger."

Sion refused the full shot glass Jac was pushing onto him.

"What about Annie?"

"What about her?"

Jac knocked Sion's shot back in one.

The place was buzzing. Students were out in force. Jac hadn't felt like this in a long time. Like lads again, on a night out.

"Come on, mate. We're the last men standing."

Sion looked at the state of his friend.

"Just about."

A group of girls, who'd been eyeing them for a while, began making their way over. Soon, they were sidled up next to where Sion and Jac were standing.

"I've not seen you here before?"

One of them had started to make conversation with Jac.

"Wanna drink?"

She was tall and blonde, not a patch on Annie of course. But she'd do, for tonight.

She strained to hear him over the music.

"Tequila?"

"Whatever."

Sion found Jac by the bar waiting to get served.

"Mate, I'm off. Come with me or you'll miss our taxi."

"Nah, I'm good."

"Mate, what you doin'? Come on. Let's go."

"Leave me be, Sion."

He sighed and smacked Jac on the shoulder.

"Alright. See ya, bro."

Turning towards the exit, Sion began battling his way out of there, towards his taxi home.

Jac jostled his way back over to the table with his tray of shots held high. Then, with the group of girls, they began slamming them down together.

As a fourth round was being bought, taking the tall girl's hand, Jac moved with her into a booth where they made-out until her friends came to find her.

The club was closing.

Staggering a little uneasily, arm in arm, they made their way back with the group to a student flat, a couple of streets behind the seafront.

"This is me."

The scruffy-looking four-storey tenement was typical student digs.

Empty spirit bottles on one of the front window ledges. A large faded Welsh flag suspended from another. And the lights were all still on, even though they were halfway to dawn.

As the other girls wobbled through the door, Jac drew the blonde back to him.

"Wanna come up?" she whispered into his mouth.

"I was hoping you'd say that."

Jac followed her unsteady climb up the stairs.

The tequila was beginning to wear off by now.

Sitting at the kitchen table under the glare of a strip-light, Jac could see that she looked young. Twenty? Twenty-two at the most.

It sobered him some more.

She made him a coffee, splashing milk and coffee granules everywhere in the process.

She was shitfaced.

Plonking it down beside him and sloshing coffee onto the table, she then boldly straddled him, pulling her blonde hair back off her shoulders as she wriggled onto him on the kitchen chair.

Her mouth drunkenly found his and her tongue hungrily explored as she kissed him hard.

What the Hell was he doing?

"Jo?" he said, suddenly pulling away.

"Jen."

"Yeah, Jen."

He moved her hand off him.

"I'm sorry, but I've gotta go. I've got a taxi to catch."

She pouted at him.

"You can stay if you want?"

"Another time. I've gotta go."

Rising from the chair, he grabbed his coat and darted from there as quickly as he dared; down the tenement stairs to the street below and into the cold night air.

Closing the door, he slipped swiftly away, until there were at least two streets between them.

Then he stopped.

It was half-past four.

He walked back to outside the club and tried the last two taxis still in the rank. But none of them would take him. They shook their heads and pulled up their side windows. It was too far.

Pulling his coat up as high as the zip would go, Jac wandered the deserted, dark streets listening out for a party. Survival training, he joked to himself. If he found one, he'd go up there, get warm, crash out on a settee.

But, by now even the students were in bed.

The March wind blasted in hard off the sea, battering his cheeks.

*Jees* it was cold!

He should have stayed with Jo.

*Damn her!* Annie had killed it for him.

He couldn't have her, and he didn't want anyone else.

He was screwed.

There was irony in that, he realised, as he found a bench in a bus shelter and tried to huddle himself warm.

He was a tough army boy. He'd lain in a fox hole in Sangin, he was sure he would survive a bitter March night in Aberystwyth. But how long could he survive living on the farm with Annie around?

Annie, who only thought the worst of him.

Alun had sought him out in The Cross Keys a couple of evenings ago. Flown a couple of ideas by him. He'd have time to chew those over some more now.

Perhaps it *would* be best to cut and run? Start afresh somewhere new, far away from here.

It had been a mistake coming home.

Leaving a message on Sion's phone, he curled himself up tightly. It was going to be a shiveringly cold few hours until the first cafés opened.

# CHAPTER 15

----------✶----------

It's a week later when I make it back to the farm in Trusty Rusty. And the old girl's loaded up to the brim with boxes, bags and bin liners. The sum total of my London life.

My apartment is now stripped bare. The furniture's been sold, and the keys are back with the letting agent.

I'm done with London. And my old career.

I'm ready for a new start.

And on my last evening there, I sent a brief resignation email to Lisa. I didn't go into any details, and despite Callista's pep talks, I held firm on my decision not to name Seb.

I haven't in any way got it all figured out, but after sitting in a London café one long afternoon, trying to decide what to do, the truth screamed at me hard.

It *was* a question of geography, after all.

My life's no longer there. It belongs, if I'm being honest, with my heart, back in Wales.

And so, with much trepidation, I've come home.

To do what?

I'm not exactly sure yet. The rent for the farm will keep me afloat, but I'll need a challenge to keep me busy and I've been bouncing some ideas around.

"*Wow!*"

I put my keys on the hook and take a good look around, noting all the changes. The kitchen's been transformed.

The old wallpapered walls have been stripped back and painted a light cream. The pine units have been painted too, a pigeon grey. It makes the space modern yet homely. And the door handles have been swapped too. They're now copper.

"You like it?"

Sion appears with paint flecked across his face.

"I love it."

"And I've made a start on the lounge."

I run my hand over the wooden countertops. They've been sanded back to a pale butchers-block finish.

"I can't believe you've done all this, Sion. It's amazing."

"Jac did that."

My eyes widen.

"He did?"

"Yeah; and picked the colours and the handles."

"I'm glad I kept you both busy."

"Been on it non-stop, apart from Sunday."

"Hungover?"

"Hmm. Went out with the boys Saturday night to Aber."

"Jac go too?"

Sion clears his throat.

"D'ya wanna hand with your stuff?"

He takes a look at the jam-packed truck.

"Travelling light?"

"I'm moving back home."

It feels so good.

For the next week, I busy myself by sorting the house out. Unpacking my stuff, buying new curtains, a rug for the lounge, and undertaking the grim task of clearing out my parents' things. It's a mammoth task, with several trips to the charity shops and the rubbish tip, but it's also cathartic. I go to the solicitors too and start the process of probate.

It's confirmed. The farm is mine.

"Jac okay?" I ask Sion, as I help him paint the stairs. "I've not seen hide nor hair of him all week."

"He's busy getting the shed ready for lambing."

Sion's making excuses for Jac, but his continued absence makes me feel nauseous.

At first, when I heard about him helping with the kitchen, I thought that I might be forgiven for what I said. But as I haven't seen him even once since I came home, I'm now convinced that I've trashed any chance that we might have of being together.

As I brush, I chew it over some more.

What if the kitchen was a subtle message from him? Helping me to sell the farm. To get out of here?

"Tell me about the army," I ask Sion, trying to push those fears away.

"What d'ya wanna know?"

"Did you enjoy it?"

"I dunno if 'enjoy' is the right word. There were fantastic times, and one or two moments of sheer Hell."

He falls silent and focuses his concentration on his roller.

"When did you meet Jac?"

"Day one. In the Welsh Guards. He's always had my back."

"He said about you both having to clean the toilets with a toothbrush?"

"When did he tell you that?"

I feel myself going bright red. It was in his first letter.

"So, you were in combat together too?"

"Yeah. Afghanistan twice. Had a couple of sticky moments. I got stuck in a building with snipers on me. Jac's truck hit an IUD."

"Were either of you hurt?"

"No. We both lived to tell the tale. Helped us get on, to be honest. We both got selected to try out for the special forces after that."

Special forces? I had no idea Jac was an elite soldier.

"Do you miss it?"

"Honestly? Yes, I do. When you're in the army, everything's structured. When you leave, you've suddenly gotta fend for yourself."

"I guess Jac's got the farming. What about you?"

"I was a bit lost for the first few months. It took time for me to adjust... but I... uhh... I retrained."

I get the vibe that Sion's not too comfortable talking about himself.

"Have you spoken to Jac since you got back?"

"He knows where I am if he wants to talk."

"Funny that. He said the same thing to me."

"Yeah well, that's the problem. Neither of us will back down. Like, *ever*."

He likes you, Annie. I've known Jac for years and I've never seen him like this about a woman."

"*Hmph.*"

"Talk to him. His moodiness is doin' my head in."

"He knows where I am," I repeat, focusing on my glossing.

No way am I going grovelling to him, if he can't even be bothered to come and say hello.

"But, can you say thank you from me, for the work he did in the kitchen?"

Sion shakes his head in exasperation.

"I've got a better idea. Why don't you tell him yourself?"

I'm surprised a couple of days later when Alun, my next-door neighbour, pulls up on the yard in his new Range Rover. I haven't seen him since my mother's funeral when he'd said again that he'd be calling.

And now he's here.

Peeking at him through the window as he marches purpose-fully towards the front door, it doesn't look like he's making a social call.

He pulls a face as he steps into the refurbished farmhouse.

"Someone's been busy."

He scans the kitchen approvingly.

"You're safe. The walls and woodwork have just dried."

I can see him making the calculations in his head. How much the place is worth. With, then without, the land.

Clearing my throat slightly, I draw his attention back to me.

"I've been dying to spruce the place up for years."

"Getting ready to sell?"

"No. I'm keeping the farm."

I say it firmly and his eyes meet mine, staring at me hard for just a second as if I'm spoiling his plans.

He looks good. Successful. I take in his expensive country-gent designer clothing, and the new top-of-the-range Range Rover parked in the yard.

But, I can't shake off the shadows of the past. I shudder. Lizard Man.

"You cold?"

He's being perfectly charming and polite. I've made him tea and we sit in the kitchen at the big pine table, now scrubbed clean with a bowl of fruit on it.

"You've not been tempted by the money, then?"

He thrusts into the real meat of the conversation, cutting to the chase.

"You could get a fair bit for a place like this."

"No. I'm staying."

Alun's face twitches.

"But, what about your job in London?"

I don't want to go into that with him.

"I've left. Time for a new start, back here."

He sips his tea and stares at me intensely.

"And what you gonna do when Jac goes?"

"What?"

Taking in my blank stare, he continues, smugly.

"Sorry, Annie, I thought you knew... He's asked me to buy his sheep off him. We've agreed a price."

"When?"

I'm summoning everything I have within me to retain my composure, although I'm certain that Alun's noticed.

"He'll be gone by June."

I gulp my tea.

"If you're interested, I'd like to rent the land after?"

I shrug noncommittally, my mind still reeling.

"Sure."

Now he's said what he came to say, Alun rises to leave. He has no time to waste.

"How about we talk it over again after you've had time to think it through? Over dinner?"

I nod, numbly.

"I'll be in touch."

Alun's car has barely left the farmyard, when I grab my coat and hastily leave the house, scouring the place in search of Jac.

I scan the yard, then rush through the old stone sheds.

He's not there and the tractor's out.

The lambing season will be starting any day now. Then, he'll be working around the clock. I was going to offer to help him, but after Alun's bombshell, everything's up in the air.

And if Alun's right, things are more than a little broken between us. Unfixable even.

But, I *can* break this stupid silence.

I need, at least, to have it out with him. And apologise for what I said.

I spot him over in the field we call Windy Corner.

He's by the tractor, in the middle of the mud, forking the silage bale around the feeder. It's soggy and boggy as I stomp across the field, my wellies squelching as I soldier on over the sodden ground.

"Jac!" I call out, as I approach him.

He carries on.

Perhaps, he hasn't heard me. Perhaps, he has. He's working with purpose. Determined. Head down.

"Jac Jones!" I shout over to him again.

I know that he's heard me, and I'm furious with him. He can't ignore me again.

Even his dog is running over to see me.

This time, he does have the courtesy to stop and glance up. *Hallelujah!*

I pat Jess.

"What d'ya want, Annie?"

His hostile tone dampens my spirits worse than the rain.

"I'm sorry," I sniff, swallowing a huge lump of pride.

"I'm sorry for what I said. I was wrong."

He stares at me coldly, and then starts to work the silage again, ignoring me.

I wait there a good while as he carries on. The rain stings my face as I stare at the bleak, bare fields. Only the tough sedge tussocks brave the barren ground.

And I stand there, still. Holding out. Expecting him to stop. Watching him forking the feed furiously. Deliberately and defiantly he ignores me until it's too uncomfortable any longer for me to stay.

He's punishing me.

Humiliated, hot-faced and defeated; at last, it's my turn to break.

Fighting back the tears, and holding my head up high, I squelch my way quickly back towards the farmhouse.

It's over.

It's only the memory of that kiss; the electricity that's so thrilling between us, that makes me even consider a final throw of the dice.

That, and Callista and Sion's assurances that he *more than likes me*. Whatever that means. They didn't hear me shooting my mouth off, accusing him of being a gold-digger.

*Argh!* I scream into the wind.

I've only one option left, and if this doesn't work, then I need to give it up and let him go.

Getting back to the farmhouse, I find a pad of paper and an envelope in the kitchen dresser drawer. Sitting down at the table, it's now my turn to write him a letter.

It takes a while, and plenty of failed attempts, until I'm happy with the words. Sealing the envelope with a kiss of hope, I go about collecting up all the screwed-up balls of paper from off the floor around my chair. The whole thing has taken ages.

Before I can change my mind, I take it down to the cottage, posting it through the letterbox before he gets back. After that, I'll wait for him to come to me.

And wait, I do. All evening.

I've had a shower, done my hair, even put on some make-up. And there I am, like Miss *flippin'* Havisham, sitting alone in the kitchen, fidgeting, flitting restlessly to the window, watching furtively for a flashlight on the yard.

I try to settle down with a book, but I can't concentrate. My ears are still on alert for a knock at the door.

But, there's nothing.

And the call that I've waited for all evening never comes.

Eventually, giving up, I retreat miserably to bed.

My heart aches and I feel empty and rejected for a second time.

Sion came in as Jac was taking sausages out of the oven. It had become an odd domestic arrangement, with Jac cooking dinner for Sion most evenings. Sion repaid him now and again with groceries and meals in the Cross Keys, but Jac was happy to cook. He liked doing it and had to make food for himself anyway, he told Sion.

Sion grabbed two beers from the fridge and prised off the tops.

"Busy day at the office, dear?"

Sion passed Jac a bottle.

"You see Annie?"

"No. Why?"

"You two are driving me nuts. She's sulking up there, and you're moping down here. If you don't do something soon, she'll be gone, mate."

Jac said nothing as he mashed boiled potatoes and swede together vigorously in the pan with some butter.

Since the deal he'd done with Alun, he'd assiduously avoided seeing her. And he'd been surprised when she turned up by the feeder. She never backed down.

And she'd apologised.

He'd made her pay for what she said to him, all right. He'd been a bastard to her. There were no other words for how he'd behaved.

*Jees!* She'd looked so beautiful too, with her golden hair blowing wildly around her wind-stung cheeks. And those brilliant green eyes of hers, sparkling angrily as he carried on with his work, punishing her.

And she stayed standing there for ages, furious with him, waiting to see if he'd crack first.

But he hadn't, he'd carried on. He'd stood his ground.

And anyway, it was all too late. They were done.

"I'll be out of here by June. All the hours I've put into this place, for *bugger all*."

"Where you going?"

"Dunno. As far away from here as I can. A beach. Somewhere hot. Somewhere, where there's no mud."

There hadn't seemed much point in carrying on, after she talked about selling the farm.

"Has she had any estate agents round yet?"

"What?"

Sion looked at him confused.

"You're not tarting the place up for nothing."

"No, mate. You've got it wrong. She's staying."

Jac stopped mashing.

"You guys seriously need to talk."

"She came to see me," he said, rubbing his face.

"When?"

"Last week."

"Why didn't you try and make up?"

"You think a few words will make it sweet? We're way beyond that."

Sion was silent.

"You're not gonna defend her, then?" Jac sniped. "Like you usually do, whenever I mention her."

He'd been out all day hiking in the hills and he was too tired for this shit.

"Whatever, Jac," he yawned. "You're probably too late, anyway. Annie's going out with Alun tonight."

"Butt out, Sion."

"Yeah, I know, mate. It's complicated."

"I've done the deal on the sheep. It's over between me and Annie."

Alun had snapped his hand off. Renting Annie's land meant Alun could instantly double his farm.

But, he was a tough cookie. And when they'd talked in the mart, Alun got a pen out, there and then, and scribbled a number on the back of a receipt. It was half what the stock was worth.

Jac had taken the pen off him and crossed it out, writing another figure below it. They went like that four times until finally the amount was agreed.

It was more than a fair price.

Jac would stay till June, to finish the lambing, then they'd exchange the stock for money. It was the end of another chapter. Jac had no idea where he was heading next, and his stomach felt hollow every time he thought about it. It was not what he wanted, but as things stood, there was no other option.

After they'd eaten, Sion loaded the dishwasher.

"Who's that from? It's been sitting there for a week, mate."

He pointed up at an envelope on the kitchen windowsill.

"No one."

The envelope had appeared on the doormat a week ago. Jac knew who it was from, and like her, he'd willed himself not to open it.

"I'm gonna check on the ewes."

They were due to lamb anytime now. He put on his big waxed jacket and found the large torch. Not that he needed it. A full moon had been out earlier on that evening. Its silvery light reminded him of the night, once upon a time, when he'd walked through the fields with Annie.

"I'm glad I took that torch," he said from the door, taking off his boots, an hour later. "It's clouded right over, and we've had a fair few flakes. The forecast's right, we're in for a dump of snow tonight."

Sion was sitting in the kitchen, waiting for him.

"You're one dumb bastard, you know that?"

Jac looked at him confused.

"You're sitting here sulking, selling your stock. And she's up there, all cut up, 'cos she's written to you telling you how much she loves you, and how she wants you to stay. But, you're too chicken shit and stubborn to even open the bloody envelope."

The letter lay opened on the kitchen table.

"You've crossed the line," Jac shouted at him angrily.

"No, Jac. I'm pulling you over it."

Sion put his hand on Jac's shoulder as he stared at the letter. "Read it."

Sitting down, Jac heaved a sigh and did as he was bid.

*Dear Jac,*

*Me and my big mouth. Everything I do and say I get wrong these days.*

*Please forgive me. I got confused. I've been feeling so lost. It's all come at once; losing my parents, my job, the people who I thought were my friends.*

*But, the one thing I can't bear to lose again is you. You've been lost to me before, and even though you'd gone, I could never let you go in my heart.*

*And, before you say it. I know. It was my own stupid fault that I didn't read your letters. We're both too stubborn for our own good, especially me. And we both need to work on it. Or not argue ever again.*

*I want to stay here, Jac, on the farm. But, there's no way I can farm this place on my own. I've got plans too, but I need your help. Maybe, it's just as a friend? Perhaps, it's as something more? That's up to you.*

*I'll be telling Alun that I've no intention of renting my land to him without you giving me proper notice that you're going.*

*Jac, I love you too much to let you drift away without telling me, again.*

*So there. I've said it.*

*The ball's in your court now.*

*Annie x*

Jac lifted his eyes towards Sion, who was quietly watching his friend.

"She's staying, mate."

"Yeah. Looks like it."

"D'ya wanna leave?"

"No. But I can't stay here, as things are."

"D'you want her?"

"'Course I do."

"So, what's stopping you?"

"You know what."

"Mate, that rule you've lived by, it might've served you well in the army, but Annie's different. You're already way beyond rules with her. Don't lose her again."

Jac put the letter in his shirt pocket and stood up straight.

"I'm going for a walk."

"I'm off out too."

Sion got up and slapped him on the back.

"Good luck, pal."

Jac strolled slowly through the fields up to the farmhouse, mulling over exactly what he was going to do next.

The sky had clouded over in a thick blanket, and the air felt expectant and thick. Snow was coming. And as he walked towards the farm, big, wet flakes began to fall thick and fast, sticking quickly onto the ground. Jac had already moved the sheep to the most sheltered fields between the farm and the cottage, but snowfall meant that tomorrow would be a busy day.

# CHAPTER 16

----------✳----------

It's been a week since I wrote that letter, and his continued avoidance of me forces me reluctantly to conclude that I'm not forgiven. We're over. And I won't approach him again.

The letter was enough.

Alun came around to see me yesterday. He looked handsome as he stood on the doorstep with a bunch of tulips in his hand, asking me to have dinner with him.

And at that moment, I thought, why not? Play the game in front of me, right?

Unlike Jac, he wants me. And there's no harm in us having dinner together, I convince myself. I need to discuss my plans with him, anyway.

With my ego and confidence well and truly bruised by Jac, I go all out in trying to look good. After much dilemma and indecision, I've chosen to wear a green silk dress that I bought in New York. It shows off a little bit of cleavage and the colour goes well with my hair, which I've curled especially.

When I'm done, I examine myself in the mirror.

I haven't looked like this since London.

What am I doing? Am I seriously considering starting something with Alun?

I think about it coolly as I'm applying my makeup. Perhaps, it is time to start being led by my head, and not my heart?

Our farms lie side-by-side to each other. If I was a business, I'd be prime merger material. And with Alun, I'd never need to worry about money.

Where has passion got me? In a whole pile of problems with Seb. And now, in a far worse heap of heartache with Jac.

My stomach knots as I think about Jac again. A wave of sadness engulfs me until I feel like I can't breathe. The trouble is, I've always felt too much for him. And that's blinded me to the truth, that he doesn't feel the same way about me.

If he did, he'd be here right now.

"I'm a little early," Alun apologises as I open the front door to let him in.

He stops speaking as he appraises me.

"You're looking very beautiful tonight, Annie."

"Thank you."

I'm flattered that I meet with his considered approval.

He's dressed well and has another large bunch of flowers in his hand.

I take them gratefully from him and put them in a large jug of water in the kitchen sink. They're lilies; stylish and expensive, and they remind me of Alun. They look fantastic, but they always make me sneeze.

"I've reserved a table at La Galloise."

I reach for my faux-fur coat.

"I've always wanted to try there."

It's a smart restaurant down the coast that has gained quite a reputation for its delicious food and its breathtaking location, high on the cliffs above the small village of Freshwater Bay.

"How did you get a table? They're usually booked up weeks in advance."

He doesn't answer but gives me a smug smile. He's obviously a regular.

And in that smile, and without arrogance, I see how my life with Alun would be.

And he's interested. His hand touches the small of my back as we cross the yard to his Range Rover. He opens the passenger side door for me, holding my hand as I climb up in my strappy high-heeled sandals.

We could easily start dating.

The images flash through my head. The big wedding. Our perfect kids, of course.

It chills me to the bone.

He's polite and attentive all evening, ordering us apple martinis as we chat. And I hate to admit it, but in spite of myself, I am quite enjoying his company.

He's been away too, studying farm management, working on large estates in England, then in New Zealand. He doesn't brag, but I can tell he's well connected. He mentions the shooting weekends he goes on with his friends from university. I never took him for the horsey type, but he's active in the local hunt. The circles he moves in; they're all wealthy landowners. It's a far cry from sheep farmers like my dad. And Jac.

The food is French and fabulous. We feast on scallops with a pea purée, followed by a delicious crispy-skinned duck in a bitter cherry sauce. And we drink a little wine.

I cover my glass with my hand as he tries to top it up again.

"Are you trying to get me drunk?"

I'm starting to feel a little buzzed.

"I'm driving and there's still some left."

"If it's alright with you, I think I'll switch to water."

We order coffees together with an unctuous chocolate mousse gâteau that we share.

Time passes easily, as we talk about people from school, about farming, about his business deals. My life in New York and London.

It's all pleasant enough, but deep down, that is the problem. As I sober up, I know too that this isn't enough.

And yet, Jac's stubborn silence screams like an alarm in my ears. Alun might be all that I could ever hope for now.

"Have you had a chance to think about the future?"

I look up from studying my coffee.

"I have."

"About renting the land to me?"

"Yes."

His eyes catch mine, and I glance away.

"I'm sorry, but at the moment I can't."

"Annie, why not?"

His voice has a note of tetchiness I've not heard before, and I can see the strain in his face.

"The thing is, Alun," I launch in, "I'm not sure if deep-down Jac wants to sell his sheep. If he tells me to my face, or in writing, that he's giving up his tenancy, I promise, I'll give you first refusal."

I read his face, which is set hard against me.

"I can't be fairer than that?"

"Without the land, Jac has no deal."

He stares at me, like he's studying a chessboard.

"So, you're trusting that hippy drifter to come through for you?"

"No. There's a tenancy agreement."

Until Jac tells me he's going, until he's gone, there's still a grain of hope. There has to be.

His narrowing eyes unnerve me, and I let out a deep breath.

"Yes. I am."

We don't stay long after that. We drive home through the snow showers that are getting steadily heavier as we head from the coast back into the hills. Like the snow, a sour mood is settling silently between us.

Pulling up outside the farmhouse, I undo my seat belt and stretch over for the door handle. He makes a half-hearted attempt at a kiss, but anticipating the move, I peck him on the cheek before diving out the door.

Skidding across the white carpeted concrete, it's not until I'm locked inside the farmhouse that I can finally breathe easy.

Whatever happens, I vow to myself, Alun is not the one for me.

A knock at the front door startles me.

"Hold on."

I kick off my wet sandals and go to unlock the door as the bell

TRUST ME

rings this time.

Nothing, if not persistent. I thought Alun had got the message. I was sure he'd driven away. He must have come back. I obviously need to spell it out to him straight that I'm not interested.

"Jac!"

He's covered in the white snowflakes that are blowing and swirling around us on the Arctic winds.

"I read your letter."

I'm taken aback.

"What?... *Tonight?*"

His face cracks into a disarming smile, that only exasperates me further.

"It's been a week, Jac."

I'm determinedly refusing to thaw, despite his charms.

"That's still less time than it took for you to read mine."

He shoots me a smirk, brushing the snow off his head with his hand, and making my heart thump hard.

I give him my best glare, unwilling to break.

"You're my tenant." I stick to my guns. "If you want out, you need to give me fair notice."

I can feel the snowflakes blowing in and landing on my face. And my bare feet are turning numb from the cold.

"Oh, yeah?"

"Yes."

His eyes burn into mine as he edges closer towards me, making my traitorous body thrum.

"In writing," I tell him, my resolve cracking.

He grins wolfishly at me, grabbing my waist and pulling me to him, out onto the icy doorstep.

"Is that so? Like, in a letter?"

"Yes, a letter would be acceptable," I gasp. "I've told Alun there's no deal. And he won't buy your ewes without my land."

"You sure?"

I stare up at him searchingly.

"Unless, you still wanna go?"

I feel his hot breath on my snow-flaked hair as his face lowers towards mine.

"Well then, can I let you know my intentions now?"

"Now works for me."

He covers my lips, drawing me into a hot, long, lustful kiss.

Feeling me trembling against his wet coat, he pulls away.

"Annie, you've got nothing on your feet!"

In one swift move, he scoops me up into his arms. Holding my legs firmly as my hands stretch up around his neck, he carries me inside the house, setting me down on the thick carpet.

He gets out of his coat, and I get back my breath.

I need to know for sure.

"Are you still leaving?"

"You still staying?"

He gently takes my shoulders. Lifting his hand to my face, he brushes the wet drop of a melted snowflake off my cheek with his thumb.

"Yes."

"Then, if it's alright with you, I'd like to stay too."

His warm mouth is on mine again and I feel all the tension between us melting away, consumed by the heat inside us, as we kiss.

"Let's never fight again."

He covers my face, then my neck in hot, steamy kisses. His mouth moves to my ear.

"I'm sorry, Annie, for being so mean to you."

"Me too," I say, struggling to think, to breathe.

"I should never have doubted you. I got so confused, back there."

"You still confused?"

I pull away and gaze up at him.

"I meant every word I said in that letter."

"Every word?"

I nod as he inches closer.

"That you love me?" he rasps, encircling me again in those strong arms.

"Yes."

"I love you too, Annie. I always have."

He runs his fingers along my jaw, his eyes smouldering as his lips lower towards mine.

"Where were we?"

"You were staying and I was kissing you."

"Was it like this?"

My heart pounds as he takes me ravenously by the mouth, pushing me back against the freshly painted wall of the hallway with all the pent-up passion that's been building between us.

"Yes, like that," I gasp, our tongues dancing greedily together again, my lustful longing for him rocketing to new heights.

"I love this," he murmurs, moving his mouth hungrily over my throat, his avaricious hands exploring under my silky dress.

I lead him up to my bedroom, where our eyes meet in thrillingly nervous anticipation.

Standing by the bed, he takes both my hands.

"You sure, Annie? Once we do this, there's no going back for either of us."

He's right.

"I trust you, Jac."

His deep chocolate eyes fix on mine. "I'm in new territory here with you."

Pulling me down with him onto the bed he begins tentatively to undress me, unzipping and shimmying my silky dress down over my hips.

"Your feet are cold."

Taking them in his hands, he rubs them, trying to warm them up.

I turn my attention to his jumper, and he helps me shuck it off him, along with his T-shirt.

"I feel like a teenager again."

I giggle nervously, then pause as I take in his muscular shoulders.

"What are these?"

He turns and shows me his back. Across it is a huge tattoo. An osprey. It's a work of art, detailed and intricately drawn.

"Your favourite bird."

I trace the outstretched wings with my fingers.

"You designed this?"

He nods, as my lips lightly brush over the lines.

"It's fabulous."

He turns, and on his chest I recognise another bird.

"A lapwing!"

His lips break into a grin as I examine the smaller bird delicately tattooed on his muscular left pectoral.

"Your favourite."

He whispers into my ear, "Inked forever on my heart."

"When did you get it done?"

"After my last letter to you."

"I want one too."

I cover the lapwing with my mouth, trailing my hands over his corded torso.

"God, you've got an amazing body, Annie," he murmurs against my skin, smattering me with insistent kisses.

Working his mouth and fingers, slowly and hungrily, he greedily feasts on every part of me, consuming me again in flames of desire. And it's like I'm finally home as we wrap ourselves tightly around each other, eventually becoming one.

"Annie. You're the only one. Ever."

"Draw me a bird. I want your art on me too."

"How about here?"

His mouth nuzzles my shoulder blade, feeling the indented marks of my past that I always cover from view.

"Yes, there."

The sky was full of snow, but Sion, alone and bored, decided to head for the pub rather than face the long evening flicking through the only four terrestrial channels that Jac's old television picked up.

He needed to check his messages anyway, and he had a feeling that Jac wouldn't be back anytime soon. At least he hoped he wouldn't be. He chuckled to himself, who knew with those two? At least now things would get sorted. One way or another.

A wall of warmth hit his face as he walked into the bar, where the fire was banked up high with logs. Claire caught his smile, her face lighting up as he walked in. And *boy* was she looking good tonight. Her tight, patterned tunic dress and leggings hugged her petite frame in all the right places, showing off her delicious curves.

Behind her, Kevin was staring at his laptop, earplugs in, oblivious to any customers. And by the reflection of his screen in the mirror behind the bar, Sion could see it was the football he was studying, not a brewery spreadsheet.

"Quiet tonight?"

He scanned the empty bar as Claire poured him a pint of real ale.

"Dead," Claire yawned. "The weather's put people off coming out. It's a night for sitting by the fire."

"Or snuggling up?"

"Hmm. Who would you be doing that with? Jac?"

"I think he might be a little preoccupied tonight."

Sion gauged her reaction carefully.

Unflinching, Claire's eyes met his.

"So, you'll be all alone, then."

"Perhaps."

He looked at her hopefully.

She broke into a laugh, shaking her head, "You're a cocky bugger, you are. D'you never give up?"

Sion clocked Kevin's piggy eyes on him. He had one ear-pod dangling, sneakily earwigging.

"Evening," he signalled, raising his voice.

Kevin instantly dived back into his laptop. Fiddling with his ear-pod, he positioned it hastily back into his ear.

"Spend some time with me, Claire. How about we go for a walk by the coast? When are you off next?"

"Not until midweek."

"Think about it?"

"Okay," she crumbled, smiling.

"That's a yes, then?"

"You don't give up, do you?"

"Never when it comes to you."

"I better get on. Someone says I need to talk less and do more cleaning when it's quiet,"

"God forbid, you should be sat watching football and online porn behind the bar all evening."

"Exactly. Or doing dodgy deals with the kids 'round here."

She rubbed the tip of her nose and sniffed; then gave him a wink, before disappearing into the kitchen.

Cocaine. He'd noticed Kevin taking cigarette breaks with random strangers a few times. It made sense now. He was dealing drugs on the side.

Taking his beer, he went over towards the pool table.

In the corner, there was a large screen that usually showed sports matches, but tonight it was playing a satellite news channel. The muted newsreader on the screen switched to a piece to camera from a London housing estate.

A unit of helmeted police were rushing up to a scruffy-looking tenement door. Lining up behind a ram, two of the police officers then knocked the door down, and they all piled inside. Another drug bust in the capital.

Sion got his laptop out of his backpack. He fired it up and checked all his sites. There were no new messages in his secure mail. No jobs or new contacts.

He'd be staying here for a while longer and that suited him fine.

He thought about Claire, who he'd just caught a glimpse of, cleaning in the kitchen area. This was the kind of place where he could easily stay a little while longer.

Especially if she was here with him.

From his chaotic early life to the army, *home* had never been a place. For him, *home* was a feeling that you got when you were with your truest friends, where you felt that you belonged.

# CHAPTER 17

-----------*----------

As dawn breaks, the first light streaming in is brighter than usual.

I sense Jac moving his arm from under me as he slides naked out of bed to look out of the window. I pull the quilt over my head. We've not slept much.

"Annie."

"Hmm?" I stir.

He nuzzles me with his stubbly face until I'm awake and squealing.

"I've got to get going. There's deep snow, I need to check the sheep."

"Hold on."

I cover my body up a little self-consciously with the quilt.

"I'll give you a hand."

He tosses the covers from me, kissing me fervently.

"Much as I'd love to stay."

I giggle, batting him away.

"We can pick this up when we finish."

We're soon dressed and in the yard. A good foot of snow has fallen, and our feet leave deep powdery tracks as we wade through it to the shed, to get Jac's Land Rover out.

We pile hay, shovels and feed into the back, and then slip and slide our way down to the cottage to pick up Jess, on our way to the fields.

First, we check the ewes that are expecting twins, near the cottage.

When we get there, they're huddled in one corner. They've kept the snow off them by keeping close together and they're in good condition.

"I need to get these into the shed after we've done feeding."

"What's that there?"

I draw his attention to a ewe with a bloody tail.

Jac examines it more carefully.

Nearby it, he spots a pool of afterbirth and we slowly edge towards the sheep, keeping Jess in check. Kneeling beside the pool, I dig away the snow with my gloved hands. Submerged beneath, twin lambs lie motionless in the cold.

Quickly, I pick up the two lifeless lambs, wiping their mouths clear of any mucus and putting them wet and mucky inside my coat to warm up. Meanwhile, Jac works with Jess to catch the ewe, putting her carefully into the back of the Land Rover.

Checking that there are no more lambs, we hastily feed them and then drive back up to the farmyard, where Jac pens the ewe in the shed, while I go to work on the lambs.

Both are still alive, just about. They're cold and very weak.

"Can you milk the ewe and get some colostrum?"

"I'll give it a go."

I line a plastic storage box deep with hay. Then, I carefully place the limp lambs in there, taking them into the farmhouse to put them under a heat lamp.

Both are starting to stir and have raised their heads when Jac comes back into the kitchen with a small tub of thick, creamy sheep milk.

"I think these two will come."

Taking the tub from him, I extract a syringe-full and try unsuccessfully to get them to drink the colostrum.

"*Damn.*"

I go clean a tube we use for the worst cases, and then feed it gently down the throat of one of the lambs.

"You done this before?" I ask him.

"Once. But it didn't work out."

Taking the flat of Jac's hand, I place it on top of the tube.

"Feel any air?"

"No."

"Me neither. We're in the stomach, not the lungs."

Carefully, I attach the syringe and then slowly squeeze the colostrum straight into the lamb's stomach.

"You're doing the other one."

And he gets it right. Like the first lamb, it begins to respond immediately once the thick milk is in its belly.

"That's amazing."

"We'll need to make sure they warm up properly before they go back to the ewe."

Four hours later, and we've dug sheep out of drifts and made sure all the animals have plenty of food. The ewes due to lamb soon are now in the shed, and the twins we've saved are back with their mother and feeding.

Jac takes off his wet coat and boots. It's mid-afternoon, and we've not stopped.

"Thanks for your help. Anyone'd think you've done this before."

"Any time," I yawn.

"I think you need to sleep."

"And who's fault is that?"

"You know as well as I do, Annie Evans, whose fault it is," he says nipping my waist with his hand.

"I'd say we're both as bad as each other."

The smell of death hung as heavily as the rows of dead pigs hanging from the meat hooks. At night, this normally busy abattoir was eerily silent, even for Connor O'Dwyer, or 'Irish' as he was known.

He moved through the shadowy regiment of carcasses towards

the empty kill room and waited for his men to bring their live pig, the bent copper, from the boot of the BMW.

Windowless, white-tiled walls, a concrete floor gently sloping to a middle drain. Power washer to the side. It was the perfect place for a kill. And he'd been here plenty of times before.

He pulled out his blade of choice and snapped it open. The straight razor gleamed under the harsh electric strip-lights. It had been his dear old daddy's. Back in the day.

Everyone had their kinks. He liked to watch them bleed.

First; a finger. Or two.

The horror on their faces.

The hot gush of desperation as they bent back their head and saw blood pooling below their suspended body. Then, the dawning realisation that it was their ear lying on the floor.

And, the deliciously slow seeping of life that spilled from them with their screamed-out secrets. Anything and everything he wanted them to tell him. Always much more.

If he'd got what he wanted, and he was feeling merciful, he'd let them go.

Stun gun, bolt, a bullet? It didn't matter which, by then.

Afterwards, the place would be hosed down, the body weighted down. Waiting for its final ferry across the Mersey, and its resting place in the deep tidal scour.

He heard his men coming through, carrying the useless plod. The pig was still lively, even though he'd been bound and gagged.

He was fat too. Detective Bob Smith was a taker, not a giver. He'd had his nose deep in the Scousers' trough for too many years, with only scraps of low-grade intel cast back their way.

His men hung the wriggling bundle upside down onto the meat hook off the central gantry.

This little piggy tried to run away, when he should have been telling them what was going on. He was in the operation room. He knew about the sweep of raids that the National Crime Agency was planning on their outfit.

No way could he have missed it. There'd been hundreds of arrests across the country. Thirty of his men had been locked up. Including Tony. They'd found kilos of coke, meth and seventy grand in cash lying around his kid brother's apartment when they'd raided it without warning. It didn't matter how good the lawyers were, his baby brother was going down for a long stretch.

Irish bristled as he felt the cold fury of his anger rising inside him. No call. No notice. This little piggy had broken their agreement.

He hated cops. Especially swaggering bent ones, like Bob Smith.

He listened to the muffled sobs coming from the tied-up detective. It wouldn't take long before this snivelling scumbag told him who the grass was.

It had to be one of their own. Someone high up, on the inside. Someone who knew about Prifti, and how they planned moving in afterwards onto his patch.

"Take his gag off."

His men retreated as Irish advanced towards the inverted policeman swinging on the hook, trying to wriggle free.

"How did the NCA know about our plans to take over Prifti's patch?"

"I don't know. Let me go, Irish. Please. I can help you."

He could indeed. But, not on his terms anymore.

The detective's eyes widened in horror as he took in the twenty-five centimetre razor in Irish's hand.

"No. I beg you."

His cries were pitiful.

Out of habit, even though it was immaculately clean, Irish wiped the blade along his leather coat sleeve.

"Who's the informer?"

The detective squirmed as Irish bent towards him. The steel edged closer, then gently caressed his face.

"Don't hurt me! Please! All I know is his code name Si."

Irish's face remained implacable.

Si was the hitman's username.

That was surprising. And disappointing; he'd been a very effective team player.

And disappointing too, that Spineless Bob Smith had squealed before he'd even got to the business end of their meeting.

*Ah well*, there'd be no dillydallying with finger removal for this gutless little piggy. He'd get straight to business too.

Irish moved around the bent copper, kneeling behind him; his free hand cradling the detective's head like a barber about to give him an upside-down shave. He angled the head into line, stroking the razor against his chin, his cheek, and then carefully removing a little of the gingery hair around his ear.

"No! God help me! Please! No!"

"Shh... it's okay," Irish whispered into the bent copper's ear. "Now tell me everything you know."

His voice would be the last thing these ears would hear.

One by one, he'd slowly slice them away; the detective's secrets spilling out with his blood. Then he'd remove the snout.

And then... He felt the thrill of anticipation as he considered how this little piggy's face would writhe and contort, how the hot gushing blood would spout, when Bob Smith became separated from his balls.

"I can't believe that I've never been here before."

Claire paused to gaze out at the estuary and the spring sunshine dancing on the waters, creating ripples of silver as the opposing tides battled.

They'd parked by a popular pub and were walking a trail along the estuary to the sea.

"You ever kayaked this?" she asked Sion.

"Yeah. A couple of times. The tide's a bit tricky."

"I think I'd be scared."

"I'll take you some time, if you want?"

Claire didn't respond. She focussed her camera on a cormorant spearing itself into the waters below.

"Yes!"

"Let me see."

Sion studied the shot. The bird held itself in a perpendicular dive. She'd caught it arrowlike; headfirst with its beak skimming the water's surface, its wings arched back like an Olympic diver.

"This is really good."

"Y'think?"

"Definitely."

Embarrassed, she pointed to a quaint whitewashed cottage on the shoreline opposite.

"I could live there."

Sion agreed. It was the kind of place he'd choose too. Right on the water's edge. Peaceful.

They walked on. The wild garlic springing up from the ground formed an aromatic carpet of green as they walked alongside the bank of the widening estuary.

They were heading to the Victorian wooden bridge that spanned the sea and led them to Barmouth and the huge beach beyond.

"We came here to the seaside as kids, but I've never done this walk."

"When you live somewhere, it's easy to forget to see the beauty of the place."

"You from around these parts, then?" she asked.

"Caernarfon."

Venturing across the bridge, seeing the water way below her in the cracks between the boards made her queasy.

Sion stopped in the middle to look out at the sea, and then back up the estuary.

"I moved about a lot as a kid."

"Me too."

She took another shot with her camera. This time, it was of the snow-dusted grey Snowdonia mountains that rose dramatically from behind the mouth of the estuary.

"Mum came here from Birmingham," she explained, "And we

lived on the caravan sites. Mum remarried, after a bit. Moved on. I moved out when I was sixteen."

He'd been right about her. She'd had tough times too.

"But, this is the best place. I'm glad we came here."

Sion took her hand as they walked through the seaside town, past the booths that would soon be selling buckets and spades and bait for crabbing. They walked past the empty fairground, and the waltzers that had been Claire's most favourite thing in the world, before carrying on out onto the vast beach beyond.

The tide was far out, and the flat bank of rippled sand stretched before them as they wandered on together, leaving a faint trail of footprints between the lugworm casts.

It was almost early evening by the time they got back to the pub by the car park. Even though it was out of season, the place was crowded.

Ravenous, they ordered crab from the specials board.

Sion checked his phone. There was a message in.

Rising from the table as she came back from the toilets, Sion excused himself.

"I need to make a quick call. Work. I won't be long."

Claire shrugged and got her camera out, flicking through the shots she'd taken while she waited for their food.

She looked up as he disappeared outside. He'd come across as a little cocky at first, but he was actually quite shy. Quiet, even. If anything, a little closed off. She liked him. That mystery about him was part of the attraction. Hidden depths she wanted to explore.

But, one doubt niggled her. Who was he on the phone to?

She hoped it wasn't another woman.

Sion came back to the table.

"Everything alright?"

The food had just arrived, and she began to wonder if she'd made a wise choice, tackling a crab shell on a first date.

"Yeah. I'm off on a job next week."

"Where to?"

"Wrexham."

"That's not too far, a couple of hours, tops."

"I'll be gone for about a week."

He studied her face. Was that a flicker of disappointment?

"I've enjoyed today."

Her lips curved as she took a sip of her gin and tonic.

"Me too."

"When I come back, d'ya wanna do this again?"

Her eyes caught his before she shyly looked away.

"Yes. Okay."

# CHAPTER 18

----------*----------

He'd packed his gear into the Volvo and was all set to go.

The mark, this time, was Welsh. From Irish's email, it was clear that he was a dealer who'd started shopping around, using other suppliers.

He was certainly offering exotic lines to the good people of Wrexham. Lemon drops, chocolate balls; the gear this guy was offering hourly by text sounded more like sweets than drugs.

But, that was the point. And he had kids running them straight to the punters in a classic county lines operation. Delivery within thirty minutes.

Sion had arranged a meet with him. The mark was offering to show him samples, and if he liked them, he'd said, they'd then discuss supply, price and routes to market.

They'd be having weekly targets and sales reports next. Since when had drug dealing gotten so professional?

At least, the venue they'd arranged to meet at was what he expected. A rough-looking boozer near the football ground. It'd be match day, so there'd be a crowd around them.

That might be perfect for a meeting about drugs, but it was riskier for him. It meant that he had to be swift and subtle. And kill at close range.

He couldn't risk bringing a gun with him into the busy pub. So, that meant a fatal knife wound would be best. It wouldn't be out of keeping, either. Random stabbings between fans were not unknown in the local football derby. But knife wounds were messy, and he was a sniper.

From his training, he knew there were two options.

The first was to stab him in the kidneys. Pinpoint accuracy and jabs like a sewing machine to get him to bleed out and die. Not easy to do unnoticed in a crowded bar.

No, the second option was best. A stab wound to the back of the neck at the base of the skull. He'd spring him from behind and deliver one hard, accurate stab upwards, severing the brain stem.

He cast his mind back to his training. It required speed and power.

And a specialist knife.

He searched through one of the reinforced cases until he found the misericorde. Its French name meant 'act of mercy.' He removed it from its sheath. Fifteen centimetres of thin stainless steel, designed to deliver death wounds. The triangular blade had three edges, sharpened for precision piercing and penetration.

He packed it into his tubular travel bag, along with a semi-automatic, bullets, rope, some plastic ties and a few other essential items that no discerning contract killer would be without.

It was midday by the time Sion strolled over to the farmhouse to find Jac. He hadn't seen his friend in days, and he didn't want to leave a note. Even Jess was spending her nights in the dog kennels at the farm.

He found his friend in the lambing shed, holding a new-born lamb. Clearing the birthing hood off its face, he put it back with its mother.

"If it's alright with you, I won't shake your hand."

Sion looked at his friend.

"You look knackered, mate."

"Delivered ten sets of twins and two sets of triplets this weekend."

Sion grinned.

"That must be it. I've got a job on. I'll be away for a bit. Not, that you'd notice I'm gone."

Jac climbed out of the pen.

"Been a bit busy, mate."

"Sure. But... If you *do* ever decide... *like*... to be here on a more full-time basis... *to be closer to the lambing shed, an' all...* d'you think Annie'd rent the cottage to me? I wouldn't mind sticking around for a while longer."

"I'll ask her. But, I don't want to push it. Things are good between us, right now."

"I can see that," Sion smirked, knocking Jac's shoulder.

Driving from the cottage, Sion swung by The Cross Keys. The car park was busy, and it looked like they had a fair few customers in for lunch.

As he opened the door, he saw Claire behind the bar, serving a large round of drinks. Kevin passed him carrying two plates of food out.

There was something about that guy that set Sion on edge. Call it a sixth sense, but Kevin reminded him of some of the semi-feral survivors he'd grown up with in care.

"Wanna drink?" Claire asked, grabbing a glass.

"No, I'm off to Wrexham. Should be back Sunday, if you'd like to go out somewhere?"

"Sounds good. I'll book it off. They got wifi where you're staying?"

Sion nodded.

"Perhaps, we could talk later, then?"

"Yeah. I'd like that."

He wasn't sure what was happening between them, but he couldn't wait to get back.

Before he left the pub, he fired off a message to his NCA contact about this new Scouser job that had come in from Irish.

He wasn't sure if they'd be interested in such a small fish in a provincial pond like Wrexham, but the message would cover his arse if he got arrested.

Irish sat opposite his kid brother Tony in the visitor's centre. Up above them, he noticed the damp ringed patches on the ancient polystyrene roof tiles. The paint was bubbling and peeling up in the far corner by the grilled high windows. This was a shitty prison to be on remand in. Old, damp and bleak.

"How yer doin', our kid?"

He gave his younger brother a smile. Trying to cheer him up.

Tony looked away.

The Brief said he was looking at ten years. Intent to supply and dealing. On account of who his brother was, no doubt. Not that they could ever touch Irish. Connor O'Dwyer was far too smart for that.

"Has Britney not been to see you?"

Tony blinked. She hadn't

"How's she doin'?"

"Gone back to her mum's."

The police had seized all of his brother's assets. The cars. The apartment. Even his designer gear.

Tony's heavily pregnant girlfriend scarpered the morning of the raid with his Rolexes stashed in her bra. Or so she'd bragged to her mates, that night in the pub.

Britney would never wait for his brother. He'd guarantee that now.

But, when the baby came, he'd make damn sure that kid would always know who their real dad was. If, indeed, it was Tony's. Cheap tart, that she was.

"How you getting' on fixin' that leak?"

"The job's in the pipeline, and I've arranged for delivery. Very soon."

He couldn't say more. Not here. But, Tony understood what he meant.

And Irish was very much looking forward to his forthcoming visit to the abattoir. And to making his next little piggy, the hired hitman, bleed out and scream.

"We should've done this ages ago," Claire mumbles into the towel as she stretches face down on the bench beside me.

"Totally."

My back is being deliciously massaged, the tension in my neck disappearing with every touch.

Claire found a discount code offer on a spa in a local hotel, after we'd got talking a few evenings before. We formulated our escape plan, there and then.

After the massage, we relax in the sauna, and then dip ourselves into the fierce bubbles of the jacuzzi.

"I definitely could get used to this."

I close my eyes, enjoying the waters fizzing around me.

"If I get any more relaxed, I'll be asleep."

"You up at night a lot with the lambs?"

"Yip. How do people cope with babies? This is killing me."

"So, it's official now, is it? You and Jac?"

"I guess."

"Thank God for that."

We've not spent a night away from each other yet. In fact, with lambing now in full swing we've been pretty much together twenty-four seven. He's not complained so far, but it is nice to have some girl time.

Claire dips down into the water to cover her shoulders.

"I'm not being funny, Annie, but it's been brewing since school. You two took your time, that's all I'm saying."

I grin and put it back on her.

"But, what is far more interesting is what's brewing now."

She throws me a look.

"Meaning?"

"You and Sion? And don't start telling me nothing's goin' on, 'cos I don't believe you."

"*Nothing*, is about right. Honestly! We've been out once. For a walk. That's it."

"Jac says he goes to the pub every night, so he can see you."

"So he can get on the wifi, more like."

"Don't be daft, he's definitely interested."

"He's a nice guy."

She giggles then screws her nose up at me.

"But, d'you think he might be a player?"

I pull a face at that.

"So, why's he always so secretive on his phone, then? If he's not talking to other girls?"

"No! Jac would've said."

I'm certain he's not seeing anyone else. But she's right; I don't know him that well, either.

Claire sighs, then stands to get out of the jacuzzi.

"I'm not sure it's going anywhere. Shame though."

"'Cos you like him?"

"Yeah, that. And, 'cos he's got a very nice ass."

Sion spent a third day studying his mark.

Mid-thirties with a wide-boy look. He had a flashy sports car and he wore dark sunglasses even though it was pouring with rain.

Sion sat all day in the back of a hired blacked-out van studying his movements.

He'd come outside on his phone every now and then; having a stretch, a fag, getting something from his car. Most days, he'd walked to the parade of shops in the middle of this large council estate, returning some fifteen minutes later with more cigarettes or a bottle of pop in his hand.

Even though it was Friday morning, a string of school-age kids on bikes had been coming and going through the day. Delivery mules. He was obviously dealing. And he was raking in the cash, judging by the number of visits he was getting.

At five, a moped rocked up. Dinner had arrived. Pizza by the look of it.

Then, at about eight p.m. the man left the house and Sion followed, watching from the shadows as he disappeared into a rough-looking sports bar by the parade of shops.

Sion reached into his jacket, answering a burner phone vibrating in the pocket.

It was his handler.

"Go-ahead with the hit. Intel says the Scousers are a tad tetchy after the London raids. The hit'll take the heat off you."

"You sure know how to show a girl a good time."

It's our first day out since lambing started, and we're sitting on a bench on the Aberystwyth seafront, eating fish and chips from the paper with a chip fork.

The spring sunshine warms my back.

There are groups of university students out too with a sunny determination to enjoy the first few spring rays by the beach, despite the chilly April breeze.

"This is the life."

Jac stretches his legs out and scrunches up the empty greasy paper into a ball.

"Ah! He's got it."

An arctic skua wheels into the sea, stealing a fish from a tern.

"Cheeky beggar."

I finish my chips.

"It is nice to get out."

He puts our papers into the bin beside the bench we're sitting on.

"You and me, we've never been on a date."

"What about the Cross Keys?"

"Doesn't count."

"Those hundreds of woolly babies we have might put paid to date-night, any time soon."

A quick stop like this, when we get supplies, is the most we can hope for.

"I promise, Annie, I'll take you out properly once we're finished lambing."

"Sounds good, 'cos all my free labour's gonna cost you. Big time."

"Is that right?"

"Yeah. At least a weekend in Paris? Or… Prague?"

"How about Porthmadog?"

I shove my elbow into his ribs.

"Jac, you need to go out with the boys too."

He puts his arm around me.

"I will. But right now, I'm enjoying our early nights in."

A crowd of students approach, sauntering up the promenade, giggling together about something.

"Let's go."

Jac jumps up off the bench, lowering his baseball cap and lifting his jacket collar.

"You cold?"

"A bit… Sun's in my eyes."

"*Hey! Jac!* How you doin'?"

One of the girls calls over to us, as I'm standing up to go.

She's blonde and wearing denim cutaway hot pants with thick black tights and boots.

Jac turns towards her.

"Uh… good, ta."

He shifts uncomfortably, "This is my girlfriend, Annie."

I put on a smiley face, even though an icy shiver is shooting right through me. She's pretty. Taller than me. And quite a few years younger.

Jac coughs.

"Nice to see you… uh… Jo."

"It's Jen."

"Sorry, yeah, Jen."

"Hey! We better get going."

He hastily makes to leave, taking my hand and dragging me away with him.

She's all smiles as she moves quickly away too, re-joining her friends who've walked on.

"Who was that?"

She's laughing with another girl, now she's checking her phone.

We walk along the beachfront towards our truck. Without speaking.

"I met her one night when I was out," he mutters, breaking the moody silence.

"When?"

I stop and watch his eyebrows furrowing.

"When you were in London."

"*What?*"

"I thought we were all over. I was drunk, and she came on to me. At the club on the pier. Nothing happened. *Honest.* Except I missed my taxi and Sion had to pick me up the next day."

He adds a little nervously, "Ask Sion if you want. I spent a freezing cold night on a bench in a bus shelter."

"Good... I hope you froze your nuts off."

He sniggers and I huff, walking on.

"Annie?"

Catching me up, he goes off in front, jogging backwards to face me.

I stop and stare out to sea, refusing to engage.

He grabs both my hands and I can feel his dark eyes on me.

"We good?"

Are we good? It's a fair question.

Slowly my eyes lift towards his, and the fear I can see clouding them immediately douses my smouldering jealousy. It's painful, but I swallow my wounded pride.

He squeezes my hands.

"Annie, please."

I hear his voice catch, extinguishing the final embers of anger.

Stretching up, I find his lips.

"Thanks."

"What for?"

He looks a little surprised.

"For not spinning me some bullshit line. For telling me the truth."

"Yeah, well, she made me realise I was still in love with you. Which was a bugger at the time 'cos you hated my guts... Again."

I can't be jealous after that.

I really like that girl.

# CHAPTER 19

---------*----------

It was after eleven when Sion lay flat back on his bed in the small budget hotel. It was not the kind of room you wanted to do more than sleep in.

As he lay there, he reflected on his contact's words. What did he mean when he'd said that the Scousers were *'tetchy'* and that the job would *'take the heat off him'*?

Did that mean that the heat was *on* him? And what did it mean to have the heat on you, anyway?

It was probably just sloppy wording, but it bothered him.

He checked his phone, Claire was online. He clicked to chat, and she came on immediately.

"Hey!"

"Hey."

"You okay? You sound flat."

Claire yawned, stretching her arms above her head.

"Just tired, that's all. Kev was drinking with his Scally pals and left me to rush around like a blue-arsed fly, taking orders and serving on the bar. What've you been up to?"

Sion scratched his nose.

"Sifting through data all day and testing network systems."

He needed to do more research into what IT networking consultants did, but no one else appeared to know either and he'd not been busted yet.

"The crazy life you lead, eh?"

"You wouldn't believe it, if I told you."

"Bit of a change to spending your days with a gun slung over your shoulder?"

"Hmm. This work's very dull."

"I bet."

He shifted awkwardly, he needed to switch the conversation off his cover story. He hated lying to her.

"At least now, I don't have people worrying about me when I'm away."

She took the bait.

"And did you have people worrying about you? Someone special?"

"Yeah."

He saw her eyes widen on the screen.

"You did? Who?"

"My mam."

She paused, and he could see her nose scrunching up.

"Hold on... You told me you were in Care? And, that your mam's dead?"

"Got ya!"

"Ah, Sion, that's rotten! Plus... you can't give me half a story."

"I might've had one or two girlfriends near where we were stationed."

"And no-one now?"

"No, 'course not."

He stared straight at her on the screen.

"Why d'ya say that?"

"It doesn't matter, forget I said anything."

"No, come on, tell me, why? What is it, Claire?"

"Okay. When you're on the phone, you always go out to take the call."

She was observant. He'd never even thought about how that looked.

"Is that why, every time I asked you on a date, you said no."

She nodded.

"Believe me when I tell you, there's no one else. The calls I get, they're all about work."

He saw her studying his face. She looked embarrassed.

"We are the only place with signal, I s'pose."

"Exactly. It's the only time I get to make calls. But, what about you?"

"Split up from my boyfriend last year."

"Why?... Sorry, that's none of my business."

Claire smiled at the screen.

"It's alright. We wanted different things."

"Like?"

"Like, he wanted to get married, and I didn't."

"Ah."

"I couldn't go through with it. Was that wrong?"

"No. It happens. It'd run its course and you were stuck."

"Exactly. Only, he didn't see it that way."

"What d'you mean?"

"He proposed and when I said no, he got upset and asked me to leave. So, I did. That night. Slept on a friend's sofa, until I got a place to stay."

She was renting a room in a flat above a hairdresser's with a single mother now; a friend from school.

"You glad you left?"

"Best thing I ever did."

Claire shrugged.

"Sounds silly, but I've always wanted to travel. I've spent the last six months scraping every penny I can together, so's I can go off, with a pack on my back, travelling the world."

"Where to?"

"Everywhere."

He caught her smile.

"I've never been abroad. My first ever passport came through last month."

Sion couldn't help but laugh at her animated face.

"Where to first, then?"

"I wanna... I wanna...," she said excitedly, "I dunno, eat pasta by the leaning tower of Pisa. Swim with dolphins. Lie on the beach in Thailand. Surf in Bondi… And I wanna find my dad."

"Your dad?"

"He's from New Zealand, my mum said. I've never met him, but I'd like to look him up."

Sion nodded.

"All great things. You should definitely do them."

"Wanna come?"

She threw it out casually; by her eyes that shyly studied his on the screen, he could see she was serious.

"I'd love to."

"You see that?"

I follow the direction of Jac's pointed arm and study a heavily pregnant ewe on her own in the field. She's swinging her head about wildly, disoriented but still trying to eat the grass.

"It's like she's dizzy."

"We've got to get the vet out, Jac. Could be a couple of things, but we need to hurry."

"Like what?"

The ewe is now circling aimlessly in the field. *Dammit!* I've seen it before a couple of times, and it's not good news.

"What is it, Annie?"

"It could be listeriosis."

Jac looks at me concerned.

"Do we need to check the silage?"

"Definitely."

It could mean many more sick sheep and stillborn lambs. That would be a disaster.

"If it is listeriosis, she'll need a big dose of antibiotic, and even then she might not make it."

Jac rubs his face with his hands and lets out a deep breath.

"What did I do wrong, Annie?"

"Hey, we don't know what it is, yet. It might be twin lamb disease, or a brain thing? I'm no vet, I could be totally wrong."

"But, I should know this."

I can see he's upset.

"I'm a rookie, and this poor animal's suffering because of me."

"Stop it, Jac," I snap. "This is not your fault, okay? It happens. It's farming."

He's quiet as we go about getting the ewe in, only speaking to give Jess commands. I can see that he's privately beating himself up about it; shutting me out, making me feel helpless.

The vet arrives later in the afternoon, approaching the pen to check her out.

"Well, she's sitting up. That's a good sign. And you gave her glucose, you say?"

" thought her breath smelled sweet."

The ewe gets a little twitchy and shifts as the vet goes in. She's more lively than earlier on; but she's still glassy-eyed.

"You were right to give her glucose. I'm pretty sure it's twin lamb disease, not listeriosis."

A wave of relief floods through me, even though the diagnosis isn't great for this ewe. Twin lamb disease is usually fatal unless treated early.

I move to stand alongside Jac. He's barely uttered a word to me all day.

All afternoon, he's been checking and rechecking the silage bales for holes.

"I'm gonna induce her so we can get these lambs out."

"Lambs?" Jac utters. "They were all scanned, and this one's having a single."

"Well, I'm pretty sure she's carrying two at least. That's probably the reason she's lost condition."

I touch his hand and he takes it in his, locking his fingers tightly in mine.

"I think your quick actions with the glucose drench might just have saved this one," the vet says, administering the injection to induce delivery, "Though, it's early days yet."

I can't help but notice the palpable relief on Jac's face.

"Keep an hourly watch on her," the vet advises as she walks back to her truck. "She's weak and she'll need help getting those lambs out."

Jac nods.

Another sleepless night.

In the end, we delivered triplets at two in the morning. They're healthy, and they've each taken a drink of the ewe's colostrum from a small bottle.

Mum's still pretty weak, and Jac's given her another dose of glucose. It'll be touch and go for a day or so. And in the meantime, the three will be kept with her but fed on a bottle every couple of hours.

Jac looks exhausted as we head back to bed.

"What if I do the seven o'clock feed," I offer. "So you can lie in?"

"Deal."

I end up dozing in and out of a light sleep, conscious that I'm going to be woken up too soon by the alarm. And I am. Just as I'm drifting off into a deep slumber.

Sleepily, I step into my wellies, and with the bottles clinking against each other in the bucket, I head over to the shed.

In the morning light, as I approach the pens I can see that the sick ewe is standing up. And under her, two of the triplets are feeding. I stand well back, amazed; watching her making small beckoning grunts as she bends her head towards her tiny lambs.

It must be from exhaustion, but my eyes are welling up.

She's made it, and she's such a good mother.

Trying not to disturb the ewe, I pick up the little lambs one by one and give them a little of the formula colostrum. It's a top-up because I'm not sure how much milk she's got and three is a lot to feed, even for a healthy sheep.

Next door, there's a lamb riot going on, as five, not so little boys and girls have heard me coming and are going mad, calling out for milk and my attention.

I go into their pen next, a bottle in each hand.

The lambs jostle with each other until two succeed in grabbing the bottles and begin sucking hard on the teats, making the milk gurgle. Behind me, the three other lambs are pounding their heads on the back of my legs, trying to get my attention.

"Wait your turn," I tell them.

I switch bottles and feed the two others, then find number five.

Full to bursting, at last, the lambs move away, and I gather up the detritus of their feed.

The recovering ewe is now nuzzling one of her babies and my heart's about to burst.

It's not a bad life here.

Feeling extremely thankful and more than a little smug, I wander back across the yard to the gorgeous man who is fast asleep in my bed.

# CHAPTER 20

----------*----------

I've made us a special meal that evening, as a celebration for saving the ewe and her triplets.

After more glucose and some general TLC, she's on her feet the whole time and feeding again. The triplets are still strong too.

I thought he'd be happy about it.

And I've tried to make an effort. I've cooked us fillets of salmon with hollandaise sauce, some asparagus and new potatoes. I've even found a bottle of chilled Pinot Grigio.

But Jac is still out of sorts, and is sitting in a sulk, moodily eating his food.

That's it. I've had enough.

Taking a good gulp of the chilled dry wine, I launch in.

"Are you gonna tell me what's up, or do I have to put up with your smacked arse face all evening?"

"Leave off, Annie."

"Fine. Whatever."

Maybe, we *have* spent too much time together over the last weeks. It doesn't help that we're both working from the crack of dawn all day, and getting up in the night. When you think of it like that, I reason trying hard not to cry, it's not surprising he's grumpy. We're both way beyond tired.

I push my plate away.

"Alright. I'll do the feeds tonight. Gotta do something to improve that foul mood of yours."

He takes a drink of wine.

"What is it, Jac?"

A tear escapes despite my best efforts.

"Tell me what's up?"

He plays with the stem of his wine glass.

"It's you."

"Me?"

"Yeah."

I stare at him, dumbfounded. Is he ending it? How have I not seen this coming?

"What've I done?"

"Nothing."

He glances up, surprised to see me upset.

"Hey, Annie. What's up, hun? Just ignore me, I'm knackered."

"Is it over between us?"

"*God!* No."

He stares at me shocked.

"How could you think that? I want to be with you always."

"You do?"

"Yeah...I can't imagine my life without you."

"Nor me."

I swallow a sob of relief.

"What is it, then, Jac? Tell me what's wrong. What've I done?"

He stares at the straw-coloured wine and takes a drink.

"You've not done anything. It's... I..."

He struggles to find the words.

"That ewe could've died. They all could've had listeriosis. And I didn't have a bloody clue."

His bitterness makes me shudder, and I stretch my hands across the table, finding his.

"Jac, it's alright. How could you've known? I spent most of my childhood in that shed. There are loads of things you've done on the farm that I could never do."

"Like what?"

"Like, all that fencing for a start. And the stock rotation. The work you've done on improving the grass. You've researched it, you've found better ways of doing things. I'd never have done that."

He shrugs.

"And those new rams?"

"I guess... But, I couldn't have done the lambing without you."

"We make a good team."

I get up and take our plates over to the sink, wiping my tears away.

He comes over to give me a hand, more relaxed now. I scrub the pans, his words echoing in my brain.

This is the real deal, and it hurts.

"Have you heard from Sion?"

"No. Nothing. Still on that job, I reckon."

Jac wipes the saucepan dry.

"Before Sion went, he asked me if you'd be interested in him renting the cottage? How d'you feel about me moving in here properly?"

"Makes sense. You spend all your time here anyway."

His clothes are hanging up in the wardrobe and he's commandeered one of the chests of drawers.

He puts the pan on the worktop and looks at me steadily.

"Are you sure, though? That you want me here? Like, permanently?"

"Are *you* sure, Jac?"

He draws me to him. The bubbly suds from my hands cling to his jumper.

"I love you, Annie. It's a big step, though."

His hands slip around my waist.

"It's your farm, it's your decision."

"No, Jac... it's our farm now."

Enveloping me in his arms, he gazes down at me.

"But how is that a good deal for you?"

I try to speak the words that are singing in my heart.

"I love you and I want us to be together. That's the deal... You cool with that?"

Leaning down, he kisses me deeply.

"I'm cool with that," he answers huskily. "Lucky I opened that letter."

"That's not quite how Sion remembers it."

The pub was packed with a sea of red football shirts. It was derby day. Wrexham had a midweek evening cup draw, playing an arch enemy. It was a classic rivalry. Red versus blue. Wales versus England.

When such honour was at stake, tensions were high; and a little trouble inevitably spilled out between the diehard fans. Even with the heavy police presence around the ground, it was the perfect backdrop for Sion to carry out his mission.

He scanned the crowd. Everyone wearing the same thing made it difficult to spot the dealer. His mark.

Sion was wearing a red and white striped football scarf over his leather jacket, especially for the occasion.

The long, thin misericorde was sheathed and taped to his shin, and a flick knife secreted in his coat, in case of any upfront bother.

His burner phone pinged in his pocket, and his stomach lurched. He was a professional, but still, he'd never done this before.

Death by stabbing.

His hands covered in blood. Literally.

*'I'm at the table by the window. Where are you?'*

Sion spotted him. In the far corner; he was sitting on his own in a booth, staring meanly into his phone.

In front of him was a table of used pint glasses, and beside him a pile of coats, dumped by the punters who preferred to stand.

His mark clocked Sion jostling his way out of the throng of the footie fans.

"About *bleedin'* time."

Sion held out his hand and gave him a disarming smile.

The mark stared at it and reluctantly shook hands.

Shifting the coats, Sion sat down, across from him in the booth.

"So, where you from?"

"Out West. The coast."

"What? Got no suppliers there, then?"

"Yeah. Plenty," Sion bluffed. "But I'm building my range. The punters these days, they've got more diverse tastes. Coke 'n doves don't cut it no more."

"What you after?"

"Lemon drops?"

"Yeah, easy. I can do you M-cat, Ket, Monkey Dust, Meth… whatever, man."

"Sweet. You got samples?"

"Yeah. But not here. Bogs in two minutes? Second stall from the door."

The mark grabbed the zipped bag beside him, and gulping the last of his lager headed without another word through the crowd to the toilets at the back of the pub.

Sion watched the football fans parting, letting him through, sometimes with a nod of acknowledgement. Sion was on this dude's turf.

The next moves were critical.

He had visualised it so many times, but it was an entirely different thing to do it for real.

His gut twisted again. He wasn't a hand to hand fighter; he was a sniper.

So, do what you always do before you take the shot, he told himself.

Regulate your pulse. That's it, slow and steady breaths.

He took his time, breathing in and out, visualising his next steps.

Retrieve the blade.

Open the door.

Spring him.

Grab him and hold his neck fast from behind.

Then stab.

Go on, do it. Do it quickly before he can wriggle out of your grasp.

One blow. Powerful. Precise. Straight through the base of his skull and up into the brainstem.

That's it. Do it - boom!

Now, stop fannying about, he told himself.

Go get him.

Revved up, Sion sliced swiftly through the crowd to the back of the pub, cutting across to the door by the toilets, pushing through into the corridor.

No one was around.

Perfect.

By the door to the gents, he bent down, as if tying his laces, to retrieve the blade strapped to his shin.

*Whack.*

A bottle crashed hard into the back of his head as three men burst from the bar and jumped him from behind.

His mark had set a trap.

Pinned to the wall by a mountain of muscle, Sion stood helpless as the pockets of his leather coat and his jeans were ransacked, and his flick knife and phone confiscated.

"S'that all he's got? Where's his wallet?"

But Sion had nothing else on him. And, no ID. Everything was safely stored in the boot of his car, parked up on a side-street.

The mark swaggered out of the toilet and snorted loudly as he took in Sion with his hands bound behind his back with a plastic tie.

"Fancied yer chances whacking me did ya?"

He drove a hard punch into Sion's stomach, winding him.

Sion gasped for breath, then bent and coughed.

"You've got it wrong, mate. I'm a dealer, like you. All I wanna do is make us rich."

"Yeah, whatever."

Grabbing hold of his collar, he smashed Sion's sore head hard, cracking the glass-framed picture hanging on the wall behind him.

"*Aargh!*"

"Yer lyin' prick."

The mark nodded to the men.

One grabbed Sion by his tied up arms and shoved him roughly through a door next to the toilets, signed as 'private.' It was the old pub kitchen, disused and filthy. Three men and the mark walked behind him, pushing him on, out of the back door into a concreted courtyard.

Amid a row of beer barrels and an industrial bin filled to the brim with empty bottles, a black BMW saloon was parked up. Sion took in as much as he could. It was dealership new. Top-of-the-range with blackened windows. This was a professional outfit.

"Where you taking me?"

"Irish wants a word in your ear," one of the goons said in a thick Liverpool accent, making the others snigger.

The mark rammed Sion forward, causing him to stumble into the car.

"*Oi!* Gerroff the car, tosser."

Another pile-driving punch. This time to the kidneys, sending him staggering sideways.

"*Aaahh!* I don't know any guy called Irish. You've got the wrong man. What does he want me for?"

"Don't lie. You screwed us over, you grass."

Sion looked at him, confused.

A kick to the shins.

Sion stumbled to the ground, unable to put out his arms to save himself.

"Pathetic piece of piss."

On the ground, one of the men kicked him in the ribs.

"Lucky for you, you don't wear specs."

"Where he's headin', he's better off with swimming goggles."

His mind was whirring as he staggered back up off the concrete and stood up.

He'd been set up. They knew he was an informer. He was being hauled in by the Scousers, he surmised grimly.

To be killed.

The mark took his watch off. That wasn't good. It meant that he was about to get smacked again. This time properly.

He needed to think. Fast. How was he going to get out of this? Convince them that they'd made a mistake? That he wasn't a player.

"*Shit!*"

A heavily ringed fist crashed into his cheek sending him reeling back onto the BMW like a boxer on the rope-a-dope.

"Watch the car, I told ya, dickhead!"

The fist smacked into him again, this time slamming into his shoulder.

"I... I don't understand."

"Tosser."

Another blow. This time, a sharp stinging pain made Sion flinch, and he cried out dramatically as a hard kick was delivered into his shin giving him a dead leg.

Two of the henchmen grabbed his shoulders and held him firm.

"Ya done?"

The mark sniffed.

Not yet. Another heavy blow into the solar plexus made Sion moan out in pain again. This time for real.

"Yeah, I'm done."

The mark rubbed his knuckles and put his watch back on.

The third man, who Sion presumed to be the driver, popped open the boot from his key fob. The two who were holding Sion, pushed him towards it.

"Easy way or hard way, buddy?"

He groaned as he moved to stand straight.

"Easy way... Please.... Easy."

"Get in the boot, then. Go on, ya piece of shit. Gerrin."

With his hands bound behind his back, Sion falteringly leaned his body forward and tipped himself shoulders first into the boot of the BMW. Rolling and squirming to find enough room for his legs, he formed a foetal position on his side.

The men gathered around the boot, staring in.

"I'm not a grass. I just sell charlie. Please…You've got the wrong man."

The mark spat on him.

Unable to wipe it, Sion felt the phlegm trickling stickily down the side of his cheek.

"Where are you taking me? I'm not good in small spaces, I get really claustrophobic."

One of the men raised an eyebrow at that, making the others chuckle.

"Best have a little snooze, then, dear."

Sion cried out and one of the heavies slammed the boot down, causing another one, who Sion presumed was the driver, to shout again.

In the darkness, Sion heard them still bickering around him.

"It's not your motor. What d'you care?"

"Irish'll *fuckin'* care."

"You sure we got the right one?"

It sounded like the mark speaking.

"This muppet's a right limp lettuce."

It had worked.

He'd live with the loss of his street cred if they were underestimating him. And, he still had his blade strapped to his leg.

The guys hadn't noticed either the full features of their new top-of-the-range BMW. German engineering, the best. There, glowing a fluorescent green in the blackness, was the safety pull tab. An emergency lever to get out.

His next car would be a BMW, he vowed.

Things were grim but could have been a whole lot worse. The thugs in the front didn't realise it, but his chance to live depended on what they did next.

# CHAPTER 21

-----------*----------

Sion summoned all his will and skill to keep calm and not panic. He was a professional soldier; he could get out of this. He needed, above all, to keep his head clear, and push away the terrifying thoughts that kept seeping in uninvited. They were taking him to Irish. And they were planning to drown him.

He'd been in some scrapes in his time, but this was about the worst. And this time, Jase wasn't waiting in the chopper for air evac, and Jac wasn't covering his back with rounds of fire.

He had to get out of the boot before he was delivered to Irish, that was for sure. Once they took him out of the car he had limited options.

Judging by their speed and the straight direction of travel, he was fairly sure that they were on motorways. That meant they were probably headed towards Liverpool or Manchester.

The tightly bound ties cut into his wrist and his arms were aching from them being stretched back behind him. But from the foetal position he lay in, his fingers could still reach his ankle and up the side of his shin. And when he wriggled his feet upwards, he could easily touch the sheath and remove the blade with his fingers. Plus, he was certain he could hold the dagger fast with one hand and rub his other against it to break the ties.

He could escape.

He glanced up at the fluorescent lever. His lifesaver. He

couldn't pop the boot while they were driving, the car was going too fast. And if he did it when they slowed, they'd be after him straight away.

He couldn't risk a straight chase with them, either. He'd be too easily outrun, and these guys weren't mucking about. They were sure to be carrying handguns.

Sion ruled out a surprise attack when they opened the boot, for that reason too.

It went against his instinct, but rational evaluation told him grimly that his best option was to stay tied up for a little while longer.

He hoped the gamble would pay off.

The darkness of the boot and the rhythm of the tyres pounding against the tarmac beneath him drew him deeper into his blackest thoughts.

What if these were his last hours?

He would never grow old.

The tyres drummed out a hypnotic rhythm.

What if... he'd never become a father? Would never be with Claire?

Claire.

It hurt to think about her. That had never happened before.

Even though they weren't together, there was a magnetic pull between them. It wasn't what they said or did. It was like a connection. A shared bond.

She'd had a tough early life like him. But, it was more than that. She had hidden depths; qualities and talents that even she didn't fully understand the potential of. Like her photography. And it fascinated him.

He had to stay alive. If only to see Claire again.

To feel her lips on his at least one time in his life. To have all of her. He couldn't think about that. The thought of not seeing her again was too painful.

The car slowed, and he was then thrown sideways when it turned sharply. He guessed that they were at a junction. Then, there were what he surmised to be a series of roundabouts. And after, yet more turns flinging him about.

He sensed now that they were starting to slow. Sion felt the car moving right down the gears. Rough bumps sent jolts of pain through his hip. They were off-road.

Sion's heart pumped hard; he felt the adrenaline kicking in. They were getting closer. The next few minutes would determine if he'd live, or die.

They rolled to a stop.

Car doors opened and then clicked shut.

This was it.

The boot lid suddenly popped, and Sion squinted as torchlight from a phone blinded his eyes.

"The squealer's not going anywhere."

"Probably pissed himself by now."

Then, blackness again. The boot shut smoothly over his head and he heard their voices around the car.

"Since when did the abattoir start doin' late shifts?"

"Overtime to meet demand. Started last week, the guard on the gate said. Boss'll be bouncing."

"Thought you paid 'em to tell you shit like that?"

"Yeah, well. He's new."

"So, who's gonna tell Irish?"

"Guess that'll be me? I'll put him off 'til midnight. The place'll be empty by then."

Back in the darkness, Sion drew a deep breath. Thank God he'd not cut himself free.

*'He's not going anywhere... Midnight.'*

Did that mean that they were leaving him alone for a while?

*'Abattoir?'*

He'd be hung up for some ritual humiliation, torture even. Was that the ear thing? A video then posted up. Stitches for snitches.

But, he had a small window of opportunity, if he acted now.

Wriggling his shoulders, he stretched his hands downwards, feeling for the bottom of his trouser leg and finding the sheath stuck to the side of his shin.

Five minutes passed.

No voices. No footsteps. No shuffling around the car.

Deadly quiet.

He was convinced that the men had left him alone in the boot.

Perhaps, they'd stopped for food or a drink?

Perhaps he'd been delivered, and was outside the abattoir waiting for the shift to end?

Either way, he was getting out.

Working blindly with his hands behind his back and arms painfully extended, he carefully pulled the knife free of its holder. Wriggling into a more comfortable position, it slipped in his fingers. He shuffled it back with his palm and thumb.

He had to be more careful. Time was too precious to waste scrambling for it in the darkness.

With his fingertips, he carefully positioned the thin blade in his right palm so he could rub the plastic tie against it with his left.

Holding the blade tight, he worked swiftly, pulling against the tie until he was sure that it was nearly ready to snap.

He tried; using all his strength, willing his hands apart.

Nothing.

He rubbed away at it again. And again.

The misericorde, designed for puncturing, was not the ideal tool for sawing through the tough plastic.

Surely, he was nearly there by now?

Exerting as much pressure as he possibly could, he tried again. Pushing his hands together he thrust them outwards with all the force he could muster.

It snapped.

His hands flung free.

With no time to spare, knife in hand, he tugged the internal fluorescent lever and heard the catch mechanism release.

He froze, ready to stab out with the blade.

Nothing.

But, still, they could be watching the car.

Easing the boot open a fraction more, he peeped out of the crack.

His eyes took a minute to adjust to the sodium streetlight nearby. From the tiny gap, he saw the black mirror of a puddled pothole in front of him. There were no feet, and no one reflected in it.

Gingerly, he inched the boot open a little wider. Weapon ready.

He was in a makeshift car park.

The puddled ground was gravel and mud, and around the edge of the car park there was a high perimeter wire fence topped with a rolled line of razor-sharp barbs.

To the side, and inside the fence, were rows of metal boxes; containers. They were smaller than shipping ones, more the type that people hired for storage. If he got put in one of those, there'd be no fluorescent lever to pull.

The coast was clear.

In a split second, the boot lid was up, and Sion sprang out, softly closing it behind him.

Sprinting on the balls of his feet, he dashed silently across the yard towards the first row of the storage units. He flung himself out of sight, hoping desperately no one had seen him.

Out of view, he slunk back further into the shadows, recovering his breath as he tried to find where the men were.

He spied them at nine o'clock. It was bad news. They were all holed up in the security guard portacabin by the entrance to the compound. The light was on, and he could see them through the open portacabin door. They were sitting together, presumably around a table. One was drinking from a can. And were they playing cards?

Sion couldn't see, but they appeared relaxed. They were waiting for that call from their boss. Their midnight rendezvous.

One of the gang suddenly appeared at the portacabin door.

He went around to the side of the cabin to pee. After, he walked back, pulling up his fly, taking out a cigarette and lighting it.

Words were said to him, he caught an object in his hand.

Now, he was walking across the empty car park towards the BMW. The man was already pointing at the boot, presumably with the key fob. He'd been told to check their captive.

Sion had ten seconds to find cover.

There was no way out of the compound without going past the security box. And once they found him gone, they'd be straight out, after him. And the perimeter fence was too high to scale quickly. He'd be too exposed. An easy shot.

The metal posted corner of the storage unit rubbed against his shoulder. He only had one reasonable way out of this place. And that was upwards.

Creeping around to the back of the container, he fixed his foot into the jam between the metal posted corner and the corrugated wall. Pushing upwards in one steady motion, he summoned all his upper-body strength and began to shimmy up the post like a lumberjack until he was on the top.

He didn't have a choice. He knelt down and then lay starfish flat, his head to the ground on the wet rusty top.

Then, the alarm was raised. Literally.

Seeing Sion was gone, the heavy had started pressing random buttons on the key fob. He'd set the BMW off.

The high-pitched shrieking car alarm and flashing indicator lights brought the two others bowling out of the security guard portacabin. Coats half-on, guns in their hands, they dashed chaotically over to the car to shut it up.

"Wha' the fuck you doing? Shut it up now!"

Sion listened to them. More shouting when they found the boot empty. More recriminations as they anticipated the shit that was about to go down when Irish found out they'd lost his man.

Then, feet shuffling about.

Sion lifted himself a fraction to see what was going on.

He'd been right about them being tooled up. By the way they were waving their handguns around, there was no way they were professionals. This bunch were more of a danger to themselves, but he was taking no chances. The thugs were fired up and in deep doo-doo with their boss.

He lay back flat as he saw them turn towards the containers.

He heard their steps as they got closer. Explosive expletives were still being fired off into the soggy April night air as the men scouted around the units.

"Any sign?"

"Nah… Looks like he's vanished."

"What d'ya mean he's vanished? He's not soddin' Houdini. He's about here somewhere. Go fuckin' find him."

Sion raised his head again. One of the men was back near the portacabin. He'd been sent to check down the road.

That meant there were two left, below him; scouring the area around the containers. His head back to the floor, Sion heard them shuffling now, around the boxes nearby. If they looked up, would they see him?

Should he slide down and chance an escape? Not with one of them by the exit. It was too risky to run across the open car park space. They'd be sure to take a pop, even if they were crap shots.

The unmistakable sound of a safety catch clicking confirmed that they'd use their guns, and it made his stomach churn. They were below him, to the right. Real close.

"Where the Hell's he got to?"

"Think he could be up on the roof?"

The pulse in the side of Sion's eye pumped. Arms spread, face flat to the floor, he kept dead still.

He could sense them, gazing up, searching the tops.

He gripped his puncturing dagger tightly. If they climbed onto his unit, he was confident he could fight them, but he'd instantly make himself a target for a clear shot.

"Can't see owt."

"Get your arse up there and have a proper skeck."

"Ah! Wha'?"

His unit shook as it was kicked. Or had someone tried to climb up it, then fallen back down?

Ears pricked, he listened out for the sound of boots scraping on metal. His hands on the box roof feeling out for any vibration, however small.

Nothing.

Then, a noise over to his left. The container next to his. The metal made a heavy drumming sound as one of the men attempted to clumsily climb up the side again.

Sion bristled. If they made it to the roof, they'd be sure to see him.

Another staccato of boots on metal. Then a couple of heavy thuds. And a loud skid in the gravel.

"*Fuck!*"

"You alright?"

The slapping noise of hands hitting leather clothes.

"Even soddin' Spider-Man would struggle to climb up that."

Sion breathed a little easier. But he still kept pancake-flat until he was certain they were moving away.

Then, edging himself up on his elbows he wriggled soundlessly across towards the edge to gain a good viewing point.

All three had met back up at the portacabin and were standing around uneasily, waving their guns about. Deciding what to do next.

Two disappeared back inside. Leaving one outside.

He put his gun away and lit up. After a few long drags, he got his mobile out.

It was easy for Sion to guess what was going on. This one had been given the honour of telling Irish.

The call took longer than Sion expected. How were they explaining it away? Would they try to bullshit their way out of it? That the guys were on it, hunting him down at that very moment? That they'd get him soon.

And what was Irish, the Scouser General's reply? Threats? Orders?

Even from the top of the container, he could hear them all shouting at each other when the man eventually went back inside the portacabin to debrief his co-workers.

Irish had, no doubt, kicked his arse.

Because, they were soon out there again, repeating exactly what they'd spent the last half hour doing. Chasing shadows, getting cold.

Sion had the darkness on his side, for now. He'd wait it out, but he needed to move from there before dawn broke.

A couple of other cars turned up. A range rover and an Audi.

There was more shouting and more sweeps around the storage units. This time with torches. There was more kicking of the boxes and a thorough check of the fence. One of them went off in the BMW for a time, presumably to scour the surrounding area.

Then, in the wee small hours, they finally gave up their search.

The other two vehicles were long gone.

Stiff from the wet, cold and bruising from the punches he'd taken, Sion watched the men getting sheepishly into the BMW. The rear lights faded finally from view as it disappeared up the road.

He'd wait for a few, long minutes more before rising. It could still be a trap.

Twenty minutes passed until he was confident that it wasn't. Brushing the water off his leather jacket, he shook himself. His upper body had stayed dry, protected by his leather coat, but his legs had stiffened up and his jeans were sodden.

He shook them, stretched and rubbed one of his shins, trying to avoid a cramp he could feel building. He didn't have time to worry about that. Or about his face swelling up. Or his sore head where the bottle had smacked him.

He needed to get out of there.

Sliding himself off the corner of the container, he lowered himself down, then jumped clear.

Back on the ground, he scanned the compound. He felt the hackles on the back of his neck rising. It was very late, and he was certain they'd gone, but he was still wary.

The main gates had been locked together with a thick chain and a sturdy padlock. Like the perimeter fence, it consisted of diamond-shaped metal wiring, ten-foot-high and topped with a razor-wire roll.

There was no other way for it. His only way out of there was over the top.

Despite the cold, he took off his leather coat and fixed it, by the sleeves, around his neck. Placing his hands high on the diamond mesh, he started to climb. The mesh holes were small, and his toes kept slipping in the spaces. But he kept on, powering his way to the top, clinging on with his hands, using all his upper body strength and climbing skills.

As his face neared the wire roll, with one hand he pulled the leather jacket from his neck and covered over the spikes.

Ignoring the fatigue, the muscle pull in his calf, the burning in his biceps, he summoned all his strength and hauled himself over. The leather protecting his skin from the razor-sharp barbs.

Lowering himself to the ground on the other side, he did another careful check up and down the road. In front of him and behind. Listening out for the ticking over of an engine. Checking for any concealed cars.

The place was deserted.

The car park was in an industrial zone. And he could smell the sea.

Beside the road there were brick warehouses with units for small businesses. There was a sign for a backstreet garage advertising car battery deals. And there behind him, another sign he'd not noticed until now, 'Meat Fresh'. The abattoir.

Trying to remember which way the men had left the compound, he moved off the road towards the buildings.

What he would give for a map app, right now.

Then he heard it. A rumbling; getting louder.

Beyond the abattoir there was a raised hump in the ground running parallel to the road. A railway line. And if he was correct, what he'd heard was the sound of an early morning train.

Running towards it, he rapidly cleared the low fencing onto the raised track. It was away from the road, and a perfect escape route out of there.

Following the side of the metal tracks, he began to jog. In the distance he could see the glow of streetlights. There, hopefully, he'd find a station and a train back to Wrexham.

This morning, I'm full of beans. We both flaked out early and slept through the night with only one feed stop, that we did together. And I'm feeling human again instead of half-zombie.

It helps too that the sun is shining.

"What d'you think about us converting some of these buildings?"

I pass it by Jac as we carry our buckets of empty bottles across the yard.

"We could do with a more modern shed. But that won't be cheap. Why?"

"How about we turn some of the old stone sheds into holiday cottages?"

He stops, then examines the buildings as if he's seeing them for the first time.

"And we could put some yurts and teepees up in the summer too."

His face cracks into a broad grin.

"You ever lived in a yurt?"

"No. Have you?"

"Yeah. I have. In a protest camp near Brecon. And it was bloody freezing."

"When was that, then?"

"Before we came here. Cal spent a year campaigning against the gas pipelines, d'ya remember?"

I pull a face.

"Yeah, well I do. And it was the muddiest, wettest and most miserable year of my life."

"You make it sound like a trench in the first world war. People like it. They call it glamping."

He humphed.

"Bet they only do it once."

"Okay, so the yurt idea's a bit out there, but holiday cottages? Might be good? There are places nearer the coast, but nothing up this way."

Jac scuffs his toe on the concrete and studies the sheds some more.

"The Cross Keys is nearby, and there are some great biking trails and walks 'round here."

"Not up to the ledge though. That's our place."

His face cracks into a grin.

"If you wanna do this, you're gonna have to share. Visitors'll be on the yard and in the fields every day."

"That's alright. It'll be fun to meet new folk. And we could offer it as a retreat. How many places these days are so off-grid?"

He rubs his stubbly cheek.

"Turn a negative into a positive."

"Cal visited a place like that in Spain."

"*Aha!* I thought she'd be involved in this scheme of yours, somewhere along the line."

"Well? What d'ya think?"

"We should definitely do some more research. Might be grants available."

I agree. It's a big investment and we need to be sure people will come. But, I can tell he likes the idea.

# CHAPTER 22

----------*----------

Irish stared at the grainy CCTV photograph he had of Si, the hitman, and felt the cold chill of hate running through his veins.

Their outfit was compromised, irreparably damaged because of him. He'd lost some of his best boys, and his brother. It'd take months to get the county lines operation back up and running in the south again. Precious time that meant loss of trade and valuable London turf.

And worst of all, the hitman had made a mug out of him. Giving his men the slip that easily. He'd have them on *feckin'* car park duty for the rest of their days. No way was that bunch of amateurs ever getting near his ops again.

Britney's baby had been born last night and Tony should've been there. Instead of being a proud dad, carrying his little boy home from the hospital, he was banged up in a cell awaiting sentence.

Irish added some details to the post he was putting up. The pub camera had picked up his full face. You could see his features, but it was black and white and blurry. But, the best he had.

From the height of the door and the men by him, he'd say Si was six foot. He was white. Athletic build. Ex-Services, obviously. His hair was light; sandy brown possibly ginger, hard to say. Around thirty, give or take? That was about it.

He pressed send.

He didn't care about the security on this one. He'd sent it straight out on the wider chat group.

Now, every Scally, ex-con and chancer looking to make a few quid would see it and take an interest. Especially when they saw the reward he'd set.

The instructions were clear. Capture and collect. All they had to do was hold onto him and wait for his men. He'd send professionals, this time.

Si was in his sights, and pretty soon he'd have him hanging from a hook.

Jac's been holed up in the living room all evening while I'm snug in bed, reading on my Kindle.

It's a filthy night. The weather should be improving now it's spring. But rough winds are shaking the April buds, and the rain is battering relentlessly against the bedroom window.

The telephone ringing out in the hall makes me start, and it's an effort to pull myself out of my book to go answer it.

It's Claire. We've been calling each other regularly and she's come up to see me a couple of times since we had our spa day.

She's usually quite chilled out, but tonight she's frantic. I promise to call her tomorrow and find out what's going on.

"What are you up to?"

Jac's sketching in front of the fire in the living room.

"You'll see."

He gives me a teasing grin, making me all the more curious to see what he's drawing.

"Who was on the phone?"

"Claire. She's worried. She's not heard from Sion."

Jac pulls a face.

"Something definitely going on there, then?"

"They've been talking to each other every day. She says that they'd got real close, and then he suddenly stopped calling. He was meant to be back last Sunday. She's not heard from him for a week and he's not answered her messages."

"He's not contacted me either, but Sion's not flaky. He's probably working all hours to get the job finished. I'll try him tomorrow."

"Jac; d'you think he's okay?"

"Yeah. It'll be work or his phone's broke; there'll be a good reason. Look, if I can't get hold of him, I'll try Jase."

"Claire asked him to go travelling with her. She's worried she's scared him off."

"No way. Not Sion. He's spent months chasing her. He's drunk a lot of beer for that woman."

"I'll tell her that."

Sidling up towards him, I sit by the fire and try to sneak a peek at what he's sketching. But he's too quick; he clutches the pad tightly to his chest, then holds it away from me in the air.

"Ahh, come on, Jac. That's not fair. Lemme see. Please."

I wrestle and tickle him to free up his arm so I can see the paper, making him laugh.

"Okay, nosey. You really wanna see?"

He liberates himself from my clutches and shows me the sketch pad.

"You wanted me to design you a tattoo. Thought we could both have this done."

On the paper is the most delicately sketched bird.

"A swallow?"

"Yeah. I started playing around with ideas, and the bird I kept seeing was a swallow. Seeing as we've both come home."

"You'd better not be buggering off abroad every winter, then."

"Not unless we go together."

He smiles and my heart melts. *Dammit.*

I study the delicately pencil-etched swallow with its feathered wings, into which he's added a faint hint of blue and a slightly reddened throat. Its wings are set back and the bird is plummeting downwards, except for the head which arcs, as if it's about to soar up again.

He unbuttons my pyjama top and pulls it down, exposing my

shoulder blade.

"It'll be discreet, 'cos it'll fit low on your shoulder and then go up to here," he says, tracing over my back with his fingers.

"And it'll cover the marks?"

His eyes burn into mine.

"Yes."

"It's beautiful."

"It's a part of me on you forever, Annie. You sure you want to go ahead?"

I nod and he kisses me tenderly.

"What happens next?"

"I'll make a stencil. Then, after lambing, we'll go see Matt."

"Matt?"

"The guy who did my other two."

It suddenly feels like it's happening.

"Annie, if you change your mind, you need to say. 'Cos once it's on, it's not coming off."

"I want to get it done."

"You sure?"

"Yes. Give him a call."

"You're going into witness protection."

The way the NCA officer said it, there was no argument to be had. But still, the words reverberated in Sion's ears. It was what he'd been dreading.

It meant that it was all over. He was being decommissioned.

He watched a pigeon with its beak in the dust in front of their park bench. He'd be like that from now on, spending the rest of his life pecking around, trying to survive in an unfamiliar world. His career, his life, was over.

The officer fired the ring pull on his can of Coca-Cola and the bird flew away.

"Irish has put the word out on the street. There's a hefty price on your head. You're a walking target, and there's plenty who'd jump at taking a shot."

"London's safe enough."

The officer opened his phone and clicked on an app.

A grainy picture of Sion's face popped up on screen together with details of the finder's fee.

He then clicked open a map and four friends pins suddenly popped up on it. They were all within a one-mile range.

Rattled, Sion pulled his baseball cap down low over his forehead and lifted his hoodie over the top of it.

"I need forty-eight hours."

"No dice. You're leaving right now."

"I can't. I've got to see my mam before I go."

His handler shook his head at Sion's weak attempt at emotional blackmail. Did he take him for an idiot?

"C'mon man, this is it for me. You know the score, once I get a new identity I'm dead to everyone. Forty-eight hours, what's that?"

"The difference between you living and dying, for real?"

"What's the worst that's gonna happen to me? That I get jumped? Think I can't handle myself against a couple of Scallies trying to make a few quid?"

"Sion; don't underestimate them. You had a lucky escape. In their eyes, you're a police informer and you've made them look like fools. If they catch you, it won't be pretty."

"I'm a skilled operative."

"Thirty of them are banged up because of you."

"See? I'll be fine."

"And they're royally pissed off. Mainly with you."

"So, do I get my two days?"

"And what if I say no?"

Sion looked away.

The officer sighed.

"Monday morning, National Crime Agency HQ with your suitcase packed. And think hard about where you wanna go."

"Oh… *and Sion*?"

"Yeah?"

"Don't bullshit me again. I read your bio. If you want a plus one, you best give me a call."

"Appreciate it."

Sion moved off the park bench and pulled his hoodie even lower before walking away.

How many people were after him? How many already had visuals on him? Did they know his car?

The photo was from the Wrexham pub. He'd been careless, arrogant even. And now he was paying the price.

And, was he being arrogant to have begged for time? He could have been on a plane in a couple of hours escaping to safety.

But not without seeing Claire first.

It was a fair old drive back to Wales, but one he had to make.

"He's been with you? No... Nothing's up. Hadn't heard from him, that's all."

Jac wraps up the call.

"Definitely... yes, you'll get to meet her, don't you worry. We're planning a trip down after lambing. Gonna see Matt... Yeah, having another one done... Yeah, both of us... Thanks bro... See ya soon."

"Is Sion alright?"

Since Claire called, I've been worrying too. Why would someone suddenly go offline for a whole week? Even if they were mad busy, they could still send a quick text. Make a call, surely?

"He's fine. He's been crashing at Jase's place in London."

"Why's he not phoned her?"

"Jase says he got into a fight on a night out. Got a few bruises on his face. He didn't want Claire to know. Or to see the state of him."

It made sense, but it wasn't going to please Claire.

"What you smirking about?"

"Nothing. Just wouldn't like to be in Sion's shoes, that's all. Claire's pretty pissed off with him and that's not much of an excuse not to send her a text."

"Jase says Sion's gonna call and see her on his way back."

"Brave man."

"Jase said we can stay at his place when we go see Matt."

A nervous knot forms in my stomach.

"Cool... I can't wait to meet Jase. Get all the dirt on you from your army days."

"Hmm, on second thoughts, p'raps we should stay with Cal. Less you know, the better."

Hearing her ringtone, Claire rushed over to her bag stowed under the bar. She'd been waiting over a week. If it was him, she'd tell him to do one.

Her pounding heart told her she wouldn't.

"Gotta take this, sorry."

Kevin frowned, but she didn't care what he thought anymore. The lunch shift was nearly over. Anyway, he was always on his phone. And no way was it always work-related, either.

She moved into the recess by the glasswasher. Her stomach was suddenly full of butterflies. And dread.

"Sion?"

It came out too enthusiastically, she reigned herself back in.

"Everything okay? Where the Hell have you been?"

"... Yeah, right."

He'd explain it all and he wanted to meet up.

"Why should I, when you can't even be arsed to call me?"

He wasn't making much sense.

"Look, Sion, I've gotta go. I'm at work."

He was persistent, she gave him that. He really needed to see her, he told her. It wouldn't wait.

In the end, she relented.

"Alright, alright. I'll see you at seven."

She turned back towards the bar.

"*Shit!* You gave me a fright."

Kevin was standing there, right in front of her. Had he been listening in?

Staring indignantly, she put her phone back into her bag.

Thank God she was off for a couple of days after this shift.

"Yer boyfriend back?"

"Sion's not my boyfriend. But since you ask, yes he is. I'm seeing him tonight, so I'll need my wages before I go, if that's alright?"

"No can do, sweetheart."

His scouse drawl irritated her even more than usual.

"You know the score. I do the wages Monday."

"Any chance I could have it sooner, Kev? Please?"

Kevin considered it

"Alright, darlin.' Seein' as it's you. Come pick it tomorrow before the lunch shift."

"Great, see you at eleven."

◆ ◆ ◆

Sion drove fast.

His heart raced when he thought of Claire and he couldn't wait to see her again. But, the call he'd made to her, she'd sounded upset. Angry, because he hadn't called. He could understand why. He'd seen all the times she'd tried to contact him and had listened to the messages she'd left.

After he'd dodged the train guards and got himself back to Wrexham, his boss at the NCA had told him in no uncertain terms to get his arse to London. They'd put a twenty-four hour detail on Jason's flat and strict instructions for him to lie low. No contact and no calls. He'd felt bad about that, but he had spared her seeing his badly bruised face and beat-up body. She'd have freaked out.

It had been a crappy two weeks. He'd screwed up his job, his life.

But he had found Claire. In their late-night chats, he'd shared more about himself than he'd told any other woman. He hoped she'd understand when he explained it to her; face to face.

He glanced over at the small sports bag on the passenger seat beside him. It was his toolbox and his security for the next forty-eight hours. In it, he kept the essentials for his job, knives, rope, ties and a handgun.

And how would she react when he asked her to come with him? It wasn't exactly the backpacking around the world she was planning, but it'd be a one-way ticket out of here to somewhere far away.

He still wasn't sure what to say to her. If she knew the whole truth, what were the chances that she'd go with him?

# CHAPTER 23

----------✳----------

"Claire."

She stepped into the street from her flat above the shop looking like she wasn't sure what to do next.

And for the first time ever, Sion wasn't either. Her large dark-brown eyes were stormy and proud as she approached his car, talking to him from the pavement through the driver window.

"You go quiet for a week, and then you show up wanting to see me?"

The sulky challenge was deserved. He knew how it looked.

"Like I told you, I had a spot of bother."

"You never answered my messages."

"I lost my phone. Got a new one, but my contacts were wiped."

"Don't sell me that horse shit, Sion. You could've got through to me, messaged me off your laptop. You work in IT for Christ's sake!"

She had a point. She was the first person ever to blow a hole in his cover story.

"Look, I get it. You don't wanna come travelling with me. You've thought it through and decided there's no point carrying this on if I'm going off for a year. You could've just told me. Instead of ghosting me."

"Ghosting you? Claire, it's not about you going travelling. I wanna go with you too. I've got something I need to fly by you.

Get in and let me explain properly."

She came closer towards the window.

"*Jesus*, Sion! What's happened to your face? It's all bruised."

"Get in. We'll go down to the beach."

"What? Now?... It'll be dark soon."

"Come on, Claire. We need to talk."

She shook her head, but moved around the car and opened the door, warring against her better judgement. Sion quickly lifted the sports bag off the passenger seat, got out and stowed it in the boot.

She sat silently by his side all through the drive down to his favourite cove. This wasn't quite the reunion he'd had in mind, but he took her moodiness as a good sign. The fact that she was upset meant that she must like him, at least a little.

Parking up, they walked over the dunes to a small beach, a perfectly formed crescent set in between the headlands. By now, the moon was high in the sky, and it was light enough to walk without needing a torch. The weather had been warming up a little, even though they were both wrapped up against the chill sea breeze.

Tentatively taking Claire's hand, they walked without speaking along the shore, and she didn't pull away. They headed across the cove over to the far side, where a pile of rocks jutted out from the sand.

There, they climbed and sat side-by-side on top of a clump of smooth black boulders.

"Claire?"

She remained fixed on the waves lapping insistently onto the shore.

"What I tell you, you gotta promise you won't repeat it. Can I trust you?"

"'Course you can. What is it, Sion? What've you been hiding from me?"

She was the only one who'd ever seen him for who he was.

Taking a deep breath, he told her everything. About the work, the contracts and his job undercover for the security services.

About the Helbanianz and the Scousers. And he explained why he'd not been able to call her.

And then he told her how he'd thought about her when he was tied up in the boot of the car, and how he'd been determined to stay alive so that he could see her again.

She sat, listening intently.

And when he was done, he waited in the quiet. The rhythm of the rolling waves, a drum-roll prelude to her response.

"How did you get into it?"

It was a valid question. Not one he'd anticipated.

"A friend of mine, from the first care home. The one I told you about. He was in the shit. He'd racked up some massive debts, got in deep with some well dodgy types. I was his only way out. They were after a specialist to do a job, and I was fresh out of the army. He asked me, explained it all and I agreed. It meant getting the heavies off my mate's back, and he agreed to go away after, to start fresh. In Spain."

This was the friend he'd talked to her about. The one who'd protected him from the two violent bullies who'd set on him on his first night in care. With a razor and ink, they'd performed an initiation. Tattooed his arm and beat him. His friend intervened before the next part, thank God. He'd been spared from being violated unspeakably. After that, Sion had been safe, under his new friend's wing. And he'd owed him.

"The gang got me a contact where I could source the equipment I needed."

"What? Like weapons?"

"Guns. Anyway, on the ferry back from Dublin, I was hauled in. Turns out, I'd been under surveillance the whole time. They'd read my army records, saw my skill set and wanted to keep me in play. So, I ended up working for the NCA deep undercover."

"But, you've killed people?"

He couldn't hide from that.

"Yes, I have."

"Shouldn't they have been arrested? Put on trial?"

Her voice rose.

"What about their right to defend themselves in court, Sion?"
She had a point.

"Look, everyone I've killed's been a street soldier. A real villain outside of the law. Guys like Prifti, Irish even; they're far too smart to get caught. They're untouchable. And they hire people like me to bump each other off, settle scores in their battles between each other over turf and control. And the information I've passed to the NCA has saved many more lives. It's given them the evidence they needed for arrests. I've helped close down whole operations, sent lots of really bad people to jail."

"No wonder the Scousers want your ass."

"Yeah. I screwed things up for them. Big time. *Argh!* The Scousers are the worst of the lot. They're using kids as drug mules, Claire. Nine, ten years old. Across the country, kids like we were, they're skippin' school or out late at night on their bikes making drug deliveries, like it's pizza. And what kills me, is that it's only a matter of time before they're hooked on the stuff too."

She put her hand over his and he turned to her.

"So many young lives ruined. I hope what I've done has helped save a few."

She reached up and touched his face, then examined the yellowing around his eye and the purple bloom on his cheek.

"They hurt you bad?"

"No. But they're not the type of bruises a computer geek can explain away."

He took her hands in his. Bending his head he gently brushed his lips over her fingers as he held them. He could hear her breathing. Did she want him too? Or was she afraid of him?

"And now what?"

"I begged two days to come up here. On Monday, I'm going into witness protection. A new identity abroad. Far away from here."

"Does that mean no one'll ever see you again."

"Pretty much. Yes."

Silence again.

"What about me?"

She was gazing up at the moon, avoiding his eyes.

"Come with me."

Pulling her hand away from his, she shook her head.

"All the things you've told me…"

"Claire."

She sniffed.

"I need to think about it. Please, Sion. Take me home."

He pulled into the bus stop on the high street, opposite her flat. She'd been quiet all the way back.

"I'm good from here."

She went to undo her seat belt and he touched her hand.

"Is this goodbye?"

Pivoting, she faced him.

"Honestly? I don't know yet."

Her eyes met his, and behind their bright blueness, she saw his pain.

Leaning towards him, in spite of all the doubts and fears of who this man was, she couldn't help herself. She kissed his lips.

"Am I safe with you?"

He gazed deep into her eyes.

"I'll always protect you, Claire. I promise you that. I was stupid, I should've done something else with my life after the army."

"Like, computing?"

A hint of a smile flickered across her face.

"Yeah, like computing. But it's done now and I'm starting again. A new life in a new country. Come with me."

She had no words for him yet, so she kissed him.

This time, her lips opened as she felt him respond to her. His hand lightly caressed her shoulder as she leaned in closer, and she felt his desire for her as they both became wrapped around each other. Whether it was a kiss full of promise and hope, or regret and sadness, Claire didn't yet know.

She ended it, and drew herself apart, reaching for the door handle.

"I've gotta go."

"I'm leaving tomorrow. Even if it's a no, can I see you?"

She leaned back into the open passenger door.

"I'm picking up my wages tomorrow morning. Then I'm free."

"Alright. I'll meet you by The Cross Keys?"

"Fine. See you in the car park at eleven."

Shiny vivid-green leaves were popping out from the hawthorn hedges. The celandines and stitchwort flowers were peppering the hedgerows in waves of brilliant yellow and white. The bluebells had started peeping out. Their heads pushing up like asparagus spears, soon they'd form a bright blue carpet across the woodland behind the cottage. This was the best time of year, and it filled Sion's heart with sadness. He'd never be here again.

Reaching the farmhouse, he checked the outbuildings. It was Sunday morning, but still, Jac was sure to be doing jobs about the place.

"Hey! Sion!"

Spotting him on the yard, Annie had come out from the house.

"Hi, Annie."

"Long time no see. There were a couple of people wondering what happened to you

"You seen Jac?"

"He's just got back in. Kettle's on if you wanna brew?"

Sion hugged her as he met her by the porch.

"*Shit, Sion!* Your face! It's still yellow and green. Jase told us about the bar brawl."

Sion hastily bent down and pulled his shoes off.

"Has Claire seen the state of you?"

"Not in the daylight. It's much better than it was. It'll be gone in a day or two."

He changed tack quickly.

"Looks like you're still flat out. Your shed's full."

"Turning most of them out into the fields today. We're hoping this fine weather will last. Couple more weeks'll do us."

"Sion!"

He surprised Jac with his strong embrace.

Jac was staring at him too, when he noticed his face. Good job they couldn't see the rest of his body. From his ribs down, he was still a deep shade of purple. He'd been lucky, nothing was broken. The medical officer they sent to examine him, said it was a miracle he'd not cracked a rib or burst his spleen.

"Great to see you back. What does the other guy look like?"

As they drank coffee and chatted, Sion grew quieter. Their banter began to dry up.

"What's up, mate?"

Annie got up to give them some space, but Sion held his hand out towards her.

"Don't go. I need to tell you something. Both of you."

She sat back down.

"I'm going away."

"When?"

"Today. Right after I see Claire. I've got into some strife."

Jac rubbed his face.

"What kind of trouble you in, mate? Did they arrest you for fighting?"

He regarded his friend cagily, then hung his head.

"I won't bore you with the details, but let's just say that I was stretching it a bit when I said I was in computing."

His eyes met his best friend's.

"I was on ops, Jac."

Jac leaned back in his chair.

"*I knew it!* I knew you'd never sit behind a desk all day. Why didn't you tell me?"

"I couldn't, mate. It wasn't safe."

"*Sion!*"

His friend shrugged.

"The bruises?" Annie asked quietly.

"Things went tits up on my last job. Which is why I couldn't call Claire. We talked last night. But, the mess means I've got to get outta here, and I can't come back."

"What? Like... not *ever*?"

"They're putting me in witness protection."

"A whole new identity?"

"Yeah. And place. Far away."

Annie looked at him in disbelief.

"What about Claire?"

"I've asked her to come too. She's still thinking about it."

Jac stared at him, his face frozen.

"So... we'll... we'll never see you again? Is that what you're saying?"

Sion rose from his chair, unable to speak anymore as he faced Jac who was up on his feet too and standing by him.

Jac had been there from the start. Through it all. Thick and thin. Almost half a lifetime together.

"You're my brother. I'll always have your back."

Sion nodded and placed his hands on Jac's shoulder. They hugged each other hard.

"Get word to us, bro. Find us some app, or some code to use. When you're safe, tell us where you are and we'll come see you."

Sion nodded.

"I've gotta lay low for a bit, but as soon as I can, I will."

Sion kissed her cheek.

"Look after him, Annie."

Jac put his arm around Annie as Sion made to leave.

"And none of that stubborn bollocks, alright?"

His laugh cut through the melancholic air.

"'Cos I won't be here to sort it, so don't go screwin' it up. Either of you."

Annie's face reddened. Jac coughed and rubbed his face.

"Take care, bro. Send word."

Sion gave them a wink.

"I'll see you again. I promise."

# CHAPTER 24

----------*----------

Claire had been up all night. At four a.m., she'd made up her mind categorically that she wasn't going. She didn't know the guy. He'd consistently lied about himself. Plus, there was the teeny-weeny, microscopically-minuscule fact that he was a professional assassin. Even if he was working for the good guys.

No, Sion Edwards was not exactly ideal boyfriend material.

Yet, there *was* something between them that she couldn't deny. It wasn't just she could talk to him about stuff and he made her laugh. It was more than that. And more than an attraction. It was something visceral between them.

She'd felt it in their kiss. He'd held back at first, she could tell, and he'd let her kiss him. But then his guard dropped, and when she sensed his passion for her it had thrilled her to her core. No-one had ever made her feel like that before.

This enigma of a man was too confusing, and no matter how hard she tried, she couldn't make up her mind.

So, in the middle of the night she'd dumped her things into her backpack anyway. She didn't have a lot. But it was heavy enough; lying propped up against the wall, waiting. Waiting for her to finally settle on what to do.

She'd decide when she saw him, she told herself, as she parked her old two-door Suzuki in The Cross Keys car park.

Locking the car, she walked across the tarmac to the pub's kitchen. Glenda, the cleaner, had finished mopping the floor in the bar and was carrying the bucket to empty down the drain outside.

"Is Kevin about?"

"Upstairs, chuck. If you see him, tell him I'm off now, will ya?"

"Yeah, no worries. See you soon."

"Kevin?"

Claire called out his name again, then started up the stairs to the accommodation wing above the pub.

"Kevin?"

The door into the flat was ajar.

Slowly, she pushed it a little wider, opening into the kitchen area.

"Hiya? Kevin? You there? It's Claire. I've come for my wages."

Sion spotted Claire at the back door of the pub as he drove into the car park. He was certain that she hadn't caught sight of him before she quickly disappeared inside. And he didn't want to look like he was stalking her, so he stayed in the car.

Turning on the radio, his stomach churned again. He'd been on tenterhooks all night wondering what she was going to do.

He couldn't call it.

Her eyes had been clouded with doubt. And he didn't blame her for that. He'd be the same too, in her situation.

But then, she'd put her soft lips shyly on his. And then more passionately. *Wow!* He'd been right about her. Claire had hidden depths he was desperate to explore. He'd have to accept it if she didn't want to go with him. But it would be a damn shame, all the same.

Claire's car was next to his. A battered old Suzuki one litre job. His heart sank. He couldn't see any travel bags on the seat. They could be in the boot or back at her flat? Or, the sinking feeling returned; she was staying.

Something over by the pub suddenly grabbed his attention.

A middle-aged woman had come running out of the kitchen door and was now scanning the car park frantically, looking like she needed help.

Without hesitation, Sion rushed out of the car.

Something was up.

Jogging over, he called over to the woman. She was in a state.

"What's up?"

"Help! He's hurting her. I heard her scream."

"Who?"

"Claire."

Sion's blood ran cold.

"She went to see Kevin. And I was puttin' my mop bucket back and there was this loud thump on the ceiling. And then I heard her scream."

"You got a phone?"

The cleaner nodded.

"Call the police."

Squashing his instinct to race up there immediately, instead, he bolted back to the car. Grabbing his bag from the boot, he then raced swiftly across the car park, into the pub, to the door of the upstairs flat.

Why did Kevin want to harm Claire?

At the base of the stairs, he unzipped his bag and loaded his handgun. Checking the safety catch, he slipped it into the back of his jeans.

Grabbing a handful of cable ties, he shoved them into his front pocket.

Bag in one hand, gun in the other, there was no time to waste.

"*Arghh!* Please! Let go of me."

The voice was unmistakably hers. And she wasn't far away. Another cry.

Fury rose up within him. If he touched her again, *God help him!*

He had to keep it together. He needed to stay calm. Focussed. For her sake.

Creeping soundlessly up the stairs, he stole forward and peeped in through the open door into the kitchen area. Kevin and Claire were both directly in front of Sion facing at ninety degrees away from him and about twelve steps towards the middle of the kitchen area.

Kevin had Claire pulled down onto her knees. He'd grabbed her from behind and was now holding her tight with her head yanked back by her ponytail, exposing the full length of her neck.

*The bastard!*

She was struggling to get free, trying to resist him but he could tell that she was wary too of the sharp, steely blade held firmly at her throat.

Fierce, primal anger welled up again, and he battled hard to quell it. It pained him beyond words to see her like this. But losing his temper would do more harm.

He stood out of their sight by the open door. He needed to bide his time.

"Where is he?"

Kevin sounded revved up. His movements were agitated too.

"Who?"

"Don't gimme that, you dumb bitch."

Kevin pressed again.

"Where is he? You got your phone? Call him. Get him to come here. Now."

Yanking her hair harder.

*"Oww!"*

Sion watched silently. So that was it. He was one of them. He'd seen the Scouser's wanted post. He was trying to get hold of the reward money.

A wave of nausea washed over him as he saw the back of Claire's head pulled back. He'd told her last night he'd keep her safe. And here she was, with a knife to her neck because of him.

Kevin had definitely been sniffing something. Coke or Meth? If he sprang the gun on him, he was wound up so tight, he could easily slash Claire's throat. And that could be fatal. His only chance was surprise.

He crept up further to the door jamb.

"Why d'ya want Sion?" he heard Claire say through gritted teeth.

"Friends of mine wanna word with him."

Taking a deep breath, he stole forward into the middle of the room, stepping soundlessly behind Kevin's back.

Claire hadn't seen him, either.

The closer he was, the easier it would be to spring himself on him and get the knife.

"Sion's a computer geek. He works in an office."

"Don't gimme that, sugar-tits. There's a finder's fee out on him for twenty big ones."

"You've got the wrong man."

"He's a grass. And I'm the lucky son of a bitch who gets to cash him in. Now where's your phone?"

He kicked at her legs, spurring her to check her pockets, get out her phone.

"I'd hate to spoil that pretty face of yours. So for the last time, where *the fuck* is it?"

"It's in the car," Claire screamed at him.

He had to stop him, but he couldn't get any closer. If he jumped him, she'd be scarred for life.

He had no choice.

"You looking for me?"

The pig-eyed manager spinned around, Claire with him.

Sion was five steps away, towering over them.

The gun was in the back of his trousers. Could he grab it? Shoot him at close range?

"Let her go and then we'll speak."

He was trying to be as calm as he could be, taking in the man's amphetamine-wired state, and the sharp blade that was still hovering by the side of Claire's face.

"Why do you want me, Kevin?"

"Friends of mine wanna speak with you."

"So, you'd like me to wait here for them, with you. Is that it?"

He stepped closer and Kevin grabbed onto Claire hard.

Sion froze.

"Let her go."

Kevin ignored him, clinging onto her hair.

"Are they on their way? These mates of yours?"

Beads of sweat began forming on Kevin's brow and Sion noticed his hand by Claire's nose beginning to twitch. He was cracking.

But the blade was a proper bit of kit. The flick knife would cut deep if it sliced into her skin.

He tried again.

"I promise to stay with you and wait for them. Might take a while, though, to get here from Liverpool. This is between me and you. Let Claire go."

Kevin shifted nervously, looking down at Claire, considering it.

"She's going nowhere."

He uttered finally; and held onto Claire with renewed determination.

Sion shrugged. He'd had the choice.

He'd just taken the hard way.

One hand behind his back, he eased his hand towards the gun in his belt until he could feel the metal of the handle. With the knife so close to her he couldn't afford any sudden movements, so he inched his fingers discreetly until finally he had the gun securely in his hand.

"Give it up, Kevin. No one's coming. The cleaner's called the police."

Kevin's eyes darted towards the door.

"They're outside right now and they'll be treating this as a hostage situation. The only reward you'll be getting is free lodgings in a twelve by eight cell, courtesy of her majesty."

"You're shitting me."

"Did ya not hear the sirens?"

He was agitated now. His pupils like black saucers.

Frantically, he looked around and checked the door. Then, over in Sion's direction. Then, the space around them.

He was about to crack.

Sion took his chance.

"There's blue lights all over the car park, Kev. You can see from the window. Go see for yourself."

Pulling her up with him, knife at her neck, Kevin started to move; dragging Claire across the room towards the window.

Sion pulled the gun from behind his back and pointed it, trigger poised, ready to shoot.

But Claire hadn't seen that.

She took her chance too.

Slamming her elbows back, she drove them fiercely into Kevin's solar plexus. Snapping herself upwards. Coming right between Kevin and Sion's clear line of fire.

*"Claire!"*

*"Argh!"*

A vicious slice.

Sion stashed the gun quickly back in his belt and leapt into the air, but it was too late to stop the line of crimson beading up behind the knife as it sliced its way angrily down Claire's neck.

*No!*

Grabbing Kevin's fist, Sion smashed it down to the ground.

The knife bounced free and scuttled across the floor, out of their reach.

Claire flung herself after it, scrambling clear of the two men wrestling on the ground. Grabbing the knife tightly, she brandished it at them in self-defence.

"Claire? Honey? You alright?"

Taking advantage of Sion's momentary distraction, Kevin, wriggling an arm and fist free, slammed a punch with force into Sion's face, sending him reeling.

Seeing Kevin coming at him again, Sion snatched for his gun in the back of his jeans. Flicking free the safety catch, he fired a deafening shot upwards into the air, flinging Kevin backwards.

*Smack.*

The handgun came crashing down into Kevin's face, shattering his nose and stunning him.

That one was for Claire.

Like a bear catching a salmon, Sion expertly flipped him over onto the floor. His face covered the carpet tile in a pool of dark blood. In one swift move, Sion then skilfully had the barman tied up securely, with his hands and ankles secured tightly with the plastic ties.

"Claire?"

She was behind him cowering in a corner, frozen from shock. Her knees were hunched tightly into her body, her arms wrapped tightly around herself. And he saw too, the steady stream of blood running freely down her neck onto her collar bone and into her hair.

She snapped out of her daze and touched her neck; her hands becoming covered in blood too.

"*Oh my God!* Help!"

"*Shh*. It's okay."

She began shaking with shock. Kneeling beside her, he took her in his arms and held her tightly.

"Let me see it, Claire."

Pulling back her hair for him, he could see that the gash was deeper than he realised, and there was a fair bit of blood coming from it. It ran from the base of her ear right down the side of her neck and she was damn lucky that it had missed an artery.

Still, it was bad enough.

Sion found her a tea towel and sat her down on a chair.

"You need to get that stitched. Keep pressing on it to try and stop the flow."

"They'll have you sooner or later," Kevin growled into the carpet. "Watch yer back, 'cos this ain't over yet. Not by a long shot."

"One more peep and it will be for you," Sion snarled.

Claire was still shaking a little, but she held the towel firm as Sion quickly retrieved the rope out of his bag.

Hauling Kevin to the other chair, far enough away from Claire, he bound him up fast. If he heard another peep out of him, he'd gag him too.

Then, after storing his gun back in the bag, he phoned the farm. Annie was on her way to take Claire to hospital while he waited with Kevin for the police to arrive.

# CHAPTER 25

----------*----------

"What d'you mean, I can't go in?"

"There are reports of gunfire. It's an armed siege. You need to shift your vehicle from here, Miss, and stay behind the tape."

The whole of the car park is crowded with police and a black BMW is blocking the road behind me, trying to turn around too. Sunday city tourists in big, flashy cars that are far too big for our narrow country lanes.

"Annie!"

Detective Ellis Roberts recognises me and comes over.

"What you doin' here?"

"I got a call from Sion. He's in there, with my friend, Claire."

"Is Sion who the cleaner said ran in there?"

"All I know is Claire's got a knife wound. He phoned and asked me to take her to hospital. It's not serious but she needs stitches."

Ellis gives the uniformed officer a nod.

"Park up."

I swing Trusty Rusty into the back of the car park, while Ellis waits for me.

"What's going on?" I ask him breathlessly.

"There's been gunshot. We're waiting for the armed response unit. So, tell me what Sion said to you?"

I repeat the phone call word for word.

"And is this the same Sion who was staying with your mam's tenant?"

"You mean Jac? Yes, it is. You do know Mam passed away?"

Ellis stares at me.

"I'm sorry. No I didn't. How did...?"

"Cancer," I cut in, "A couple of weeks after Dad. She was dying and hadn't told us."

There's an awkward pause; and the way his eyes bore into me, makes me feel uncomfortable.

"Sorry to hear that. How you managing with the farm?"

"Jac's been a big help."

"Jac and Sion? They were in the army together, right?"

"Yeah. They're both ex-special forces. Look, can you let me go in and see what's going on? What's the worst that can happen, eh?"

"You could get shot and killed."

"There is that... But Sion's a friend. He called for me to come, so it must be safe."

Ellis rubs his face.

"It goes against all our protocols."

"Please, detective. I can phone him?"

It sounds reasonable and he's considering it.

"Alright, but if we do this, you need to stay behind me and do exactly what I say. Understood?"

"Absolutely."

He shakes his head and goes over to clear it with a uniformed officer who's speaking into his walkie talkie.

I can tell that they're disagreeing about it.

Eventually, Ellis beckons me over.

"Give him a call."

He answers immediately.

"Sion? It's Annie. The police are here, they've heard shots. Is it safe for us to come in?"

He tells me it is. I pass the phone to the detective, and afterwards he's happier with the situation and we get the green light.

I follow him towards the kitchen door. Then, moving into the pub behind Ellis, he checks out each room first before we go further inside. I can sense that he's not convinced that this isn't a trap.

Near the bar, we approach the open door and see the stairs up to the flat.

"Sion? You up there?"

There's a movement of feet above us.

"Is that Detective Roberts?".

"Yes. And Annie's here too."

"Hi Sion. How's Claire?" I call.

"She's shook up."

He appears at the top of the stairs.

"She's a bit sore. Gonna a need a fair few stitches down her neck"

"What happened?"

"Her manager attacked her. I ran in to help. I've tied him up."

"We'd better come up, then," Ellis says a little stiffly. He's still wary.

We both climb up the stairs towards Sion, who backs off into the kitchen.

"Annie!"

Claire rushes to me with a bloody towel on the side of her face, and I hold onto her tightly.

"It's alright."

"Kevin cut me. What's it like?"

She lifts the towel tentatively away from her face, and I guide her over to the window so I can take a proper look at it. I can see the deep, thick line that's been slashed right down her neck.

"It's nasty but we'll get you sorted, don't worry."

"Will it scar?"

When I don't answer, I hear her sniffing back tears.

It's only then that I notice Kevin tied to a chair. His face is covered in blood too, and he looks mean.

"Yes, you can enter the flat safely, over... Roger that."

Ellis' voice into his police radio cuts through the air.

Then, silence.

The detective appears frozen for a second. I'm not sure why. Surely, he must have dealt with worse incidents than this?

"If it's alright with you, I'm gonna take Claire to Accident and Emergency."

"Stay put for a minute."

The detective's eyes are fixed on Sion.

"The gun? Where is it?"

Sion looks at him innocently.

"Gun?"

"Yeah. The police outside heard gunshot."

Ellis scans the room, then points upwards to his left.

"The bullet's probably embedded in that hole. Right there, in the ceiling."

"It's in his bag."

The detective swivels around towards Kevin, who's piped up for the first time.

"Annie, can you hand me that sports bag, please?"

Sion watches on impassively, as I take the bag over to the detective.

"Open it, please."

I put the bag onto the ground and unzip it fully for the detective. Inside, we can all see a handgun.

Ellis' eyes meet Sion's.

"I'm arresting you for possession of an illegal firearm."

He produces a set of cuffs from his pocket and places them around Sion's already outstretched wrists. Locking them shut, he continues.

"And on suspicion of murder."

"Murder? Who's murder?" I ask, dumbfounded.

He motions to Kevin bound to the chair in front of him.

"Your father, Glyn Evans. It's the same rope."

Claire and I watch speechless and shocked, as both Sion and Kevin are handcuffed and taken away by the police.

Sion doesn't speak either. His head is bowed, but as he leaves, I see his eyes fixed on Claire's with unshakeable imploring intensity.

"I didn't do it."

Claire lets out a loud sob when we're finally alone.

Placing my arm around her, I take her out of there and on to the hospital. After that, we've got a trip to the police station to make a statement.

While she's getting treated, I call the farmhouse and talk to Jac.

I don't believe it. Why on earth would Sion, Jac's best mate, murder my father?

# CHAPTER 26

----------✳----------

"Are you sure that you're up to this?"

Detective Ellis smiled kindly at Claire, who was sitting across from him with large sterile pads taped along her neck up to her ear.

"Yes. I want to get it over and done with."

"So, you went to get your wages?"

"Right. And Glenda, the cleaner, told me that Kevin was up in the flat. So, I went up the stairs and he attacked me from behind as I went in. He held a knife to my face, and he threatened to use it on me if I didn't phone Sion."

"Why?"

"Why what?"

"Why was he interested in Sion?"

Claire shifted in her chair.

"I dunno."

She felt Ellis' eyes searing into her.

"It doesn't make sense. Why would Kevin grab you, so you could call Sion?"

"You need to ask Kevin that."

"But, why Sion?"

"No idea," she repeated, her voice rising with emotion. "He had a knife, and he slashed me when I tried to get free."

She was getting upset. He pushed the paper pad and biro towards her.

"Interview terminated at five-thirty. Write out your statement here, Claire, and then you can go home. It's been a traumatic day. Is Annie waiting for you?"

She nodded.

"And Jac's here too."

She began to jot down the sequence of events as they ended the recording.

Ellis leaned back in his seat. She was holding out on him. It didn't matter, for now, it would all come out sooner or later.

After a wall of silence from Sion, he'd given him his phone call.

But, he'd spent a very productive hour with Kevin, while Sion was left to stew back in a holding cell.

Kevin had sung like a canary.

According to him, Sion was a wanted man. The Scousers, the notorious Liverpool drugs outfit, had put a large price on his head. They had their tentacles in Wales. But, out here too? In the Cross Keys pub? In the middle of nowhere?

The Baikal IZH-79 confirmed that Sion Edwards was no angel. His bag was full of professional kit, and his gun was *the* semi-automatic firearm of choice on the black market.

The picture was becoming clearer.

This ex-SAS soldier was a professional gangster.

So, what was the connection to Glyn Evans?

Ellis picked up the vending machine cup of cold, sweet black coffee and knocked it back like a shot.

"Annie and Jac?"

Ellis threw out casually as Claire finished up writing her statement.

"What's going on there?"

"Back together," Claire responded, not looking up.

Ellis nodded pensively.

Two deaths. A large inheritance. Two elite ex-soldiers.

Motive, opportunity and means.

It was going to be a long night.

Taking Claire's statement, he signalled to the uniformed officer by the interview room door.

"We'll get someone to take you home."

Claire was confused.

"But, Jac and Annie are waiting for me in reception?"

"They're going to be a bit busy, I'm afraid. Helping us with our enquiries."

"How the Hell could I have known that Sion murdered my father?"

He's drilling again.

"I was away in London. I was hardly ever back home."

"No, I didn't meet him when I was back at Christmas. *Or Jac*.... That's right, I was home for three days.... No, I'd never heard of Sion Edwards, back then.... I hadn't spoken to Jac before my father died for twelve years.... Detective, where are you going with this?"

I can't believe what I'm hearing.

First, Jac and I are called in from the front reception area. Then, we're then taken to different interview rooms to give statements. And now, all of a sudden, I'm sitting here, listening to all manner of lies being knitted together about us.

Ellis presses on, aggressively.

"You and Jac? You're lovers now? Isn't it, kinda perfect how it's all worked out for you?"

"Yes. It is. It's the one positive outcome from weeks of pain. The shock of dad; then, watching my mother die. Have you any idea what that's like?"

I'm getting angry and upset.

"*So what*, about Jac and me? We were together when we were eighteen, and we are again now. Ask Claire or Cal? Even better, check with Jac? They'll *all* tell you how we got together after Mam and Dad passed."

"Cal?"

He reads off his notes.

"Is that Callista Jones?"

"Yes."

"Jac's mother?"

He's staring smugly at me. *Jees!* Now he thinks she's in on it as well. Whatever *'it'* is.

I throw my hands in the air in exasperation.

"You can keep on with your conspiracy theories all night, *but you're wrong!* I hadn't been in touch with Jac for years. In fact, not until you guys asked him to call me."

"So, you and Sion go way back, right?"

Jac raked his fingers over his head and took a deep breath.

"Yeah. We joined up at the same time."

"And you say he's like a brother to you?"

"Yes."

Jac paused to find his words.

"When you're on the front line with someone, dodging a bullet, watching out for snipers and IUDs every day, you develop a bond. He saved my life one time. And I saved his. We're like brothers."

"So, you'd say that you really know him?" Ellis pressed. "About as well as anybody could?"

"Yeah, I'd say so."

Ellis swung back on his plastic chair.

"So how come, then, you knew nothing about his gun?"

Ellis leaned in, eyeballing him.

"Or his involvement with the Scousers?"

"Who?"

Jac glanced away.

"He didn't tell me," he uttered quietly.

"Didn't tell you? Why's that? I thought you guys had..."

He checked his notes.

"A special bond?"

Jac studied the table.

"I don't know why he didn't say."

"For the recording, can you repeat that please?"

"I said, I don't know why he didn't tell me."

Ellis spotted the irritation in his voice; he was starting to break him down.

"No. You thought he was off mending computer networks. So… are you now telling me that you didn't know your so-called *brother* as well as you thought you did? Is that right?"

"Apparently so."

"What about the gun?"

"Never seen it before."

"No?"

"No."

"And the rope?"

"The rope?"

"Yes. The climbing rope Sion tied the bar manager up with. It was the same rope he used to hang Glyn Evans."

Jac stared blankly at Ellis.

"What happened, Jac?"

"I've no idea what you're on about… Ask Sion."

Ellis studied him carefully.

The silence bounced around the walls as Jac tensed and squirmed on the hard plastic chair.

"You've done well for yourself."

"What?"

"Beautiful girl, like Annie. Big farm, lots of potential. Very good income."

Ellis could feel him smouldering. Any second, he'd blow.

He pushed again.

"Feet well and truly under the table. It's all working out well for you, Jac. Isn't it?"

"What are you implying?"

"What d'you think I'm implying, Jac?"

"That I'm with Annie just for the farm? *That I don't love her?*"

Jac's voice rose in a crescendo of anger.

"Or that we cooked up a plan to kill Glyn between us? Is that what you're saying? And that we gave Maureen terminal cancer too? This is bollocks! *Utter bullshit!*"

"So, how did Glyn get that rope?"

"*I... don't... know!*"

Sion stared at the bare shadowy wall behind Ellis' head. The video camera was on, and so far it had recorded a whole heap of nothing.

This Sion was one tough nut to crack. Trained in interrogation, no doubt.

"Tell me," Ellis began again. "We know you're on the Scousers' Most Wanted list. Let's put that to one side for now. What I'm really interested in is this climbing rope of yours. How did Glyn Evans get a hold of that rope to kill himself?"

Sion didn't answer.

Ellis tried again.

"What did they offer you?"

Silence.

It was harder than anyone could imagine maintaining silence. Ellis thought of it as a war. Who would break first?

"How much did Jac and Annie pay you to kill Glyn Evans?"

Silence.

"For the recording, Sion Edwards refuses to answer the question."

Nothing.

"How did you do it?"

"For the recording, Sion Edwards refuses to answer the question."

This was ridiculous.

"Did you kill Maureen too?"

Sion gave him a sarcastic look but kept schtum.

"For the recording, Sion Edwards refuses to answer the question."

Fifteen minutes ticked by. Twenty. Thirty.

"Interview terminated at seven-fifteen pm. Take him back to the cells."

Ellis motioned to the uniformed officer at the door, then turned back towards Sion.

"Let's see how a night locked up improves your communication skills, eh?"

"Hey, Carol?"

Ellis called after his colleague who'd started walking back to her office upstairs.

"Yeah?"

"Can you do us a favour and dig out Glyn Evans' post-mortem report and get the medical records and death certificate for Maureen Evans?"

"Sure. Leave it with me."

There had to be a point of triangulation? Something more than just the rope?

"Ellis?"

A uniformed officer came up to meet them.

"Boss wants to see you in her office. Right away."

Dropping the files onto his cluttered desk, Ellis went to the toilets to try and smarten himself up before making his way upstairs.

# CHAPTER 27

----------*----------

"He's free to go? But Ma'am…"

Ellis stood in front of The Superintendent, who was sitting stiffly behind the desk.

Her face was fixed as solidly as her lacquered, highlighted hair. And her sour face told him plainly that she was not in the mood to argue the toss about this.

"But, he was in possession of an illegal firearm? It's obvious that he's a villain."

"He's one of us."

"What?"

"He's an undercover operative. NCA. That's why the Scousers are after him. I've arranged transportation for him back to London tonight. He's going into witness protection. Throw the book at the barman. Grievous bodily harm with intent. Attempted murder, if you can make it stick. And talk to the NCA, check out the barman's connections to the Scousers. They've obviously moved onto our patch."

"But Ma'am, what about Glyn Evans?"

"What about Glyn Evans?"

Her eyes narrowed.

"Ahh, you mean your farfetched hunch about the farmer suicide?"

"Yes, Ma'am. It's hardly far-fetched though. It's not a common rope around here, and…"

The Superintendent glared back at him and he shut up immediately.

"I've already examined the post-mortem report. There's nothing. No bruising. No toxicology. No suggestions of force. But you know that already, right?"

Ellis scrunched his face.

He did.

"But Ma'am, how did Glyn get hold of the…"

She cut across him.

"Drop it, Roberts."

"But Ma'am, with respect."

"I said drop it."

The words were articulated clearly and forcefully.

The post-mortem and Maureen's medical records would hold nothing for him. It was another one of those messy endings that he hated so much.

"Is Claire Williams still here?" Sion asked the female uniformed officer as she released him from the cell.

There was arranged transport back to London. But he couldn't leave without seeing Claire first.

"Let me check."

The officer returned to the check-in desk by the cells, a couple of minutes later.

"She's still in reception. We've been struggling to get a police car to take her home, so she's waiting on a taxi."

"Can I see her? I won't be long."

The officer took him through the building to the reception area, where Sion could see Claire slumped on the padded leatherette chairs. Her head was leaning against the wall, and she'd turned her coat into a pillow. The bandaged side of her face was covered from view. Sion could see that she was exhausted.

"Claire."

Her head rose as he called her name.

"Sion?"

He heard the nervousness in her voice. He wanted to hug her, to hold her, but he could sense her tensing up as he approached.

In the end, he sat down in the row of chairs opposite.

"How's your neck?"

"Sore."

She turned away from him as her eyes filled up.

Leaning across the space between them, he took her hands in his.

"Claire, look at me."

Reluctantly, she tilted her head towards him.

As well as tears, he saw her uncertainty.

"I'm free to go. They've dropped all their wild accusations. I'm heading to London. Tonight. Then witness protection. Come with me."

She shook her head and stared at the floor.

There it was. Decision made.

"I can't."

She was trembling. Was it from shock or was she scared of him?

"You can't deny it. We've got something, you and me. Something I've never felt before with anyone else. Tell me you don't feel it too?"

"I do," she breathed.

A tear escaped, and he let go of her hand to brush it off her cheek.

The police receptionist interrupted them.

"Your taxi's here."

Quickly rising from the chair, she gathered her coat and bag, and made to leave.

He tried to hold her hand again as she moved past him, but she pulled it away.

"I'm sorry, Sion."

With her head down, she began walking towards the front entrance, where the taxi was parked outside.

"I'm innocent," he called after her. "Please, Claire. Why won't you come with me?"

She stopped, turning back to face him.

"Because…"

Her eyes met his.

"Because, I'm not sure I believe you."

Sion stopped by the cottage to pack up his things, while the police driver waited for him outside.

He was sad to be leaving, but he could never stay. He'd be forever watching his back. Kevin may be banged to rights, but that would only further infuriate the Scousers. From everything he'd seen and heard, Irish was a dangerous sociopath. He'd never be able to breathe easy here again.

Locking the door behind him, he posted the key through the letterbox.

He gave the driver the keys to his car and told him about the secure cases he'd put in the boot. His sniper gun. A rifle and another handgun. His knives. His bag of tricks. All handed to the police.

He wasn't sure where he was headed. An English speaking country hopefully, far away. Australia maybe? Or America? If he had a choice, he knew where he wanted to go.

He put his one large rucksack into the police car. Clothes and some bits of tech. It was all he had. He'd need to delete all traces of contacts, all apps, all social media.

The things that mattered, he couldn't take with him.

His friends. His name.

And she was dead to him too.

Claire's final words had pierced him worse than his misericorde.

"You awake?"

I yawn and stretch. It's four a.m. and Jac's lying awake in the darkness beside me.

"You missing the night feeds or something?"

Jac's found the latest milk feeder on the internet. The bottle-fed lambs are strong enough to come up to the tank now and feed as they need it. And the bonus is we get to sleep through. Genius.

"What's up?"

He pulls me to him, and I rest my head on his deliciously muscular, warm chest.

"Can I buy the farm off you?"

I tilt my head upwards to look at him.

"Why d'you wanna do that?"

"If Cal lends me half, I can borrow the rest from the bank."

"Jac, stop. Where's this coming from?"

I rack my brains.

"*Flippin' Ellis Roberts*. What exactly did he say to you?"

"That we got Sion to kill Glyn. That we did it to get the farm."

"He tried that one on to me, too. I told him where to get off."

His chest rises and falls as he chuckles.

"He said I was only with you because of the farm. That's not true, Annie. Whatever our circumstances were, I've always wanted to be with you. Forever."

I kiss his chest.

"I know that. And I *did* have letters to prove it, once."

I start to feel the injustice rising inside me.

"Why is it no one bats an eyelid about a poor woman marrying a rich farmer? But swap that around, so's I'm the farmer. Then, all of a sudden, 'cos you're my boyfriend, you must be trying to fleece me."

He strokes my shoulder.

"Would it feel better, though, if I bought the farm off you?"

"No. It'd be bonkers for you to get into a whole pile of debt because of some bad-minded gossips. But can *you* live with that? Or, does it still bother you too?"

I can feel his mouth on the top of my head as he lightly brushes it with persistent kisses that are now working their way down my neck.

"Doesn't bother me at all, now you've put it like that."

# CHAPTER 28

----------*----------

The silage is baled, and the calendar marker for the appointment sits in my phone, screaming at me. Every time I think about it, my stomach knots up.

A mate of Jac's from school is looking after the stock and Jess while we're away in London.

There shouldn't be any major dramas. The sheep are sheared and are grazing the summer meadow grass, high up in the hills. It's usually a time for farmers like we are now, to go to agricultural shows, relax and enjoy the late July sunshine.

Jac and I head off to pick up Claire in our new SUV. Trusty Rusty has sadly been retired to farm duties.

She's waiting for us on the high street as we pull over, a large backpack at her side.

"Hey! I can't believe you're finally doing this. You must be so excited?"

She giggles.

"I can't wait... I've been dreaming about this trip for so long. Does this look bad?"

She's still self-conscious of the angry red welt down the side of her neck. She's taken to wearing a scarf and high necklines, but today's hot, and she's wearing a t-shirt. Her travelling clothes.

"Claire, you look great. You always do. Don't worry about the scar. Your long hair covers it."

"Thanks, Annie. You always make me feel good."

Time goes quickly as we both sit in the back, chatting about Claire's trip. She's going to be enjoying a summer in Europe, before heading over to Southeast Asia, and then Down Under. She's no real plans, just a couple of contacts and the promise of some work in a café in Crete.

We've become quite close, and she's told me about that evening when we were being questioned. They'd questioned her too, about me and Jac.

"I think I made a mistake, Annie."

She's staring out of the window at the motorway traffic in the opposite lane.

"I keep catching myself wondering how different things'd be, if I'd've gone with him."

"You can't ever look back."

I offer her a bottle of water and she takes a swig.

"Where did you get to be so wise, Yoda?"

"It's Cal. She's spent her life trying to sort me out. Must have rubbed off."

Jac flashes me an ironic look in the rear-view mirror, and I pull a face back at him that makes him smile.

"I can't wait to see her."

I've made vegan brownies for a meal we're making tomorrow evening. A thank you to Jason for letting us stay. Cal and Sam are coming over too.

"I'm quite nervous."

"About the tattoo?"

"No. 'Course not. About meeting Jase. I hope he likes me."

Jac's listening.

He's still convinced that I'm only going through with it to please him.

Irish stabbed at them with his cocktail stick.

What had happened to Liverpool boozers?

*A dish of feckin' olives?*

The intricate stained glass and Victorian tiles of the Philharmonic bar still pulled in the tourists. Even Paul McCartney had breezed in recently. It wasn't his usual choice of city pubs, but more Pete's style these days.

"So, he's cost us ten million? Is that what you're telling me?"

Peter had sent him the three-month accounting breakdown. As predicted, turnover in the south had tanked since the arrests.

"Afraid so. Your fixed laundering costs are still high. But, it could be worse. The stock's still secure. Police didn't find any of our depots. We simply need to build up our routes to market again."

Irish studied the figures in front of him. That was all very well as a business recovery plan. But, his *routes to market* were his loyal foot soldiers, his private army. He couldn't very well post up job adverts or employ a recruitment agency.

Or, could he?

He smiled to himself ironically. They'd both said from the start that they would run the operation like a corporation. Peter, the company secretary, crunching the numbers, laundering the cash. And Irish, with his contacts and his unique skill set, leading the operation on the ground.

Maybe, he needed to develop a graduate scheme? Internships, even? He had plenty to offer bright students who wanted an alternative career path.

Prestigious company car, regular staff nights out, flexible hours, performance-related pay. There were plenty of incentives for talented, like-minded go-getters who could grow their customer base. It was how he and Pete had started out.

"How's your brother?" Pete asked,

Irish stopped murdering the olives.

"Better, now he's been moved."

He'd not spoken to Tony since his sentencing, but his mum had told him that he was in the new super-prison thirty miles away. A much cushier number. Woodwork and school classes. Rehab and personal growth bullshit. Still, it was better than the place he'd been in, on remand.

Plus, he'd heard it was a cinch to get drugs in. That'd make his life a bit easier; getting some dealing going on.

Irish went back to pummelling the olives; now a pulpy mush in the dish.

"What've they done to you?"

Talking about the losses, the business compromised, his brother; it still made him tense.

Irish's face cracked into a grin. Pete knew it. They went way back.

They'd first started drawing up their county lines model as students. They'd worked out a unique distribution model that would turn their small-time dealing operation from the house they shared, to the big league. Make them super rich. And it had. If they were in any other business, they'd have been listed by Forbes by now.

"Any joy on the contract you put out?"

"A few red herrings."

Olives pulped, Irish started on the beer mat. Tearing off the corners, pulling them away, like he was slicing off ears.

"What would you do, Pete? The trail's gone cold."

"Leave it, Irish. Walk away."

"Can't."

"It doesn't matter about the money. We'll soon build the business back up."

"I can't get time back though, Pete. Sion Edwards has cost our Tony his son. My brother will be a stranger to that little boy, by the time he gets out."

Peter peered at his old uni pal over his expensive titanium frames.

"Then, what about the girl?"

What about the girl? He'd forgotten about her.

"Kevin told you that this Sion was smitten. Came every evening to see her. Was always asking her out. But she stayed."

"Yeah. She's still working in the pub."

"Get on her socials. He might get in touch. He's only got to make one mistake and you'll have him."

He'd obviously dumped her. Buggered off. Cut the rope. Still, Pete was right. Claire Williams was worth keeping an eye on.

And right now, she was the only link to Sion Edwards he'd got.

"Jase, mate!"

Jac embraced his friend, as both Claire and Annie stood behind him with their bags.

"This is Annie."

Jason was dark-haired, tall; and he had an airline pilot's air of calm authority that put her immediately at ease.

"Annie. Great to meet you at last."

"Jac's told me a lot about you."

"All good things. Nothing incriminating, I promise," Jac grinned. "And this is Claire."

Jason embraced her too, his eyes hovering on her neck as he moved away.

Thankfully, she didn't notice.

"You're off travelling, I hear?"

"Yes," Claire beamed, "Eurostar to Paris, day after next. This is my first time in London though, so while these two are gettin' inked up, I'm gonna make the most of it and be a total tourist."

"I'm off tomorrow. D'ya wanna guide? Free of charge?"

"That'd be great."

Jac thought Jason's two-bedroom flat was surprisingly spacious. And like him, he liked to keep it organised. Old military habits die hard.

Much to Claire's embarrassment, Jason insisted that she take his bed, while he took the couch.

"But that's not fair."

"Believe me, I've slept in worse places. And doing a job like mine, you learn to sleep as soon as your head hits the pillow. Any pillow."

They spent a couple of hours in the pub around the corner.

Chatting, Jason getting to know Annie and Claire.

It was a pity Sion wasn't there too, Jac thought. But who could tell what would've happened with him and Claire? She rarely mentioned him now, and her life was about to open a new exciting chapter. She'd need to have her wits about her. But, she was a survivor, he could tell. Still, it was a shame about her and Sion. She would've been good for him. Her no-nonsense sparkiness suited him, somehow.

Later, they got a takeaway. The girls drank Prosecco, as Jac and Jason reminisced over a beer about their time in the military together.

Annie put down her chopsticks and pushed her bowl away. She sighed and loosened the top button of her jeans.

"This is my guilty pleasure."

"I'm not gonna lie, if there's one thing I miss about London, it's the food. And I've eaten way too much of this."

"Certainly beats airline grub," Jason agreed.

"Must be so glamorous, though," Claire added wistfully, "Flying everywhere. Seeing new places."

"I see a lot of airports. And airport hotels. Sure, I do get to go to exotic places, but it's not much fun on your own."

Later on, Annie and Claire turned in and left the men to catch up. They sat on the sofas, both a little mellow, and Jason cracked open a bottle of malt whisky.

"So, what d'ya think?"

"The girls? They're great."

"No. You don't need to tell me that, ya idiot. Annie's the best thing that's ever happened to me. I meant about Sion?"

Jason said nothing.

Jac shook his head as Jason poured them both a finger of the amber liquid.

"Just me in the dark, then?"

"He told me too."

Claire spoke out from across the room.

"The night before he went."

They both turned towards the open bedroom door.

"Come and join us."

Jac held up his glass.

"Wanna short?"

Dressed in pyjamas, Claire shuffled up next to Jac on the sofa and Jason got her a glass of whisky.

Between them, they patched together Sion's story for Jac. In turn, he sat there quietly; listening, taking it all in, feeling more than a little bruised.

"Why didn't he tell me?"

"He wanted a safe space," Jason explained. "Where no one would suspect him. That's why you were out of the loop. He only told me the bare minimum, too. Said it was safer, that way."

"He was right about that,"

Claire unconsciously touched her neck.

"He only came clean with me at the end, when he wanted me to go with him."

"But you stayed?"

"I did."

"Why?"

Claire took a sip of the peaty liquor; it burned the back of her throat.

"At the police station, he claimed he was innocent, and he didn't kill Annie's dad. And I told him that I didn't believe him."

Jac looked at her horrified.

"Claire? *Why?* If Sion said he didn't do it, then, he didn't do it. He would never lie to you."

She stared at Jac intently.

"You so sure? After everything you've heard tonight?"

Jason poured them more whisky.

"How d'you explain the rope, then?"

"What? You think Sion strung Glyn up and killed him?" Jac muttered, "Never mind the practicalities of that, why would he do it? He barely knew Glyn Evans. Or, do you agree with Ellis Roberts, and think that we hired him? To get the farm."

"No! 'Course not."

Claire put her hand on Jac's arm.

"You'd never do that. *God! Is that what the detective said?* I was so mixed-up about it all. I still am."

Covering her head with her hands, she sighed.

"I couldn't have gone with him then. And now, I'm never gonna see him again."

"If we hear from him, we'll get in touch."

Her eyes met theirs.

"Promise?"

# CHAPTER 29

----------*----------

"Who's going first?"

"Me."

We're both sitting opposite Matt on the distressed leather sofa. It's all very hipster here. It's probably best I do go first, because I'm certain that sitting watching Jac having it done will wind me up even more.

"Completely sure you wanna have it done?"

It's the umpteenth time he's asked me.

"Okay, then," Matt announces, "Let's get started."

I take off my shirt and lie face down on the retro leather dentist chair, while Matt sets up and gets things ready.

Jac holds my hand as I wait for the buzz of the needle to begin.

"Relax and keep still. Close your eyes, if it helps."

The noise starts and Matt carefully begins scratching into my skin.

I smile bravely at Jac, trying to be tough, biting my lip, bearing the pain and discomfort of the needle cutting into me.

It's sustained and irritatingly painful; but as time passes I begin to relax, even chatting with Jac.

"You're doing great." Matt says as he works, finely etching away until the swallow takes shape. Its wings sweep upwards towards my shoulder, the head and body cover the deep indentations I don't want ever to see again.

When it's all done, Matt leans back and I rise from the chair and gaze long and hard into the full-length mirror on the wall. It's a little swollen, but already I can see that it's another amazing work of art from Matt.

"It's incredible. And you can't see the dents at all, now. Thank you."

I'm relieved beyond words. Jac is too.

He comes over and studies it closely.

"I love you, Annie," he whispers as he kisses my neck.

My cheek heats up when I notice Matt discreetly looking away. He's tidying up his kit, making like he's not seen us.

"Let's get you covered up," Matt calls over. "And I'll go through the aftercare with you both, though Jac knows the drill."

He takes a break, and we go down the high street for a coffee and some lunch, before it's Jac's turn.

By the end of the day, we're both wrapped up tightly in steri-pads and cling film, bonded forever by the matching art on our bodies beneath them.

"I've never been so high. Is this what it's like?"

St. Paul's Cathedral and London Bridge were now far below them.

Jason laughed. "If I was this close to the ground in the middle of the city, I'd be panicking, believe me. But yeah, it's pretty awesome. My absolute favourite thing is flying over The Alps to Turin."

"That's another place on my list."

It had taken some persuasion to get Claire up onto the viewing deck of The Shard's seventy-second floor. But now she could see the view, she was glad she'd come.

Jason had enjoyed the morning. They'd been to Buckingham Palace, Hyde Park and The Tower of London. He'd never done the tourist thing, and it was nice seeing the sights, especially with Claire, who'd never been to London before. It was like he was seeing everything for the first time.

There was something quirky about her. And attractive; with her dark hair and beautiful eyes. Like she belonged on a Pacific Island. Or in a Gaughan painting.

He could tell though, that she was still really conscious of that scar. Today, she'd tried to cover it up with makeup and her hair; but as they walked, he could see it plainly. The redness came back through, and he saw the pained look on her face as she subtly checked it in the reflection of shop windows.

Jac had explained to him how she'd got it. She'd been brave, fighting back like she did. He could see why Sion liked her.

She leaned up against the barrier.

"How did you meet Sion and Jac? 'Cos you were in the RAF, not the army, right?"

"We were on operations. I flew the chopper. Mainly getting them out of sticky messes they'd gotten themselves into. Unless, Sion had other ideas, that was."

"What d'ya mean?"

"He was the lead. One time, we were in... It doesn't matter where we were, let's just say it was hot and sandy. And we had to get an interpreter out of this town, right? The place had been taken over by insurgents and the interpreter was stuck there. He'd been in contact, giving us intel. And it was dynamite."

"Sounds dangerous."

"Yeah. Dodgy as. The insurgents were twitchy, so we had to move fast before he got busted. It was on the news. They were chopping heads off and sticking them on spikes on the main road."

"And, Sion went in?"

"Oh yeah. And Jac. They'd dropped in at night, undercover. But they couldn't get close. They'd been under heavy fire, and I was pulling them out the next day. The insurgents were still shooting when we set down in the chopper, and I didn't wanna stick around. They all evacced into the Apache, and I'm trying to get them the Hell outta there, when Sion tells me to veer back. It's against my better judgement. But I do it, 'cos Sion asked. So we hop around to the other side of the market square; and as soon as I set down, we see the interpreter dude running towards us. The guns fire up again; so Sion sprints out, grabs him by his coat and pretty much hurls him into the chopper. Under heavy fire."

"*Really!* He sounds fearless."

"Yeah. He was an amazing soldier. He saved the interpreter's life that day."

Claire shivered. The air was cold up here, even for July.

"Claire, he'd never kill a civilian. I know Sion. There's no way he'd kill Glyn Evans."

Claire shrugged a little sadly.

"I know that now. And it's too late."

He'd rubbed her nose in it, but she needed to know the qualities of the man she'd lost. He'd take her back down to ground level to find a coffee. And then, a stroll along the Embankment to Westminster.

Who knew what the future held? But, if there was anything he'd learned about his old mate Sion, it was that he never gave up. He always got what he wanted.

Eventually.

We're making dinner when Jason and Claire get back to the flat. And, man, do they look whacked.

"Where've you been?"

"Everywhere," Jason yawns.

"What've you done to him, Claire?"

Claire pulls off her trainer to examine a blister that's forming on the back of her heel.

"I got my money's worth, that's all. Jase, you're an awesome tour guide. London rocks!"

"It kinda fades on you after a while," I tell her.

Jac glances across at me.

"Not sad you left, then?"

"Nah. These days I much prefer the mud and rain."

"Ahh, you say that. But tell me, you don't love it, when it's just you in a field with the songs of the birds."

"Hmm. You're right. And no streetlights. A sky full of proper darkness, lit up only by the stars."

Jac smiles at me. There's no way either of us is ever leaving the farm.

When Callista and Sam arrive, Claire's had a shower and packed her bag ready, and Jason's been napping on the sofa like an old man. He really *can* sleep anywhere.

Callista's new partner is much less flamboyant than Cal, more down to earth. She doesn't say much, but when she speaks it's full of sense. Jac likes her, and they chat together on the sofa, while Cal helps me finish off making the food.

"So, let me see this wonderful work of art, then."

The bandage is off, so I slip my sloppy slash-necked t-shirt off my shoulder for her to see.

"D'you like it?"

"It's fabulous, darling... Jac?," she calls out from the kitchen, "Can you design one for me and Sam too?"

"You're not getting me anywhere near a tattoo parlour."

"Honestly, honey, you can be such a prude. You're meant to be the artistic one!"

By the end of the meal, I can see that Cal's endless travel tips have got Claire's head spinning. She's excited but getting a little anxious too.

"You don't mind me saying, dear, but that looks very red. What've you been putting on it?"

Claire flinches at Cal's mention of her scar.

"I've been covering it with make-up."

"That's no good, sweetie. Manuka honey; that'll sort it."

"I'll bear it in mind."

"How ever did it happen?"

Just as I realise we haven't told her, Jac jumps in.

"You remember Sion? A guy was after him and he attacked Claire with a knife."

"Oh! Claire, darling, that's awful. Did they arrest him?"

"He pleaded guilty and got three years. He'll probably be out in eighteen months."

Cal tuts.

"And Sion?"

Jason shoots Jac a look.

"He's gone away for a bit."

Jac takes a long swig of his beer.

"They tried to charge him with Glyn's murder, Cal. They said it was his rope. That it wasn't suicide. They had me and Annie in for questioning. Accused us of plotting to kill Annie's parents to get the farm."

Cal's at a loss for words. For the first time ever.

"Jac's only with me for my money."

I try to lighten the mood, but her face is still a stony-grey and I can tell that it's upset her deeply.

"What?" Sam asks her quietly as the table falls silent.

"I'm shocked, that's all. Shocked... that those kinds of spurious allegations could be made without any substance... It's worse than living in a fascist state, darling, it really is."

The mood has tanked, and I don't want to end the evening like this.

"Don't worry. They dropped it. It was all bullshit. Sion was free to go."

Cal stares at Claire.

"But you've still got doubts about Sion?"

Claire's fork clangs onto her plate. She mouths an apology and quickly takes a drink of her wine.

Later, as she leaves, Cal pauses by the front door. Her hand grips mine tightly as she kisses me goodnight.

"Can you and Jac come to see me tomorrow?"

# CHAPTER 30

---------✱----------

It's a teary farewell as Claire climbs the steps onto the Eurostar train, with her pack on her back. In less than three hours, she'll be in Paris at the start of her great adventure.

We're rattling along on the Northern Line in a jam-packed tube train and my face is getting squashed up against the armpit of a large man with a guitar case strapped to his back.

"D'you wish we were travelling too?"

"Nah," Jac says. "I've spent my whole life wandering. I like being home, with you."

"Me too."

Taking my hand, we follow a steady stream of people spilling onto the platform.

When we arrive at Callista's Victorian terrace, I notice the blinds flickering. Moments later, Cal is at the door, welcoming us in. And we go through the house into the spacious flower-filled garden at the back.

Jac notices it too. Cal is behaving very strangely.

Whenever either of us goes around there, we're always stepping into delightful chaos. But today, everything's prepared. Three chairs are neatly arranged around the wooden garden table for us to sit at, chilled homemade lemonade is at the ready, that she's made especially for us.

Perhaps, it's because it's such a hot day. But, she seems restless and anxious.

"What's the matter, Cal?"

Suddenly, I get a sinking feeling.

*Please, God!* Please don't let Callista be sick too.

Her deep eyes meet mine.

"I need to give you something."

In her hand is a familiar-looking cream envelope. And it's addressed to me.

"It's from Mam."

Cal nods grimly.

Hesitantly, I tear the top of the envelope, revealing a handwritten letter inside. My hand is shaking as I pull it out.

"Why haven't you given me this before?"

She doesn't answer.

"Why d'you want me to read it now?"

I steady myself as I start to read it.

*Dear Annie,*

*If you're reading this letter then something's happened.*

*A person has many friends, but only a few you'd trust your life with. They're your soulmates. Cal is one of those to me, and I love her dearly. She's promised to look after you when I'm gone, and I know she will. So don't blame her for not giving you this letter sooner.*

*I never wanted to write it down, but then I worry about that young man who's been so good to me. Without him, I'd be locked up now, instead of spending my last days with you.*

*And it's been so precious, our time together, Annie.*

*You've no idea how much I missed you over the years. Wondering what you were up to. Hoping you were happy. Happier than I've been, anyway.*

*When I first got my diagnosis, one of my hospital friends - I won't say who, they got me some insulin. I saw it as a way out if I needed it. It was all my idea. I was depressed and your father was difficult. It's not an excuse, but you saw him at Christmas.*

*The man was ill. God knows I've excused him so many times over the years. But the truth is, as you know, Annie when he was drunk, your father was a nasty piece of work. That wasn't the condition or the alcohol. It was him.*

*I'll never forgive him for that terrible beating he gave you with his belt after you came in late that time, cariad. Still makes my blood boil, it does.*

*And Sion's been good to me. He saw straight away what was going on. He's been through it too, you see, with his father. We've talked a lot. More than to anyone else, and it's helped us both.*

*The night your father died; he'd been hitting the bottle hard all day. I was making him supper when he barged into the kitchen, catching me unawares. And I could tell he was gunning for me.*

*He stood there, by the door, me cornered by the stove. There was no way out. So, I went to make him a cuppa, trying to keep things normal, calm him down. 'Course that just wound him up even more.*

*Then, I saw him going for the kettle. And it wasn't to make the tea. He'd poured scalding water on me once before and I'd had the most painful burns for weeks.*

*Thinking about that, made me flip. I'm not sure what possessed me, except survival? I knew how bad it was going to hurt, you see.*

*I'd hidden the insulin and a syringe behind the butter in the fridge. And I filled it now, sticking the needle in my cardigan pocket when I got the milk for our tea.*

*I was right. When I set the milk down and turned around for the mugs, he came at me with the boiling kettle.*

*Annie, I swear to God, cariad, it was self-defence.*

*He pushed me and I staggered back onto the floor. He came at me again, when I was on my knees. Pulling me up one-handed, he lifted the kettle to pour over my face.*

*And I stabbed him in the neck.*

*It took a couple of seconds to kick in. He was grabbing at his neck like he'd been stung, spilling boiling water all over the floor. He was grabbing at me too, but I'd ducked out of his way. And then, he suddenly keeled over onto the floor.*

*I put him in recovery, and I should've called an ambulance. But, God help me, I didn't. I can't even remember driving to the cottage for help.*

*Jac was in The Cross Keys and Sion had just got home. He drove me in his car back to the house. He checked Glyn, but he was already gone.*

*I was in a state, but Sion was calm. So, I asked him to help me. And he did. He hung him up from the shed beam and cleaned everything up tidy.*

*'Course the detective was quite right about the rope and Glyn's slippers.*

*I wanted to take this with me to my grave. But, I hope telling you what happened will set things straight.*

*Annie, I hope that you'll find it in your heart to forgive me, cariad.*

*I love you so much and I always will.*

*Mam x*

Glassy-eyed, I hand the letter to Jac. And then to Callista. The truth sits between us on the table. My mother killed my father.

"When did you find out?"

Callista fiddles with the envelope.

"That night. She phoned me."

"And you never told me?"

"It wasn't for me to tell."

"That's the thing."

Folding the letter back into the envelope, I leave Jac and Cal and take it with me into the kitchen.

In the fierce blue flames of the gas hob, the envelope instantly catches alight.

I carry it back into the garden as it begins to burn away.

The yellow flames quickly devour the letter, the words disappearing into blackness and the air.

As my fingers start to burn, I throw it onto the stone patio where the pieces lie like petals on the ground.

"Annie, darling!"

Callista stares at the charred fragments.

Jac shifts his gaze from his mother onto me.

"Doesn't she deserve to know the truth?"

Sighing, I shake my head.

It's not for me to tell Claire.

The story continues in Find Me by Nell Grey, Trust Me's exciting finale.

*Available for download now from Amazon.com and on Kindle Unlimited.*

# BOOKS IN THIS SERIES

*Trust Me Find Me Romantic*
*Suspense Series*

## Find Me

Find Me
By
Nell Grey

Trust Me's exciting sequel

What should she have done?
They'd been friends, even kissed once.
The police said he was a murderer. But, they let him go. Knowing all that, how could she go with him into witness protection?

A few months on, and Claire Williams is still bearing the scars; still chasing the ghost of Sion Edwards, even though he's dead to her now. Determined to start afresh and to find the father she's never known; she takes a big world trip. It's meant to be the adventure of a lifetime. It will be. But not the way she imagined it.

Is there anywhere safe to hide?

Sion Edwards was an undercover agent, a hitman for one of England's most notorious drugs gangs. And now there's a price on his head. They're after his blood and they won't rest until he's reeled back in and they have their revenge.

When the big fish slips the hook, it's time to use live bait.

Find Me by Nell Grey is available for download on Amazon and on Kindle Unlimited.

# BOOKS BY THIS AUTHOR

The Strictly Business Proposal

The Actor's Deceit

Their Just Deserts

The Rural Escape

Find Me

# PRAISE FOR AUTHOR

*Reviews of The Freshwater Bay Series*

'*Highly recommend the whole series. Brilliant characters, with interesting and exciting plots. Beautifully set in Wales.*'

'*You won't be disappointed. A most enjoyable read.*'

'*Really enjoying this great series, Freshwater Bay. Each book keeps you captivated, not wanting to put it down.*'

'*Ok, somebody just transport me to this beautiful picturesque location in Wales. Such a fun and delightful read!*'

'*Well written, believable characters, good storyline, and pleasant settings craftily described. I could see the places and buildings and feel the air. Nicely done. You won't be disappointed with this, and I can't wait for the next in the series.*'

Printed in Great Britain
by Amazon